THE WISDOM OF HAIR

Kim Boykin

BERKLEY BOOKS, NEW YORK

THE BERKLEY PUBLISHING GROUP
Published by the Penguin Group
Penguin Group (USA) Inc.
375 Hudson Street, New York, New York 10014, USA

USA / Canada / UK / Ireland / Australia / New Zealand / India / South Africa / China

Penguin Books Ltd., Registered Offices: 80 Strand, London WC2R 0RL, England
For more information about the Penguin Group visit penguin.com

This book is an original publication of The Berkley Publishing Group.

Library of Congress Cataloging-in-Publication Data

Boykin, Kim, 1957–
The wisdom of hair / Kim Boykin.—Berkley trade paperback ed.
p. cm.
ISBN 978-0-425-26105-7
1. Beauty shops—Fiction. 2. Female friendship—Fiction. 3. Hair—Fiction.
4. South Carolina—Fiction. I. Title.
PS3602.O95W57 2013
813'.6—dc23 2012035919

PUBLISHING HISTORY
Berkley trade paperback edition / March 2013

PRINTED IN THE UNITED STATES OF AMERICA

10 9 8 7 6 5 4 3 2 1

Cover photograph of woman © Glow Images, Inc. / Getty Images;
photograph of leather upholstery © iStockphoto / Thinkstock.
Cover design by Judith Lagerman.
Interior text design by Laura K. Corless.

"In Kim Boykin's novel, hair is not only wise, it's witty and eloquent. As we've long suspected, our hair can define us. It can also teach us things about ourselves that will surprise and change us. *The Wisdom of Hair* is a lovely, engaging novel. Zora Adams is a heroine to root for!"   —Wendy Wax, author of O

"*The Wisdom of Hair* has a big, beating heart, and I couldn't put it down. What I loved best about the book was the pervasive kindness; page after page, good people try their best, sometimes succeeding and sometimes failing. It's hard to write an engaging novel about (mostly) nice people, but Kim Boykin has pulled it off."

—Ann Napolitano, author of *A Good Hard Look*

Welcome to Beauty School

According to the brochure, beauty school was supposed to be "The Beginning of an Exciting Career That Will Last a Lifetime." But the first thing that caught my eye when I walked through the front door of the Davenport School of Beauty was a sign on slick white poster board beside the cash register. A bubble over a pair of legs said, NO MORE THAN THREE ABOVE THE KNEE. Looking down at my uniform, I didn't need a ruler to tell me that I was out of line.

I pulled at the sides of my uniform, trying to lengthen the hem like a lot of the other students. I could just picture us all after school let out, sitting around our respective homes with scissors, big red tomato pincushions, and spools of white thread scattered about, undoing our hemlines.

Nobody looked anything like the proud, confident blonde on the cover of the brochure, except for one girl. She was the only one not worrying her dress. Hers was an inch or two below the knee and had a sassy little slit up the back. From the neck up, she looked like a movie star, and the way she carried herself made you forget that she could probably afford to lose fifty or sixty pounds.

As attendance was called, we were supposed to introduce ourselves. Some of the girls stammered or giggled. My own voice came out just above a whisper, but the big girl spoke in a deep, sexy drawl with a proud confidence that every single girl in the room coveted. We looked at Sara Jane Farquhar in awe, and there wasn't a single soul in that room, even our instructor, who didn't want to be her . . .

For my grandfather, Bryan Standridge,
the greatest storyteller I have ever known,
and to my parents for their never-ending love story

ACKNOWLEDGMENTS

Attempting to publish is a lot like golf; it's an awful endeavor and just when you're ready to give up, one small good thing will happen that gives you hope and makes you believe. I had a lot of years like that until my agent, Kevan Lyon, picked me. Thank you, Kevan, for being an extraordinary agent and friend. Heartfelt thanks to Berkley Publishing and to my amazing editor, Leis Pederson, a Southern girl like me. Thanks, Leis, for loving this story to publication and nailing the title.

Thank you to Miranda Fuller, my first reader, who made me believe this was possible. To my critique partners, Wendy Oglesby, Mary Ann Thomas, Vera LaFleur, Claire Iannini, Susan Martin, Kim Blum-Hyclak, and Jes Young, all wonderful writers, thank you for your good judgment and honesty.

For Crickett Pfirman and hair stylists everywhere who really have answered one of life's highest callings, thank you for making those of us in your charge feel valuable and beautiful.

Finally, love and thanks to my family. To Kaley and Austin, thank you for sharing your childhood with me, I'm so proud of who you are. And to Mike, my husband of thirty years and counting, you are my heart. Thank you for believing in me.

1

The problem with cutting your own hair is that once you start, you just keep cutting, trying to fix it, and the truth is, some things can never be fixed. The day of my daddy's funeral, I cut my bangs until they were the length of those little paintbrushes that come with dime-store watercolor sets. I was nine years old. People asked me why I did it, but I was too young then to know I was changing my hair because I wanted to change my life.

Ten years later, I stared into my mother's dressing-table mirror, ready to shave my head. It was my birthday, and Mama was going out to celebrate. She stood in front of me for her ta-dah moment, decked out like Judy Garland, her pretty blond hair covered up with cheap chestnut color, and put up under a black fedora. The oversized men's tuxedo jacket she wore had been taken in at all the right places and didn't come close to mid-thigh. Unlike her alter ego, she'd skipped the dress shirt altogether. Regulation black pumps clicked across our bare floor like tap shoes, long legs moving in short steps to mimic Judy's four-foot-ten-inch stride. Mama wasn't going to a costume party. She always dressed like her favorite star, who died on a toilet seat the year Mama was born. Right down to the fake eyelashes.

"I'll be home directly, and we'll cut the cake," she said.

I knew that was a lie because she was already slurring her words and there was no cake.

"Sure, Mama. Just be safe."

She cocked her head to the side and looked around me to see herself again in the full-length mirror duct taped to the front of the bathroom door. Her long, slender fingers ran over the black satin lapels and then reached inside her jacket and pulled her breasts up as high as they would go. She arranged her wares until she'd achieved the maximum cleavage for a B cup, and sighed.

"*You* don't have this problem." She raised her eyebrows at me like I'd been playing dress-up with her breasts and she wanted them back. "How do I look?"

"Beautiful," I said, because she was beautiful.

"I do look good." She turned sideways, eyed her long legs and smoothed her hand over her round bottom. "You'd look good, too, if you fixed up now and then."

Mama's definition of my fixing up was making me play Liza Minnelli to her Judy Garland. Up until I was eleven, I let her cut my hair short once a year and spray it jet black with Halloween color she bought every November on clearance. I was so excited when she dressed me up like a child star and pulled the kitchen chairs in front of the TV so we could watch *The Wizard of Oz* together. I watched her mouth every line Dorothy Gale spoke with great expression. By the time Dorothy declared there was no place like home, Mama was almost two pints into the story and sobbing because she'd been robbed of her Oscar for *A Star Is Born*.

As crazy as that sounds, she wasn't always like that, not when my daddy was living. But she was never the kind of mom who wore the macaroni necklaces you made her or showed up at your elementary school play sober. She got worse after Daddy passed, so bad my uncle Heath took her to the state mental hospital in Columbia to see what was wrong with her. Other than drying her out, there was nothing the doctors could do for her. They sent her back home with a diagnosis my uncle wrote down because he couldn't remember the word *narcissistic*, much less pronounce it.

"Bet you'd like to go out with me. We could do your birthday up right." She opened the closet, pulled out two hangers, and dangled them in front of me—black satin hot pants and a halter top with a cowl neckline that plunged close to navel level.

"I made this to wear on Oscar night the year *Cabaret* came out. Bet you anything it'll fit you. What do you say?"

The last time I saw Mama in that outfit, she didn't come home for two days and when she did, two things were obvious: She'd danced the feet out of her thick black fishnet stockings and someone had roughed her up. I was only eleven years old, but that was old enough to know, no matter what it cost me, I didn't want to be a part of her charade anymore.

"Just be safe."

It was just after three in the morning, and she wasn't home. As much as I tried to make out like I didn't care, I did. With every minute that passed, the worry inside me grew. I told myself to go to bed, but it's just as easy to worry upright as it is laying flat in the bed. I pushed the door open to her bedroom. Costumes puddled on the floor, a mass of cheap satin and sequins she'd stitched together herself. The Tampa cigar box she used for a jewelry box was running over with cheap dime-store trinkets men had given her or she'd bought herself with money we didn't have. The room smelled like Ambush, her favorite cologne, thick and musky and nauseatingly sweet.

I sat down at the dressing table eye to eye with myself, took the clippers out of the drawer, and plugged them in. They vibrated in my hand; the sensation traveled up my arm and settled in my brain.

It didn't matter that I was smart enough to go to college. It didn't matter that I'd been accepted to the best beauty school in the state three hundred miles from home. It didn't make a stitch of difference that my high-school English teacher, Miss Cunningham, had found me a place to stay rent free there so I could become a cosmetologist in six months. By process of elimination, I was the only fool left on the mountain who would take care of Mama, and shaving my head wouldn't change anything.

I turned off the clippers about the same time she stumbled through the front door with a present, the first one she'd given me in years—and his name was Bob.

"It's her birthday," Mama gushed, her red lipstick smeared all over her face, while Bob groped her. "*Happy birthday*," she said completely out of character, more like Marilyn Monroe.

"You gonna tell her?" Bob propped himself up against the wall with a proud smile. Mama shook her head, elbowed him, and giggled again. He motioned for me to come closer and didn't seem to notice I'd traded my clippers for the baseball bat I kept just inside my bedroom door.

"Go to bed, Mama."

Bob leaned forward, almost toppling over, before he righted himself enough to get the words out. "How about a three-way for your birthday?"

I slammed my bedroom door and wedged the ladder-back chair under the doorknob, because mountain houses don't have locks, and if they do they don't work since nobody ever uses them. My hands were shaking so, I could barely dial the telephone number.

"Miss Cunningham?"

"Zora?"

"I'm sorry to wake you."

"What's wrong?"

Miss Cunningham had offered a thousand times to rescue me from the little bit she knew about my life.

"I can't stay here anymore."

There was a long silence, so long I was afraid she'd gone back to sleep.

"Do you want me to come get you now?"

I had a tiny flash of what normal might be like. Miss Cunningham would be on my doorstep in a matter of minutes, and we'd salvage my birthday. We'd bake cupcakes in the middle of the night, the kind she used to bring to my senior English class. The feral sounds coming from Mama's bedroom were interrupted by the crack of a hard slap against bare flesh. Mama screamed. I cradled the phone on my shoulder and grabbed the bat. Before I could move the chair away from my bedroom door, her scream dissolved into laughter.

I tightened my grip on the bat. Why couldn't I just say yes? "Tomorrow."

"Are you sure?"

I knew what she meant. Could I leave the mountain? My homeplace? Could I really leave Mama?

"Tomorrow," I said over the animal noises in the next room. "First thing tomorrow."

"I'm proud of you, Zora."

I wasn't a crier, there was never much point to it, but my nose stung like someone had swatted it. Even after all those years of waiting for Mama to grow up, there was still enough child left in me that ached for a mother who said things like that, or, at the very least, wanted to protect me from the Bobs of the world. I started to hang up the phone when I heard her voice.

"Zora?"

"Yes, ma'am?"

"Happy birthday."

2

Bob was gone when I got up the next morning. I'd debated on whether to leave Mama a note or just leave, but she was up early, and I didn't have a choice. When I said I was leaving, I said just that. She tried to guilt me into staying, but she was too hungover to muster any look that might change my mind. Still, the part of me that was ready to bolt toward freedom wrestled with the sticky part of me that was terrified for her. I could feel her wanting a drink as she took attendance in her mind. My real daddy—dead. Daddy Heyward and Daddy Leon and Nana—dead. And me, her only child, leaving her alone. Something she feared more than death.

Miss Cunningham pulled up to our little house on the side of the mountain in a Toyota Land Cruiser; you didn't see too many of those kinds of trucks back in 1983. She wore a pink Izod polo and a short khaki skirt that showed off her country-club tan.

Mama eyed the gold chains with coin-looking charms dangling from Miss Cunningham's neck.

"She don't belong," Mama said under her breath.

But she was one to talk standing there in an exact replica of the gold brocade outfit Judy Garland wore on the *Ed Sullivan Show* in 1965. Miss Cunningham pushed her sunglasses back so they rested on top of her head and gave me a hug. When I introduced her to Mama, she reached out to shake hands, but Mama wasn't having any of that.

"You must be very proud of Zorie." Miss Cunningham was from up north, and if she liked you, no matter what your name was, she'd put an "ie" on the end of it. Mama nodded without a smile and then looked at me like she wanted to know who in the hell Zorie was.

There wasn't much to load into the jeep, just an old American Tourister suitcase and two boxes Mama would throw away for spite if I left them behind. By the time I closed the back of the truck, Mama was looking at Miss Cunningham like she could cut her heart out and eat it cold for supper.

"Bye, Mama." It was a wonder those words came out of my mouth.

The pleading in her eyes made me look away, my mind screamed, *Today Mama will take care of herself—so I can have a little piece of life for myself,* punching every word so hard my body quaked. But Mama was trembling so over the fear of being alone, she didn't seem to notice.

For the first time since Nana died, she took me in her arms. Her nails dug into the tender part of my arms. The sorrow I felt for her bonded with the pain shooting up toward my shoulders, her nails drawing blood. I ached, so I buried my face in her long, dark hair, breathed in the smell of honky-tonk smoke and baby shampoo, and waited for her to turn me loose.

She let out a little whimper and ran into the house. I didn't go after her. I got into the truck as Miss Cunningham closed the door behind me. She smiled and pressed her hand against the glass before she walked around and got into the driver's seat. In the quiet, as we started down the mountain, I wondered if she knew what it was like to leave home without the blessing she wanted and needed. I wondered if she thought I was stupid for helping Mama be so weak and dependent.

As we neared the place halfway down the mountain where Daddy and Nana were laid to rest, I felt a hitch in my belly that bubbled up from my heart. It settled in my throat, quivering, pulsing hard. If I'd started crying, I would have never left.

"Zorie, did you want to stop and say good-bye?" It's bad luck to point at a graveyard, but Miss Cunningham didn't know any better.

I rubbed the acorn in my pocket for good luck, once for her and once for me, and shook my head. Leaving was not as easy as I had pictured it. I blinked back tears and sifted through her cassettes until I found the Stones' cassette tape, *Emotional Rescue*. I cranked it up and hoped Mick Jagger's noise would distract me from thoughts of my loved ones and what I was doing to Mama.

"Do you think I'm bad, leaving her like this?"

Miss Cunningham turned down the volume and looked at me long enough to make me nervous before she fixed her eyes back on the winding blacktop.

"You've looked out for your mom for a long time."

9

"She doesn't look crazy, does she?"

"No, but from what you've told me she's not the kind of crazy you can just pop a pill and be okay."

"She was bad after my daddy died, and awful after Nana passed last year."

"Where does the Judy Garland thing come from?"

Miss Cunningham let the silence fall between us the way she did in class when she knew one of her students knew the answer to her question. But what my daddy told me about Mama's obsession couldn't have been right.

He said she was sad after I was born, but it wasn't my fault. Some women just get that way. He borrowed his brother's truck and drove almost forty miles to Asheville so she could see *The Wizard of Oz* at the drive-in. At the time, they didn't have a TV set and neither of them had ever seen a movie before. So just the idea of going made her perk up a little bit.

Daddy said the minute Judy Garland filled up the screen, he felt a change in Mama, like the moment Dorothy opened the door in her black-and-white world and there was Oz in living color. He said Mama was happy again and whatever came with that was fine by him. The only problem was Mama didn't stay sweet and innocent like Dorothy Gale, she latched onto Judy Garland herself, and after Daddy died, she lived the Appalachian version of the tragic star's life to a *T*.

"I'm sorry, Zora. You don't have to answer that."

"I really don't know why Mama's that way; she can't sing a lick. Can't afford the pills, but she drinks like Judy, has the same luck with men."

The way I said it made Miss Cunningham laugh, which was

good because if she'd been quiet much longer I would have told her the truth. Mama's craziness was my fault.

Near Jocassee Gorge, we passed a scenic overlook I'd gone by a thousand times and hardly noticed. The mountains looked like a giant green goblet filled above the rim with blue sky and foamy clouds. Part of me ached to turn around and stay because I never loved them the way I should have. But they were always beautiful and wild and too much like Mama.

"People like your mom don't change, Zorie."

"And you're not mad at me for going to beauty school?"

"Stop. You're doing what's right for you, and that's enough for me."

Miss Cunningham had gone to some high-dollar college up north and had come to the mountain to teach girls like me high-school English and save us from ourselves. I remember she looked shocked, almost hurt when I told her I wasn't going to college. But how could I tell her about the last straw that sent me to her classroom before the bell rang?

So I told her I couldn't afford college. She wouldn't hear of that; I was smart, she'd said, and had a real chance to make something of myself. I just told her I needed to get away from Mama and be self-supporting as soon as possible and hoped she would understand. I knew she wanted to ask why, but I wouldn't have been able to put one word in front of the other. The image of coming home to find Mama wrapped around the boy I liked was still too raw.

But even that only made me talk about leaving. As bad as it was on my birthday when Mama walked through the door with Bob, looking back, he was the best present she could have given me.

We were almost out of the mountains, and I hadn't seen the first bluebird. I should have been nervous, but the truck was headed toward the Carolina coast. I had a government check in my pocket to pay for my schooling, and Miss Cunningham had found me a place to live for free until I got on my feet. I didn't need a bluebird to be happy. I tossed the acorn out the window and cranked the music up again.

Miss Cunningham smiled and nodded. She beat on the steering wheel in time to the music and belted out the lyrics, drawing out the words in that funny way Mick Jagger does. At least he has a way about his singing, even with that ugly face, that comes across as sexy. Between Miss Cunningham's thick New York accent and being tone deaf, she was just plain awful.

The closer we got to the coast, the flatter the land became. Without the mountains to compete with it, the cloudless sky seemed bigger, bluer. There wasn't a white pine or a scarlet oak in sight, but the palm trees were a real wonder. Even the air was different. Thick, almost musty, but pleasant. Dozens of billboards coaxed people to Myrtle Beach with advertisements for free nights at motels, restaurants where kids eat free, and a gift shop called the Gay Dolphin.

My heart beat like a record album played too fast. I wasn't pushing the river anymore, wasn't trying to save someone who didn't want to be saved, and it felt good. By the time we reached Davenport, the blanket of sadness I'd worn down the mountain left me, and I was excited about starting a new life.

Back home we didn't have a car, but in Davenport, it seemed everybody had two or three and drove them all at once. The town's main drag had its fair share of junk shops full of five-dollar T-shirts and outlet-quality beach towels, whatever those were. Liquor stores and party shops advertised their wares with huge black and yellow signs. Marquees on bars seemed to taunt the thirty-one flavors of churches on every street corner with promises of Drink and Drown night and wet T-shirt contests.

Miss Cunningham looked at me and smiled as we turned into the driveway of a neat old Victorian house with friendly gables and fancy white gingerbread. It looked like the kind of house you'd see in storybooks or on TV where the mothers lived for their children and baked cookies all day long.

"This is it, Zorie, your new home." She nodded toward the apartment over the stand-alone garage as we got out of the truck.

My legs acted like they'd forgotten how to walk on land with no pitch to it, so I stayed put while she knocked on the back door of the gingerbread house. When there was no answer, she tipped a clay pot full of sad-looking geraniums just enough to pull out a little brass key. For a second I was puzzled. Back home, folks didn't lock their doors, but the sight of that key dangling in front of me made my heart race and we sprinted up the stairs over the garage.

Both of us squealed and rushed into the main room. I spun around and plopped down on my very own couch while Miss Cunningham walked around the place checking things out. She pointed out the stain on the kitchen floor and how the threadbare couch should be the first thing to go. I nodded like I was taking notes in my head on how to make the apartment livable and pretended the apartment didn't make my homeplace look shabby.

"Oh, there's Winston now."

She pointed to a man in jeans and a faded blue shirt. He didn't seem to notice the truck sitting in his drive because he walked with his head down, like he was reading a book, but he wasn't.

"Winston." She grabbed my hand and we started back down the stairs.

He turned around to face us. The first time I saw a picture of Robert Redford, I gasped out loud because I never knew a man could look that good. When I looked at Winston Sawyer, I gasped on the inside and probably would have gotten down on my knees and worshiped him if my teacher hadn't been there.

He was beautiful, tall with broad shoulders. And that hair, thick and brown, long and dark, pulled back in a ponytail so that I could see his eyes. Sad blue eyes that would haunt me forever. At first I thought it was Winston's looks that charmed me so, but it was his own blanket of sadness—one that matched my own—that drew me to him.

"Hi, Lizzy." He smiled at Miss Cunningham like he had forgotten how.

I don't think she noticed he went rigid when she hugged him. She was too busy going on about people they'd gone to college with. When he didn't say much, she asked how his parents were and if he liked his job teaching freshman English at the junior college any better. His answers were short and didn't leave any room for discussion. Miss Cunningham, being like she is, tried even harder to draw him out. And I was beginning to feel invisible.

"Oh, God, I'm sorry. I'm terrible about introductions. Winston Sawyer, this is Zora Adams."

He let out a tired sigh and kept glancing at his wristwatch and then at his kitchen door. Finally, Miss Cunningham quit the small talk and went over the arrangement. I would cook dinner for Winston, and in return, I could stay in the garage apartment.

"You really don't have to do that." He talked to me but was looking toward the house.

"But I want to." I didn't think it was possible to sound even more desperate for him than I was.

A breeze kicked up, stirring the air between us. A piece of hair that was too short for his ponytail blew across his face. I imagined tucking it behind his ear. A jolt of electricity flashed through my center, and I could feel my face blushing hard.

"Okay, then. Here's some money for groceries. I get home around six; you can just leave the plate on the picnic table by the porch."

I nodded, thinking that if I could just find the right words to say, he would suddenly see me, all young and beautiful, and invite me into the gingerbread house to live happily ever after. Before I could get up the nerve, he excused himself and disappeared through the back door he'd been eyeing since Miss Cunningham introduced us.

While we unpacked, she reminded me at least ten times to look in on Winston.

"Cook for him, even if he tells you not to. And he loves lasagna but hates cheese."

I was too busy wondering how Miss Cunningham knew so much about Winston to worry about finding a recipe for cheese hater's lasagna.

"We lived together in college, but I was totally wrong for him. Not Emma. I remember when they met, they weren't aware of anything except each other."

I plopped down on the bed beside Miss Cunningham, wishing she'd noticed that same kind of reaction when Winston shook hands with me.

"What happened to her?"

"It was raining hard; there was a truck stalled on the highway. She didn't see it. She died instantly."

Died. Instantly. That's what the police had said about my daddy, like that was a comfort.

"At one time, I thought he might—" She looked at me and then fingered one of the baby blue nubs on the chenille bedspread. "Let's just say he was really depressed for about a year. But he's better now."

Her words planted a seed of hope in my heart, but my head knew the truth. When someone you love is snatched away from you the way his wife was from him, the way my daddy was from me, you never get over it.

"He still hasn't let anyone in the house. His only rule, and he was adamant." She kissed me on the forehead and held me close. "It's getting late. I have to go."

I nodded and promised myself I wouldn't cry.

"Do you have enough money?"

In my lifetime, there had never been enough money, so I was good at making do with next to nothing. I had a little over three hundred dollars to last me six months, a government grant for school, and Nana's ruby brooch I'd die before I pawned.

"Yes," I said. She raised her teacher eyebrows. "I'll be fine."

"I love you, Zorie. I hope you know that." She hugged me. Her smell was different from Mama's, faint, like store-bought perfume and lemons.

After she drove away I noticed a light on in the old Victorian house. The curtains were open in Winston's living room; he was sitting in an overstuffed chair with a glass in his hand. He tipped it up, stood, and went to a small table with several crystal bottles. He poured a drink, sat back down; a few minutes later, he was studying the bottom of the empty glass.

As much as I loved my daddy, I knew early on he was a funny, sweet drunk, but he was still a drunk. I remembered the feeling of his scruffy face on mine and the sweet smell of sour mash bourbon on his breath when he kissed me good night. I was sure all really good daddies were just like him.

I never asked him why he drank, and I didn't have to ask Winston to know why he did. I felt his pain all the way across the courtyard; his sadness rippled in the faint breeze that stirred the thick night air. I knew by the way he moved across the room that it wouldn't be long before he passed out. Somehow that didn't bother me the way it had when I'd helped Mama off of the bathroom floor or when Daddy had been resting his eyes for too long.

Winston took one long last look out the window. But not up at me. Even drunk, he was the most beautiful man I'd ever seen.

3

⁓

I woke up that next morning with Winston Sawyer on my mind
and started cleaning. I wiped down the countertops and cabinets
good. The steamy water full of pine cleaner cleared my head but
had a tough time cutting through years of greasy dirt on the hood
over the little stovetop. I flicked the switch on the fan back and
forth to see if it worked, but it didn't. Then I heard his car door
open. He started the engine up.

I used an old cloth with some scouring powder I found under
the sink. The thought of Winston with his hands on that steering
wheel made me scrub around the burners so hard that a little piece
of enamel about the size of a quarter rubbed off. I stood there fingering the spot, while his engine revved louder. When I peeked out
the window, he was raising the hood. I went over to the stove one
more time and wiped it down again like I was minding my own

business. Then I pulled some old pots out from the little drawer under the stove to keep busy.

I tried hard not to think of him bent over that little black sports car, with tools in his hands that would make it do what he wanted. God, I wished I'd had some sense and a little piece of steel wool that day. Maybe things would have been different.

I took a swig of sweet tea out of a glass I'd brought from home, marched myself into the bathroom, and scrubbed the toilet twice. The old tub was a sight with I-don't-know-what stuck in the drain: hair, dead bugs, dust, and dirt. A bunch of old *Glamour* magazines were stuffed in a basket; one was opened to the "Dos and Don'ts" page. I flipped through the May issue from four years ago and tried to twist my hair up like the model's on page fifty-three, but it didn't look good.

I took an armload of those magazines into the living room and arranged them on the coffee table by the couch before I started on the tub. After a while, the bathroom looked nice, except the floor looked like the toilet had overflowed at one time. A piece of the linoleum was torn off, and there were wavy lines in the exposed plywood. I got down on my hands and knees to see if it was as bad as it looked, thinking maybe I could find a little secondhand chenille rug to cover it up, maybe a blue one to match the walls that looked like they might once have been the color of robins' eggs.

It was hot for early June. Between cleaning and getting myself all revved up over Winston, I was tired. I turned my face in the direction of the box fan wedged in the bedroom window, and closed my eyes. The breeze blew across my face and ruffled about under my shirt.

When I opened my eyes, I noticed a box hidden under the bed. It wasn't a pasteboard box like you might store winter clothes in when you were sure spring had finally arrived. It was crimson with fancy gold letters across the top that were slick to the touch.

I don't know how I knew it was Winston's wife's, I just did. I also knew it wasn't right to even think about looking inside, but I couldn't help myself. So I closed my front door that was propped open to air out the musty old place and pulled down the shade on my solitary window before curiosity killed me.

The box was from a little shop in town called Serendipity. There was a layer of dust on the top of it, and not thinking that I'd just spent all morning cleaning, I blew the dust into the air. My nose stung like someone had swatted me. I sneezed twice and got on with my plundering.

The box opened easily, like Pandora's must have. The receipt was on top of the prettiest dress I have ever seen. I have to say I felt guilty going through a dead woman's things, but that didn't stop me from taking the dress into the bathroom and locking the door. I'd never touched silk before that day. I drew it up to slide my arms in and let the slippery fabric ripple over my body. The dress was the color of the sky at sunset, a perfect fit that felt like a whisper across my body.

I looked in the tiny medicine chest mirror, but not in the primpy sort of way I had earlier. It was more like the fearful expressions of those bwanas in the old Tarzan movies when the jungle drums suddenly stopped beating. I took that dress off, wadded it up in a ball, and sat on the toilet in my underwear.

After a while, I folded the dress up and put everything back the way I found it. The receipt had fallen into the bottom of the box.

$194.56. Even today that would be a lot of money to pay for a dress, but in 1982 it was a fortune. Before I was done cleaning, I found several more boxes from other stores, all full of pretty things Emma had bought and squirreled away for herself.

I left everything where I found it. I'd caused myself enough trouble just by trying on that dress. But I did step out for a little while and walked to a hole-in-the-wall of a grocery store on Main Street. Along the way, I passed three of the shops Emma liked to frequent and felt myself blush hard, like somebody might look at me and know what I'd done. Some boys about my age were sitting outside the pool hall. One of them whistled at me, trying to turn my head, but I'd seen their type with their smokes in their T-shirt pockets, looking like they hadn't bathed in a week, and just walked on.

I had twenty dollars in my pocket but didn't buy anything more than a little boiled ham and some loaf bread. Tomatoes were too high to touch, so I settled for a small jar of mayonnaise, figuring that when times were tough, I could just eat mayonnaise sandwiches. I spent a little over nine dollars of my own, so I splurged and bought myself a Coke.

I put the groceries away after lunch, rinsed off my plate, and dried it with a little checkered dishrag from home. I tried to put it on the top shelf of the cupboard but it wouldn't go. I tried again, shoving it so hard it's a wonder it didn't break; finally I climbed up on the counter to see what the problem was. Another hidden treasure. Now I did hesitate with this one because it was wrapped.

I took the box down carefully. It was small, no bigger than my hand, maybe three or four inches deep. The wrapping paper had sweet peas on it, pink and blue ones intertwined, making little hearts as they met. The Scotch tape had yellowed and looked like it might come undone if it wasn't handled just right. I sat there, turned it from side to side, shook it a little, and listened to the odd sound it made.

All at once, my senses came about me, and I threw that little box of Emma's into the silverware drawer. I slammed that drawer shut and sat down at the kitchen table, red-faced with shame. Still, I tried to fool the side of me that wasn't too far gone by saying there was no harm in taking a little peek inside. Then I thought about Mama and how pathetic she was over the men in her life. I was a part of her. As much as I hated the fact, her weakness made me look at right and wrong like they were identical twins I couldn't tell apart.

I opened that drawer three or four times, then slammed it shut. Once I nearly slammed my hand in the drawer. I was sure that was Nana speaking to me from the dead. I could just see her and Winston's wife, Emma, perched on the same cloud.

Nana would shake her head while she pleaded my case. "You know, Zora really is a good girl."

"Well, she must not be too good. She tried on my new dress, and look at her now. She's thinking about opening my present."

4

According to the brochure, beauty school was supposed to be "The Beginning of an Exciting Career That Will Last a Lifetime." But the first thing that caught my eye when I walked through the front door of the Davenport School of Beauty was a sign on slick white poster board beside the cash register. A bubble over a pair of legs said, NO MORE THAN THREE ABOVE THE KNEE. Looking down at my uniform, I didn't need a ruler to tell me that I was out of line.

I pulled at the sides of my uniform, trying to lengthen the hem like a lot of the other students. I could just picture us all after school let out, sitting around our respective homes with scissors, big red tomato pincushions, and spools of white thread scattered about, undoing our hemlines.

Nobody looked anything like the proud, confident blonde on the cover of the brochure, except for one girl. She was the only one not worrying her dress. Hers was an inch or two below the knee and had a sassy little slit up the back. From the neck up, she looked like a movie star, and the way she carried herself made you forget that she could probably afford to lose fifty or sixty pounds.

As attendance was called, we were supposed to introduce ourselves. Some of the girls stammered or giggled. My own voice came out just above a whisper, but the big girl spoke in a deep, sexy drawl with a proud confidence that every single girl in the room coveted. We looked at Sara Jane Farquhar in awe, and there wasn't a single soul in that room, even our instructor, who didn't want to be her.

"Now, ladies, I am Mrs. Cathcart, your instructor here at the Davenport School of Beauty. I'd like to welcome you, the winter class of 1983." She paused, waiting for us to applaud ourselves. When we didn't, she did, and we all joined in. "As students, you'll learn the art of fixing hair over the next six months. Along with the latest fashion trends, you will master vital skills like pin curls and finger waves. And though perms and color will be your bread and butter, if you can learn to do an upsweep, you can make a fortune these days.

"Class, if you can give a woman a good hairdo, she will crawl to you on her deathbed for you to fix her hair. A woman whose hair has been properly colored is a customer for life. Let me assure all of you, there is great honor in making a woman in your charge look and feel beautiful. This is indeed one of life's highest callings."

We stood there applauding for all we were worth, completely mesmerized by Mrs. Cathcart's address to the class of 1983. I looked around the room. There were twenty-three of us. One girl was crying. Later on, when she dropped out, Mrs. Cathcart would say she was called elsewhere.

After the applause ended, Mrs. Cathcart led us past the area with all of the dryers and shampoo bowls to a large room in the back that was both storage room and our classroom. Each workstation had a faceless mannequin head with glossy black hair. All of them were identical, except one or two looked newer than the others.

Most everyone leafed through the blue clothbound textbook at each station, except for the crying girl. She ran her hand over the top of *Cosmetology Today* and started to cry again. She bawled at the drop of a hat, every day. I think it must have had something to do with her being pregnant, although I don't think she knew she was at the time.

Sara Jane Farquhar leafed through her book, and then shoved it onto the little shelf under the top of her workstation. She looked at Mrs. Cathcart like she already knew it cover to cover and was ready to go to work. Mrs. Cathcart gave Sara Jane a dirty look and told everyone to open her text to page one.

All of Mrs. Cathcart's lessons were drawn out on the back of old maps, the kind teachers pull down like window shades. They were yellow and torn in a couple of places, but when she pointed her yardstick to "Cosmetology, an Introduction" and started teaching, it was clear that she was a very good teacher.

I was the only one who took notes; I may have been the only girl there who knew how to take notes. Mrs. Cathcart liked that. She smiled and nodded at me every time I recognized something important and wrote it down. She went on for at least two hours before she told us we could have a break. There was a rush for the

Coke machine, which by the time I got there only took exact change.

"You need dimes?"

I looked up and saw Sara Jane Farquhar smiling at me with a Coca-Cola in her hand. "Thanks." I handed her my quarter, but she gave it right back.

"Keep it. I always have change."

"Thanks. I'm Zora."

"I'm Sara Jane Farquhar," she said, the way Marilyn Monroe might have introduced herself. Sara Jane wasn't putting on; that was just the way she talked. "So what do you think about all this?"

"I'm excited and a little nervous, how about you?"

A group of girls were huddled together listening to a bony girl with a bad perm mimic Mrs. Cathcart's speech to us. All of them kept cutting their eyes around to make sure she didn't come around the corner and catch them.

"They shouldn't be making fun of her," I said.

Sara Jane nodded. "The joke's on them. Everything Mrs. Cathcart said was right."

"She's sweet, but don't you think she's a little overly dramatic?"

"Maybe, but women come to a stylist because they want to feel beautiful. Even if it's just for that one hour they sit in your chair, even if their hair looks like hell the next morning. For an hour, they had the undivided attention of someone focused on making them beautiful. They don't get that in real life unless they give it to themselves, and a lot of women just seem to give up on that." Sara Jane took a swig of her Coke. "But I don't have to tell you that. You've been to a stylist; you know what I'm talking about."

I nodded, and hoped she couldn't see my embarrassment. I'd never been to a beauty salon, never had anybody cut my hair but Mama and Nana. I didn't have a clue as to what she was talking about, but I believed every word Sara Jane Farquhar said.

"So, where do you live?"

"Just off Main in a little apartment on Beckett Street."

"You're lucky to have your own place. I live with my parents."

Mama had embarrassed me so many times when prospective friends came over, the thought of inviting someone like Sara Jane Farquhar to my apartment made me nauseous. But after two days in Davenport, I was lonely, and gawking over Winston Sawyer hadn't helped any.

"Do you want to come over today—after class?"

"Sure." Sara Jane smiled, and pushed one of her perfectly bleached blond tresses off of her face. "That would be fun."

I explained the arrangement I had with *the owner*, not mentioning my growing obsession for Winston, and she said that was fine by her. She would keep me company while I cooked. She also showed me how to pour salted peanuts into my Coke bottle during one of our breaks. She said it was a good, quick snack because you could eat and drink at the same time. The salty and sweet tasted good to me, but I almost choked the first time I tried it.

It's funny how neither of us ever really said anything about being best friends that day, the way you might on the first day of grade school, but after two fifteen-minute breaks and a lunch together, we just were.

After school, we went across the street to her parents' store so I could buy groceries to cook for Winston. The minute we walked through the door, Sara Jane started stuffing all kinds of things into her great big shoulder bag that was about the size of a pillowcase. The people in the store saw her but didn't say anything. I nearly died when she shoved two big T-bone steaks in there, and then called out to me from the opposite end of the aisle. "Zora, I think I need a cart for all this stuff. By the way, do you have a grill?"

I could feel my face turn red as I shook my head and ducked behind the Wise Potato Chip display on the bread aisle. Sara Jane's parents owned the store, but she took so much stuff, I just knew the police would be there any minute to haul me away as her accomplice.

Then, lo and behold, Sara Jane came around the corner with a big box perched on top of the cart that said "Hibachi" in huge black letters and asked me to pick up a ten-pound bag of charcoal and some lighter fluid there at the end of aisle six. Winston had only given me fifty dollars. My bill came to $27.74, including tax.

Sara Jane's cart was so full, I quit worrying about her shoplifting and started worrying about what in the world I was going to do if she expected me to help pay for her stuff, too. But Sara Jane Farquhar didn't even go through the checkout line. She flirted with the bag boys as they packed up her stolen goods and nearly gave me a heart attack when she asked the off-duty police officer to drive us to my place. I had never met anybody like Sara Jane Farquhar before in my life.

I felt guilty that we brought home at least a hundred dollars' worth of groceries. I guess Sara Jane knew this because while I was finishing up supper, she told me not to worry one bit, that it was just a little advance thank-you present for letting her hang around my apartment.

"Yes, but I only spent a little more than half of what Winston gave me to buy groceries."

She cocked her pretty head to the side and put her hands on her hips.

"Who in the hell is Winston?"

Well, it was almost like he drove up in the yard on cue, and for the first time that day, other than when Mrs. Cathcart was talking, Sara Jane Farquhar was speechless.

"His wife died in a car wreck. It's really sad." Both of us stared out the window and watched him disappear into the house.

"Oh, my God, it sounds just like *Passion Heals the Lonely Heart*."

"What?"

"*Passion Heals the Lonely Heart*, by Gussie Foyette. You don't read her books?"

"No."

She looked at me like I had just asked her to suck eggs.

"I read a lot when I was in school, not romance. My English teacher loved Shakespeare. Oh, and Hemingway. She loved him, too."

"Does Hemingway write romance?"

"Some, but not the kind—"

"Well, I didn't think so. I've read just about every romance written in the last five years, not to mention everything Gussie Foyette's ever written. I can't believe you've wasted your time reading those guys when you could have been reading Gussie Foyette.

"Anyway, what I was saying is that this situation has *Passion* written all over it. You got yourself the gorgeous grieving hunk of man, Trevor Waynewright. That would be the owner. Then there's the beautiful young woman fate sent his way, Angelina Bouvier.

That would be you." I smiled and could feel myself blushing. "It's all right here, plain as day. You got your estate in the English countryside there, your old Victorian mansion here in Davenport. If you take out the indentured servants, the horse-drawn carriages, and the bastard son by Trevor's chambermaid, it's the exact same story."

5

~

The white princess telephone by the bedside table never rang unless Sara Jane called to say she was coming over. But it was there, right beside the alarm clock, reminding me every morning that I should call Mama. I'd tried to ignore it for almost a whole week. Twice I picked it up and dialed her number, then put it back on the cradle before it rang. I was sick to death of being tormented by that old telephone first thing every morning, so I finally picked up the receiver and called home.

The line crackled with the tension, or maybe it was just because the princess phone was old. The boulder that was in my stomach the day I left the mountain was replaced by butterflies having a knock-down-drag-out. I trembled hard, holding the telephone with both hands. It rang maybe a dozen times. Somebody picked up but didn't say anything.

"Mama?"

I could hear Judy Garland in the background singing "Me and My Shadow." The song was from her *Alone* album and was meant to be more playful than sad, but the way Mama had it cranked up made it sound staticky and morbid. She'd probably put it on the record player the morning I left and had kept it on, just waiting for me to call.

"Mama, I can hear you breathing." Still no answer. "Okay then, I just wanted to call and tell you I'm okay and—"

She slammed the receiver down like she was using it to kill bugs, lots of them, and then the connection was lost. Since she wasn't standing in front of me with those great big Judy Garland eyes, I was surprised at how much I didn't hurt, how easy it was to just tell myself Mama was bat-shit crazy and wasn't worth the worry.

I propped the door to my place wide open. It was six thirty and already hot. The window beside my bed stayed open all the time because the window unit in the living room only pretended to be an air conditioner. Every time I turned that thing on, it made a god-awful noise, but I never complained to Winston about it. It would have been the perfect opportunity to see him up close, hear his voice again. Maybe present myself as a living sacrifice. But that wasn't what I had in mind for our first real conversation.

I heard the screen door to his kitchen open. It sounded like an old cat whose tail had been stepped on and would have kept right good time with the window unit when it was running. I sprinted back to my bed and peered through lace curtains that moved about in the breeze just enough for me to see him sitting there in an old swing, drinking coffee. His arm was draped over the back of the swing; I smiled as I imagined myself there beside him, tucked up under his arm with my head pressed against his chest. I could see his face, not real good, but good enough to know he was just hungover and drinking coffee.

After a few minutes, he put the cup on the ground. A fat bumblebee flew by him several times, but I don't think he noticed. He just stared at the cup for the longest time and then put his face in his hands. A while later he looked at his watch and trudged back into the house like an old man. I saw him go upstairs. The shades were up in his bedroom, which was unusual. He took some clothes out of a drawer and went into the bathroom.

I lay back down, dizzy from the thought of Winston naked in the shower with water rippling over his lean body. I closed my eyes, exhausted from wanting him. How many times had I reminded Mama how dangerous it was to fawn over a man, even more dangerous if he were to actually take notice.

I heard the screen door open again. I saw Winston turn and lock the kitchen door. He shifted some books around in his arms, opened the car door, and slid into the seat of his little sports car. With one great puff, the morning breeze suspended the curtains in the air so that if he had been looking at my room he would have seen me. I ducked down in the bed like I hadn't been spying on him and lay there with the covers pulled up to my chin and my heart racing the way it did every morning with his engine.

I'd spent so much time spying on Winston, I only had ten minutes to get ready for school. I knew I'd get the eye from Mrs. Cathcart. Everybody did when they came to school without fixing their hair or doing their makeup just right. The crying girl always got the eye, which made her cry even harder. Sara Jane and I were the only ones who didn't make fun of her, but we did roll our eyes at each other sometimes when we heard that pitiful little wail before she cut loose.

I tried to slip into my workstation unnoticed, but that was impossible. I was grateful Mrs. Cathcart didn't call me out. Then she started up again. "Remember, class, tardiness is one of the seven deadly sins of cosmetology. Your clients will not tolerate it for long, and neither will I."

Dolly, Mrs. Cathcart's German shepherd, came wandering back to our classroom for a dog biscuit. Mrs. Cathcart kept them in a glass Barbasol container, the kind you pour that blue stuff in to sterilize combs, but Mrs. Cathcart was too busy lecturing me and the rest of the class on the other six deadly sins to tend to Dolly. Poor Dolly went and laid her head in the crying girl's lap. The crying girl hadn't cried all morning, but the minute Dolly looked up at her with those sad old eyes, the dam broke.

The girl cried and Dolly cried; only Dolly quit when Mrs. Cathcart gave her a biscuit. Mrs. Cathcart must have felt sorry for that girl because she was always trying to help her, but the crying girl needed more help than Mrs. Cathcart could give.

We'd been in school about three weeks and had not touched a human head of hair. Mrs. Cathcart said after four weeks of studying, she would let us shampoo some of the customers when the girls in the class ahead of us got backed up. Every day was spent practicing on faceless, black-haired mannequins, doing pin curls, updos, and spit curls. I was horrible at spit curls, but not Sara Jane Farquhar. She could do anything with hair.

Mrs. Cathcart had the best-looking mannequin head. She

named it Dolly, after her beloved, who spent her days sleeping under the seat of any one of the hair dryers that happened to be on. Mrs. Cathcart loved to run her hands through Dolly's artificial hair and demonstrate techniques we all knew we would never do in a real salon. Things like upsweeps that had gone by the wayside ten years ago but would still be a part of our exam. Most every day Mrs. Cathcart got flustered. Before she could finish her long and involved how-to explanation, Sara Jane had done the drill on her ratty old mannequin and had done it better than Mrs. Cathcart.

One of my high-school teachers told us about little a boy, maybe eleven or twelve years old, who was enrolled at Duke University. She explained to us that the little boy was a prodigy, and that's exactly what Sara Jane Farquhar was like when it came to hair.

I don't think Mrs. Cathcart knew what to make of Sara Jane. I could see a part of her was proud Sara Jane could do the mannequin drills faster and better than her own example. Still, you could tell she was jealous. Mrs. Cathcart liked helping us, especially when we got flustered. Whenever she walked by Sara Jane's mannequin, she just nodded and smiled a phony smile that said, I'll stump you yet, Sara Jane Farquhar.

We'd taken our first written test from our ratty blue textbooks. I was pretty sure I had done well. When Mrs. Cathcart laid my paper facedown in front of me, she said, "You did a fine job, Zora."

I turned the paper over. She had circled 100 in red in a way that made it look like a happy face. I blushed and looked over at Sara Jane. She rolled her eyes at me and showed me her paper. Mrs. Cathcart had written STUDY across the top in big letters, under that a 27 was circled in the same gaudy red ink.

"What happened, Sara Jane?" I asked during our break.

"With what?" she answered. "That test? I can't pass a test to save my soul. Shoot, it took me six tries just to get my GED, and I don't think I passed. I just wore them down."

"I'll help you study."

Nina Price, otherwise known as the crying girl, and a few others who didn't do well on the test were huddled in a corner of the canteen. Some of them cried right along with Nina. In contrast, Sara Jane stood there with her perfectly colored blond hair drawn up in a loose bun on top of her head and little golden tresses hanging down around her gorgeous face. From the neck up, she looked like one of the heroines on the cover of a Gussie Foyette romance. And she wasn't the least little bit concerned about grades.

"I won't pass." She shrugged off the words with a thin smile.

"You have to, Sara Jane. I'll help you; my God, you're so talented. You can do anything with hair, even better than Mrs. Cathcart."

"I know I'm good at hair, but I can't remember much of anything after I read it, especially the names of muscle tissue or nerves in the human head."

"But you're so good at this."

"I'm not good at the books. Shoot, the stock boys and the guys in the meat market across the street are betting on how many weeks I'll last. The big money is on six weeks. I'm really trying to make it past then just so daddy's new stock boy will win. He bet I'd make it all the way. He didn't know any better."

Sara Jane Farquhar read every romance novel she could get her hands on. Heaving breasts and throbbing loins engrossed her so much that at first I just laughed it off. But it was sad that she could remember the tiniest details from books Nana Adams would have rightfully called smut, but she couldn't retain one word from a textbook.

"Sara Jane, if you don't mind me asking, why are you here if you know you aren't going to pass?"

"I wanted to do something; Mama knew I had a knack for fixing hair and thought it would be a good idea. She knows I won't pass, either. I got it from my daddy, whatever it is that makes me so I can't learn. Grandmamma let him drop out of school when he was in the eighth grade."

"I'll help you study. Every day. Please, Sara Jane."

She smiled at me and brushed one of the wispy curls that dangled seductively near her green cat eyes. "Sure we will. We'll have a real good time."

The sound of Winston's car in the driveway surprised me. Sara Jane and I had been studying so hard for the next exam, I'd completely forgotten to cook his dinner. The two of us rushed to my bedroom window and watched him get out of the car. He didn't even stop at the picnic table to see if there was a Styrofoam plate covered in tinfoil. He just went straight in the house to the living room and poured himself a drink.

"Oh, Zora, he's got something heavy on his mind."

I'd not missed a single day setting that hot plate on that stupid picnic table. I'd set it in the same place so often that the heat from the plate had made a permanent mark on the redwood table. I couldn't believe Winston didn't care his dinner wasn't waiting for him. I felt like someone had kicked me in the stomach. At the very least, it should have occurred to him to come check on me to see if something horrible had happened to me.

Sara Jane got up, went to my little refrigerator, and moved things around until she found a bottle of Boone's Farm Apple Wine she had actually bought at another grocery store across town because her parents were Baptists and didn't believe in drinking alcohol much less selling it. She poured mine in a Bama jelly glass and hers in my only teacup. "You drink and I'll talk." She took a big gulp of wine. "I'm going to tell you about Preston Hensley."

I nodded and sat down on the couch. It was impossible not to smile when Sara Jane gave me that little smirk. I was still dazed and wounded, but she had a way about her that made me lay down my cross for the moment.

"When I was four days shy of sixteen, Preston Hensley set his sights on me. He was the preacher's son, but he wasn't what you'd call devout. Now, he was at church every time the doors opened and nobody ever had to prod him. He wasn't there for the preaching, though. He was looking for virgins.

"He'd charm their mamas into letting them go out with him, then he'd charm the panties off of each and every one of them. I knew of at least a dozen girls who knew Preston Hensley. Some were in the Girls' Auxiliary, some in the choir, and one was a visiting missionary's daughter."

"No."

"Oh, honey, he was Beau Paramour all over, you know, from *Harvest of Passion*, that first Gussie book I gave you to read. Anyway, when we started dating I was determined I wasn't going to be an easy conquest.

"The more he flirted and teased, the more I flirted and teased right back, but I never let him do anything. Now this really drove him crazy because I think he just smiled at those other girls, and their legs parted like the Red Sea. He wanted me so bad, and I toyed with him until he couldn't stand it anymore. I didn't have the first clue as to what I was doing, but it sure was fun watching him pitch the tent in his pants and then sending him home."

"Sara Jane." My face blushed on and off like a stoplight.

She took another swig of wine, and there was a long pause for effect.

"Wait a minute."

"What?"

"If I tell you my story, you have to tell me yours."

"I don't have a story."

"Come on, Zora. Every girl has a story, especially one as pretty as you."

"Really, I don't."

My face was hot with shame, but not from Sara Jane's question. The only stories I could ever let myself tell were about dodging the advances of Mama's boyfriends who'd had too much to drink. I couldn't even look at her, and I prayed she couldn't look at me and know my secrets.

"Listen up now." She lifted my chin with those soft round hands of hers and smiled at me. "This story's so good, I'll tell it anyway. Like I said, Preston was determined to conquer me, and I was getting bored with him. So one night, a Tuesday night when nobody was at church, he took me to the nursery. We sat in the dark with just the moonlight coming through the windows. We whispered and giggled, played with those Fisher-Price trucks, rolling them around our bodies until he couldn't take it anymore. The moon was just right. I could see his face. He wasn't playing anymore."

She poured us both another glass of wine, sat down, and pulled her feet up under her as best she could. "He took the mattresses out of the cribs and laid them on the floor. Then, he knelt down, took my hand, and I knelt, too. He unbuttoned my blouse while he kissed me on the lips the way they do on TV when you hear that saxophone music in the background. He unhooked my bra, but I didn't stop him like I had before. I think I was as ready as he was.

"I reached to unbutton his shirt, but he backed away a little so that he was just out of reach. Then he read the most beautiful poem I've ever heard. I still have it. I even memorized it." She sat a little straighter and began to recite:

> *Who is this that appears like the dawn, fair as the moon, bright as the sun, majestic as the stars in procession? It is my lover. How beautiful you are and how pleasing, my love. I pray you will let your lover come into your garden and taste its choice fruits.*

"Well, that was all it took. We rolled around on that little bed exploring each other, and then he slipped it in, real gentle-like. Poor thing had been worked up for so long that he came in about a half second."

I laughed hysterically. Sara Jane laughed, too.

"Was it really that funny?" She was trying to catch her breath.

"No. Sara Jane, he was quoting the Bible."

"No."

"I'm pretty sure it's from Song of Solomon." I wiped tears away.

The first time my Nana showed me the family Bible, I was maybe twelve years old. I found that chapter right off. We weren't much for going to church, but I read that whole book and wondered what in the world was going on at that Bible-thumping church down the mountain.

"So, whatever happened to Preston Hensley?"

"He was big on the rhythm method; since his daddy was a preacher, I think he was afraid to go to a store to buy rubbers. Anyway, his parents got word that the missionary girl was pregnant, so Preston did right by her. Last I heard they were living in Africa with her parents and Preston was taking a correspondence course from some seminary in Mississippi. They had a little boy and there's another baby on the way."

We finished off the wine and opened another bottle. Between my tipsiness and Sara Jane's nonchalance over the loss of her own virtue, I forgot that it didn't matter to Winston whether I lived or died. After Sara Jane left, I'd catch myself smiling over some silly little thing she had said or done or how strong she was inside herself. I loved whatever it was inside her that always made her take over when I was hurting and make things better.

6

The only head of hair I'd worked on, other than that pitiful mannequin's, was my own. Students who'd graduated with the June class but hadn't found jobs yet worked on any customer that came into the school. We were all envious even though none of us, other than Sara Jane, actually knew enough to work on a human head. Besides, it helped those girls who hadn't found a job yet to get a jump on their apprenticeship.

Prudence Smart, a girl in our class who was neither prudent nor smart, didn't know what an apprenticeship was. Irene Styles, a bony little thing with a smart mouth, piped up and told everybody it was working for nothing, which wasn't true at all. It was closer to working for next to nothing.

Whenever Mrs. Cathcart noticed one of us looking a little jealous of those apprentices, she would remind us that they would be gone by the time we were ready for real patrons. But you can only work on a fake head of nylon hair for so long before you start resenting the girls with living, breathing customers.

The First Baptist Church sponsored a ministry at the local nursing home, and as chairman of the Outreach Committee, Mrs. Cathcart decided it would be charitable to provide the willing elderly with our services. Some of us went every Wednesday for about a month until we got a little clientele going. It worked out well for everybody because the school was closed on Wednesdays anyway in recognition of midweek prayer services at most of the churches in town. Everybody was thrilled at the prospect of having real live customers to work on, although they weren't paying ones. And it was good for those lonely old ladies to have somebody to fuss over them, even if it was just for a wash and set.

I remember that first day when those twelve elderly ladies toddled into the cafeteria just after breakfast. Two more were wheeled in by nurses' aides and one of them had an old baby doll sitting in her lap. As luck would have it, the crying girl got her. She took one look at that baby and started crying. Mrs. Cathcart tried to calm her down, but the crying girl told Mrs. Cathcart she was pregnant. It was the last time any of us ever saw her in uniform.

You'd think that after all of our complaining and chomping at the bit, every single one of us who stood over those wet silver heads would have known exactly where to begin, but we didn't. Sara Jane, on the other hand, had already sectioned off her lady's hair and was just chatting away like she had done this every day of her life.

"Well?" the old lady assigned to me snapped. "Are you gonna fix me up or what? I can't sit here like this; I'll catch my death."

"I'm sorry."

"I'll just bet Harold sent you here, didn't he? I know he would just love to see me six feet under, the little S-H-I-T."

"Honest, Mrs. Ethyl, I don't know any Harold. I'm just here to fix your hair. I'm Zora Adams. Remember? I'm here with Mrs. Cathcart from the First Baptist Church."

"Damn Baptists." I put a clip in a section of her hair and looked up to see if Mrs. Cathcart had heard her blasphemy. "My first husband was a Baptist, you know. What a cockeyed religion. I wish somebody would tell me just what they think they're doing during those altar calls. Whispering their sins in that old reverend's ear, and all the while he's nodding his head up and down. What does that mean? At least we Catholics have the decency to confess our sins in a dark little box, the way God intended."

I pulled another section of thin, wet hair up straight between my fingers and grabbed a roller off of the tray. Before I could roll it up, Ethyl would turn around to fuss about one thing and then another and it would slip out of my fingers. Mrs. Cathcart tried to distract the old bat by showing her a little Christian love and compassion, which made the little pulse on my teacher's forehead go crazy.

"How are you today, Mrs. Ethyl? God loves you and I love you."

Ethyl just looked at Mrs. Cathcart and stuck out her tongue.

"Humph. She looks just like my daughter, Lytle. Greedy little bitch. Walked around my house for years saying, 'When you're gone I want that, and that, and that,'" she said in a squeaky falsetto. She pointed to Mrs. Cathcart. "Get out of here."

Mrs. Cathcart wheeled around and stomped off. Ethyl was right pleased with herself and settled down enough so that I could try to finish rolling her hair. This was next to impossible because Ethyl talked with her head and I couldn't hold on to the section of hair long enough to get it on a curler. The woman didn't know how to be still, so I just did the best I could. Mrs. Cathcart stared at me from across the room with her Joan of Arc smile, rubbing her throbbing forehead.

Two of the women, who were sisters, sat side by side at the cafeteria tables holding hands, completely unaware Toni and Deana were working on their hair. They were old and thin with the brightest eyes, chatting about all sorts of things like school and whether they would go to the swimming hole that day. One of them confessed that she had stolen two eggs that morning and sold them for candy money when the rolling store came around. The other one said that she knew, that she had found the candy hidden under the house.

"The rats and bugs got it, Lottie. I'm so sorry."

"I sure hope they finish it before Mama finds it," Lottie said, and they both laughed so hard, it made the girls fixing their hair fuss.

Clara was assigned the only black woman in the group. Twice she walked across the room to talk to Mrs. Cathcart before she returned to her patron. I could tell by the look on her face she didn't want to touch the woman's hair, so I excused myself from Ethyl and told Mrs. Cathcart I would trade with the girl. But Clara had heard Ethyl carrying on, and she didn't want to have anything to do with her, either.

I finished rolling Ethyl's hair and had her under the hair dryer when I noticed Clara still hadn't gotten started. That sweet old woman sat there with a smile on her face waiting for Clara to begin.

"I'm Zora Adams. We're all so new at this. Do you mind if I help Clara?"

"Why, thank you. That would be real nice. My name is Pensacola Brown."

I was glad Mrs. Brown wasn't sitting in front of a mirror as I towel dried her hair. I would have died if she had seen the look on Clara's face when she finally put her hands in that hair. She looked at me with the most surprised look on her face and mouthed, "It's so soft."

"You have nice hair, Mrs. Brown."

"Thank you, Zora. I try to keep it up, and my daughter helps me sometimes. You know, I worked at the governor's mansion for thirty-three years. You had to look real neat every day."

"The governor's mansion." Mrs. Brown had Clara's full attention.

"Down in Columbia, but my daughter lives here in Davenport. She's the only black female lawyer in town. I'm so proud of her. You know she brought me here so she could keep an eye on me. I'm telling you, this place costs her a fortune, but she says it's worth it all to be near me. And I'm so glad to be near my grandchildren."

Clara rolled the first lock of hair on pink sponge rollers. "Did you ever see anybody famous at the mansion?"

"I saw Jimmy Carter. Got my picture taken with him. It's in my room. Would you like to see it?"

"No, I mean somebody really famous."

Mrs. Brown looked at Clara, but she was the kind of lady who wouldn't chastise anybody, no matter how rude or ignorant they were. I guess she got a lot of practice with that at the governor's mansion.

Clara seemed to have lost her fear of Pensacola Brown's hair, so I went over to check on Ethyl. She was sleeping hard with her head leaned against the front of the hood and her mouth wide open, snoring above the roar of the dryer.

Sara Jane came over with two cold Coca-Colas. "For God's sake, don't wake her up."

"You heard?"

"Most of it. She's a stitch."

Clara strolled over, popping her gum with the most satisfied look on her face. "I can't believe I'm the one who got the colored woman. Didn't think I could touch her hair, but I did it. It's so soft. Not at all like I thought it would be. And no head lice . . ."

"Clara."

"Zora, my mama told me their hair is just like a Brillo pad, and that they all have head lice. Right before I touched it, and you made me do it, Zora, you know you did, I thought I was going to die. But it wasn't so bad."

"Hair is hair." When Sara Jane Farquhar made a statement like that, people like Clara just shut up altogether.

"Are you gonna leave me here the whole damn day? I got a date, you know. Good God, I can't see Raymond looking like this." Ethyl started pulling the curlers out of her hair.

I rushed over to her and carefully unwrapped the rest of them. "I'll have you ready for your date in no time, Mrs. Ethyl."

Her hair was thinning badly on top so I teased it a little and smoothed it over the nearly bald spot. I thought her hair looked nice. After I sprayed it good, I handed her a mirror.

"I don't know why I bother with you bunch of know-nothings." She ripped off the cape and slammed the mirror down on the table. "Looks like hell." She hoisted herself up and stormed out of the room.

"It's a circus." Mrs. Cathcart patted me on the shoulder. "With its own wild creatures and funny smells. But we do it for the Lord, Zora."

I wasn't upset. After meeting Ethyl, I didn't think she was the kind to rave over her hairdo anyway, but the rest of those old souls seemed really grateful. They hugged the girls and carried on so about hair that looked like beginners did it, except for Sara Jane's lady, who looked like she'd stepped out of the senior edition of *Vogue* magazine.

Even by mountain standards, the beauty-school clientele wasn't high class; haircuts were only three dollars. Customers were allowed to tip, but hardly anybody did. Sometimes customers came in drunk or high. One lady even came in to escape the locusts that she imagined were everywhere. But after two or three trips to the nursing home, nobody ever complained about the customers that walked in off the street.

7

⁓

Love is a strange bird, lighting wherever it pleases, sometimes like a skittish little wren, sometimes like a bold red-tailed hawk. Winston's love must have been like one of those Canadian geese that choose to wander the world alone after they lose their mate. My feelings for him were more of the wren variety, stealing glimpses of him through lace curtains. Trying to say "I love you" with pot roast alongside creamed potatoes and scratch biscuits, instead of simple words.

I remember the day that red-tailed hawk swooped down and ensnared Sara Jane's heart. She'd had lots of experience with men, but I don't think she'd ever really been in love before. She dated a lot, but no one could ever measure up to the heroes she swooned over, guys with names like Lance and Derrick who lived between the pages of dime-store romances.

She was completely unaware when Jimmy Alvarez drove into

the yard where we were lying in the sun. I glanced up and saw him get out of his truck. He was the complete opposite of Winston—short, muscular, sun-darkened skin. He rolled the lawn mower off the back of the truck, nodded politely my way but didn't smile. When he yanked the pull cord, the mower started right up and that was when Sara Jane rolled over to see where the commotion was coming from.

"Who is he?" She watched Jimmy push the mower around the corner of the house.

"I don't know. I've never seen him before, but I did hear one of the neighbors say something to Winston about the yard last week, said it was an eyesore. I guess he's hired somebody to cut the grass."

"Somebody?"

"Well, I guess he's the yardman, Sara Jane." I rolled over onto my stomach. "Rub some oil on me, please, and don't forget to shake it up this time."

As the warm baby oil and iodine oozed down my back, I turned my face away from the sun and got a good look at Sara Jane, who wasn't paying one bit of attention to what she was doing.

"Watch out, Sara Jane. You're getting that stuff on my straps." She didn't say one word when I fussed at her; she just sat there and waited for a glimpse of that boy whenever he turned his mower around at the side of the yard. "My God, Sara Jane, you act like you've never seen a yardman before."

I'd only been out of the mountains for a few weeks where I grant you nobody had a yardman, and I was already jaded. I would have been mortified if Sara Jane could have seen my shabby life back home; I was living in a better place now, surrounded by good people. I let out a deep sigh and whispered the words so low I don't think Sara Jane heard me.

"I'm never going back."

The smell of fresh-cut grass mingled in the air with baby oil and the beach music that was playing on the radio. There was just enough of a breeze to make the hot sun feel delicious, like the very first time it's warm enough to lie out in early spring. Sara Jane had brought over a big Thermos jug full of sangria she made from a recipe a friend of hers got from his high-school Spanish teacher, only the teacher substituted sparkling grape juice for wine. Sara Jane made the real thing with orange and lemon slices. She even brought a jar of maraschino cherries from the Red & White for our drinks. I took another sip of the cold, sweet wine and nipped a cherry off at the stem.

"Oh, my." She stared at the yardman, her hand resting on her heart.

I popped the stem in my mouth and propped up on my elbows just in time to see the yardman taking his shirt off. I worked the stem around as I watched the muscles in his belly and his arms ripple each time he turned the mower. He never looked at us, just kept to his work like we weren't even there, which kind of reminded me of Winston. I was trying hard not to think about him.

"You think he's good-looking?" I showed Sara Jane the perfect knot in the stem.

"Uh-huh, don't you?"

"He's all right." She looked at me like I had cussed her mother. "I'm sorry, Sara Jane. I guess he's cute. I really didn't get a good look at his face, but he does have a nice body."

By the time he got to the side yard, he was cutting his eye around at her every time he turned the mower around in the opposite direction. After that, I don't think she heard a word I said, and it wasn't because of the mower.

Sara Jane had a sultry power about her that was growing with each turn of that mower, so that by the time Jimmy was done, she had him sipping sangria right along with us.

"It's hot." He downed the glass in a few seconds. "Real hot."

"Uh-huh."

"Thanks." He set the glass down.

"Want some more?"

"Better not. I've got two more yards to cut." And then he looked at her sexy little pout. "Oh, what the hell."

He included me in the conversation as far as asking my name and where I was from. The rest of the time, he sat at the foot of Sara Jane's lounge chair. By the time their conversation was over, they had planned a date and he had rubbed baby oil on her back and the backs of her legs. I felt like I was at a peep show.

"Jimmy," she sighed.

"Well, it ain't Lex or Darren, but I guess he was nice."

"You guess?"

"Well, Sara Jane, he said 'Hey' to you and it was all over after that. It was like I wasn't even here."

Some clouds rolled in like there might be an afternoon shower, so we decided to go inside. Between the time we pulled up our bathing suit straps and packed up, she said five, maybe six words to me and she hadn't looked at me once. I stored our lounge chairs under my bed.

"I'm sorry, Sara Jane. I know I'm jealous. You see a man, offer him a glass of sangria, and the next minute you have a date with him. I want Winston so bad and slave over a hot stove to prove it, and he doesn't even know I exist."

She gave me that sexy little all-knowing grin. "Maybe you need to offer Winston something sweet."

8

⌒

Sara Jane made a D+ on the next test. Both of us were proud, like she had just won the Nobel Prize for hair. I'd figured out a way to help her memorize facts she thought she could never remember, like the names of frontal facial muscles, by turning anatomy into a trashy romance. One muscle was the heroine, another the hero, and nerves and sinus cavities were the villains. Smaller, less significant muscles were the servants or animals. I swear, if Mrs. Cathcart had written that test the way Sara Jane learned it, I know she would have made an A+.

She brought some steaks over and some more Boone's Farm Apple Wine, which had kind of become our drink of choice. Actually it was the only one we could buy at our age, except for beer, which was only good for boiling shrimp. I baked three potatoes and tried to roast sweet corn on the little hibachi, but I forgot to soak it first. Neither one of us was watching the grill and the silks caught on fire. I beat them with an old wet dishrag, threw the smoldering ears in the trash, and put some salad in cereal bowls. It was a great dinner. Sara Jane said Winston would probably march right over and say so himself.

It was nice out that night. Windy. Not too hot. We sat out on the landing after dinner in our lawn chairs and opened a second bottle of wine.

"Look." She nudged me, and I shushed her because her voice does carry so.

Winston was in his drinking room. Judging from the way he looked, he was pretty far gone. He accidentally knocked a picture off the little table beside his chair and then picked it up two or three times because it didn't seem to want to stay on the table. He went to a cabinet with the liquor canisters on it and poured his drink with one hand while he held the wall up with the other.

"Oh, honey, you don't need any more of that medicine," Sara Jane whispered.

"We ought not to be watching this, Sara Jane."

The way he teetered about the room was suspenseful, like watching a high-wire act at the circus. Neither of us could budge from our seats even if we had wanted to. I was embarrassed for him, but mostly I was embarrassed for myself.

"He's just got to get over her. I'm telling you, if he doesn't, he's gonna drink himself to death. Look at him. He's pitiful."

"He is not." I knew she was right. "He's . . . he's . . . well, he's gorgeous, for one thing."

"He may be gorgeous, but I can guaran-damn-tee you he couldn't get it up if his life depended on it. I bet he's got permanent whiskey dick."

"He does not."

"Oh, just look at him, Zora. You know he gets that way every night. You could do a whole lot better than him."

The tiny sliver of moon in the sky made just enough light for her to see me all red-faced with tears running down my cheeks. She knew I wanted Winston and wanted him more than she wanted those men in her books to come and sweep her off her feet.

She laughed. "Oh, what the hell do I know? I'm dating the yardman."

After pouring me another glass of wine, she told me about their first date. Jimmy had taken her to the home of some rich guy he did yard work for. It was right on the ocean. They actually rode horses on the beach in the moonlight. Everything sounded so perfect, at first I wondered if she'd made the whole thing up. I also wondered how Jimmy knew just the right things to do to win Sara Jane's heart, but the truth was that he had won it the very first time they laid eyes on each other.

"I pretended we were Dominique Devereau and Beaumont Belliard in *Castaways of Love*. I even told him so. He smiled and told me I could imagine whatever I wanted to as long as he was a part of it. Zora, I think I'm in love."

It was obvious she was love-struck by the way her voice quivered when she said Jimmy's name, the way every tiny thing he did was so amazing to her. I tried not to sound jealous, but I couldn't believe her luck. "Sara Jane. You don't even know him."

"You don't have to know somebody to be in love with them. You just are."

We both turned back to the scene in the drinking room. Winston was at the liquor cabinet again, teetering from side to side. I guess he was trying to keep the room from spinning long enough to pour himself another drink.

He teetered too far to the right and fell. I was sure he was dead by the way his head snapped back when it hit the coffee table. We sat there on the edge of our seats, waiting for him to get up. I pounded my fist on the railing like he was a fallen prizefighter.

"Get up. Get up." As he lay on the floor, I prayed like crazy that he was only coldcocked by the whiskey.

"Oh, my gosh. You don't think he's . . ."

"No. He'll get up." Sara Jane's voice was steady. We sat there for half an hour, but he didn't move. "He's just dead drunk."

Dead drunk. It was the term I had used most of my life to describe Mama and the men she lived with. The way the sheriff described my daddy.

"We ought to do something, even if it's just put him to bed."

"It's his rule, Sara Jane. We can't go in there. He hasn't let anybody in the house since Emma died. Look, I know this all seems wildly romantic to you, but if I lose my apartment, I'll have to move back home."

"Well, what if he's hurt or dying?"

I didn't have an answer for that.

"What if I go? Then you won't get in trouble."

I didn't answer her right off. I sat there watching and waiting for some small movement that would let me know he had just passed out and wasn't in a coma or worse. I begged for another five or ten minutes, which seemed like hours, but he didn't stir an inch.

"Okay. Just go in, see if he's okay, and come right back out. Promise?"

She nodded.

"And, whatever you do, don't try to wake him up." She was halfway down the steps before I finished my sentence.

She knocked at the back door and looked up at me. I shook my head at her because he hadn't moved. She opened the door and disappeared inside the house. An eternity passed before I finally saw her tiptoeing into the drinking room. She inspected him closely, and I nearly jumped out of my skin when she picked up his wrist to check his pulse. She gave me the okay sign as she waved at me with his limp hand, before she tucked it in close to his chest.

I knew for sure there'd be trouble when Sara Jane picked up the picture of Emma that Winston held all the time and gave me a funny look. I was up out of my chair, waving like mad for her to get out of there, but she would just pick something else up, look at it, and laugh or just point to it, like I could see through her eyes.

I thought I would die when she started up the stairs. Pretty as you please, she went into his bedroom, turned the light on in the closet, and stayed in there for at least a hundred years, stepping out from time to time to flash one of Emma's frocks up so I could see it. I was sure this was God's way of getting back at me for plundering a dead woman's things.

Finally, she went back downstairs. Before she left, she threw a little white crocheted blanket over Winston and came back to the porch.

"He's fine. He's just drunk," she said, real nonchalant.

"I'm gonna kill you, Sara Jane Farquhar. I can't believe you went in there and took the man's pulse."

"Oh, Zora, he's so drunk I could have sat on him and pretended to ride him down the beach, and he never would have known it. Boy, he's tall."

"You almost gave me a heart attack going through his things. You know I told you what would happen if you got caught."

"First of all, the man couldn't wake up even if he wanted to. Second of all, we needed to make sure he wasn't dead or anything because you promised your teacher you'd look out for him, and I think she would call this looking out for him. And third of all . . . don't you want to know what I found?"

I was so keyed up over the whole life-and-death thing and the possibility of getting caught that the thought had not even occurred to me. But as soon as she said those words, I had to know what was in that house.

"Let's see," she said, knowing she had my full attention, "where should we start? Well, the kitchen looks like nobody lives there except for the unwashed glasses in the sink, good crystal glasses. Waterford. I turned them upside down and looked. There's hardly anything on the counters and the only thing in the refrigerator was an old box of baking soda his wife probably left there."

She laughed when she saw my eyes roll over her detailed inventory of the kitchen.

"There's lots of pictures in the hallway of the two of them in different places. Some of them were taken in Europe, I think, and then there were a lot taken at the beach, but not the beaches here, rocky beaches.

"The drinking room smells like a bar, but it's furnished real nice. I don't think he had much to do with that. Looks mostly like stuff that a woman would pick out. But my God, Zora, that man is gorgeous, even in a stupor."

My heart felt like it was going to jump out of my chest. "I don't think I can take much more of this, Sara Jane."

"He still has her things in the closet, and, honey, that woman had some beautiful clothes, I'm telling you. He didn't have much in there, everything was on hangers from the cleaners, a couple pairs of jeans, a dozen or so shirts, and a dark-blue suit that looks like it hasn't been worn in forever. It had dust on the shoulders, lots of it. Next time—"

"No," I said. "There can't be a next time with you going in there like some kind of detective. It just adds fuel to the fire I already have for the man. Look, I need this place. I can't afford to go and do something stupid. Tell me you'll never go in there again. Promise me, Sara Jane."

"Well, you didn't even let me tell you the juiciest part," she said and then she was purposely quiet until I begged her to tell. "Emma . . . looks a little . . . like you."

9

I woke up early the next morning and went right to work, cutting shortening into the flour. I poured a tad of salt in my hand with a dab of baking powder and dusted it across the flour before I worked a little ice water into the dough so that it was nice and firm, not sticky because that can be a real mess. I can't tell how much of this or that I put in the bowl because I always eyeball things the way Nana taught me. It took a lot of patience on her part for me to learn how to make anything that way, much less dumplings.

They rolled out real nice, not paper-thin, mind you, just good and thin and ready to boil. I took the pot of chicken broth out of the refrigerator and turned the stove on high. Even though it was cold, I could smell the sage and the little bit of thyme I had added the night before.

There was just enough time to set my hair in electric curlers before the pot came to a rolling boil. It was almost seven o'clock, already hot in that little kitchen. I stood there "glowing," as Mrs. Cathcart would say, as I dropped those strips of flour into that good broth. I settled for a bowl of cereal as I watched those dumplings swirl about for a few minutes before it was time to finish getting dressed. I remember smiling to myself that day because I was making "lovin'" for Winston. When I was little I always called it "chicklin and dumplings," but when I was real little, I called it "lovin'" because that's what it felt like when Nana made it special for me.

It was strange when I first moved to Davenport, how every time Winston crossed my mind, I felt like somebody had caught me playing dress-up in my mother's clothes. I was embarrassed but mostly ashamed that I had a little seed of Mama inside me, a seed that had taken root and was growing faster than the kudzu overtaking the trees behind my apartment. But the harder I fell for Winston, the less I thought about Mama.

I sang a little tune my daddy used to sing about the sun coming up over the mountain, took the rollers out of my hair, and twisted it up in a little knot so that only three or four curly little tresses fell across my face. I made a pouty face and put on some bright pink lipstick I had gotten from one of the beauty-supply salesmen, then went back into the kitchen to check the pot one last time.

I remember it was a Tuesday because that was the day Winston had his eight o'clock class. I checked myself in the mirror before I went out my front door and walked at a snail's pace down the steps because he hadn't come out of the house yet. I was on the second step from the bottom when the back door finally opened. He was in such a hurry, I guess, he didn't see me until he heard the gravel crunch under my feet.

"Good morning," I said when he looked up at me.

"Morning."

It was the first thing he'd said to me since Miss Cunningham had introduced us and it wasn't even a complete sentence. He had never once said thank you for all of the lovin' I spent hours making him, most everything from scratch. He said nothing more than that one little word, got into that sports car, and drove off to work. That sure wasn't the way I'd imagined our first exchange would go. Kudzu love or not, I marched myself down to the Davenport School of Beauty, worked 'til way past six, and gave that man Spam and cold grits for dinner that night.

That whole day was just bad all the way around. I'd been in school for two months and already had two regular clients, both of them Tuesday ladies and elderly. One lady, Mrs. Chute, didn't have more than fifty hairs on her head, but she came every week for her wash and set. The other one was a big woman named Miss Girtha, a retired schoolteacher who always tipped me twenty cents.

Anyway, both of them canceled their appointments that morning because of the croup. So I just sat there with the rest of the girls hoping for a walk-in to practice on and listening to Mrs. Cathcart's husband tell stories about his old homeplace.

Mother Hannah, Mrs. Cathcart's mother, worked up front at the appointment desk. She was well into her eighties, and when she wasn't nodding off, she'd walk back to where we were sitting with Mr. Cathcart and ask where all the customers were. Mr. Cathcart was always quick to promise that they'd come, but it was easy to get discouraged during the first couple months of school when the regular customers stayed away. Nobody said it, but I think all of us knew the walk-ins were hoping we'd make all of our beginner's mistakes on somebody other than them. Still, it was depressing to see a half dozen clients trickle through the door with the twenty-three of us standing around, ready to work.

"They always come back," Mr. Cathcart would remind us several times during the day, "sooner or later. We're the only place in town that'll cut a kid's hair for a dollar."

A lot of mothers brought their babies in for first-time haircuts, which Mrs. Cathcart loved. She'd ooh and aah over all of them, even the ugly ones, and give them little pieces of Zwieback teething biscuits. The kids who had teeth got animal crackers when they were done with their haircuts.

I absolutely hated first haircuts because those babies—and they were just babies—never sat still. Everybody including me was so afraid we were going to cut one of them, and one day I did. Well, this one wasn't exactly a baby; he was four years old with a head full of curly blond baby hair that had never been cut. When I wet it and combed it out, it was all the way down his back.

Mrs. Cathcart was good about teaching from our textbook, but she was also good about telling us practical things. Like if you're cutting a little boy's curls off for the first time, be sure and remind his mother that the moment you cut his hair it will most likely be straight as a board. Forever.

I ran the comb down his thin blond hair that almost touched the elastic waistband of his shorts and looked at his mama.

"This is a really drastic change. Are you sure you want to do this?"

"No, I don't, but his daddy does."

"His hair's going to be straight like it is now."

"I know. Go ahead, but give him the bowl cut. I'm not shaving it off like his daddy said." She sighed like she hated to see those pretty blond ringlets go. "His daddy's took to calling him 'Johnny Sue.'" She took a handful of his wet hair in her hand and held it close to her face. "Those curls were just so pretty, I couldn't never cut 'em myself."

I thought it was sweet the way she carried on over her little boy's hair, like somehow those blond curls would keep her baby from growing up. But it was too late. He was strong and a terror for his mama, who had to fight him just to get him in the chair. My job was to get the cape on him, which wasn't easy because he kept unsnapping it and laughing when it fell into his lap. When he wasn't doing that, he was pulling the cape over his head or flapping his "wings," as he called them. I wanted to use those pretty, long curls to tie him to the chair. Judging from the look on his mama's face, she wanted to do the same until he grew out of whatever phase he was going through.

I gathered his hair in my hand like a ponytail, held my breath, and cut the length of it off. Mrs. Cathcart kept a supply of pink and blue grosgrain ribbon on hand, and if he'd been the kind of child to sit still, I would have tied a blue ribbon around the fat lock and given it to his mama for a keepsake.

I held the little boy down by his shoulder with one hand and gave it to her with the other. "Oh," her voice quivered. She looked up at me like the veil had been lifted. "He's not a baby anymore."

As big as that child was, he hadn't been a baby for a long time. "Stop squirming now, Johnny." I said it nice. "I can't finish your haircut if you won't be still."

Without his baby hair to protect him, the little boy's mama was getting really mad. "John Thomas Baldwin, if you don't sit still, this woman's gonna cut your ear off."

And then it happened. I don't know how, I didn't even see it, but he made one wrong move, and part of that little brat's ear went sailing across the room.

Now, you would think after all of the threatening that woman had done to her son that she wouldn't have gotten so mad at me. But her baby was screaming and crying. He bled like I'd snipped a major artery, and she started shrieking at me, calling me every name in the book. Mrs. Cathcart was mortified by the whole exchange and immediately picked the sliver of ear up in a sanitized towel. The woman nearly fainted when Mrs. Cathcart handed it to her.

"Now you get hold of yourself," Mrs. Cathcart said sternly. "Zora, bring the first-aid kit, and tell Mr. Cathcart to bring some ice."

I brought the kit to her along with a large box of Band-Aids that was sitting on top of it. I expected her to bandage the boy up, but instead she took the smelling salts out of the little foil packet and waved it under the nose of the hysterical woman, who sat down on the floor but finally seemed to have come to her senses. Even the little boy had quit crying and was trying to look at himself in the mirror. Mr. Cathcart hurried out with an ice tray and cocked the handle so that the cubes spilled out on top of the piece of ear and onto the open towel on the woman's lap.

The woman looked at the towel like someone had put a bloody stump in her lap. She pointed to me. "You need to fire her."

"You ought to have raised your boy better. Even you told him to be still or I was going to cut his ear off," I snapped.

"I don't care. I want you fired."

"Shut up, all of you," Mrs. Cathcart screamed. "Nobody's getting fired and nobody can cut hair like it's a moving target. Now, you get this . . . this . . . get it on down to the emergency room right quick." Mrs. Cathcart bound up the towel with a big red rubber band. "They'll sew it back on good as new, but you've got to get over there in a hurry or it won't take."

The woman nodded her head like this all made perfect sense to her. "But we don't have no car."

Mr. Cathcart drove the two of them to the emergency room. The doctor said if it was a finger they could sew it back on; it wouldn't take because the ear is just made out of cartilage. I could have told them that.

When Mr. Cathcart came back he complained all day long about the woman being indigent, that she wouldn't be able to pay the bill. He was afraid that the hospital would make the beauty school pay for it, or that the woman might hire one of those ambulance-chasing lawyers. But none of that happened. As a matter of fact, the little boy still came to the school even after that. Everybody snickered when they saw him sitting so still in the chair, afraid to breathe, especially when the scissors glided around his ears. If I'd been his mother, I would have let him wear the bowl cut to cover up his disfigurement, but his mama always insisted the boy's ears were cut out, standing there with her arms crossed and her feet spread apart, daring him to move.

Mrs. Cathcart always gave the other children who came in two animal crackers after their haircut. "One for each hand," she would say, but she always handed that little boy the whole box and let him take as many as he wanted. I think it was her way for thanking him and his mama for not suing the school.

Even after all that craziness I still loved to cut hair. I never cared much for doing perms because they smell awful, and I'm not great at color; that's Sara Jane's forte. But it was about this time I began to feel, just like Mrs. Cathcart said, that I had been called to fix hair for the rest of my life.

10

Back home, I didn't listen to music much. Whenever Mama played her records, I'd put a fat rubber pencil eraser in each ear to muffle Judy Garland's show tunes. After a while, I didn't need the erasers to tune out the music. But beach music was different. It had a sweet, soulful sound that always made me dip my shoulders and shuffle my feet without even realizing it. Sure there were radio stations who played folks like Duran Duran, Eurythmics, and the king of pop, Michael Jackson, but if you lived anywhere near the beach in the Carolinas, beach music was still tops.

As much as I hated drinking when I was living with Mama, it never bothered me that drinking had become Sara Jane's and my favorite pastime. Every night the wine was cheap and cold, and went down as easy as those sweet piña coladas we used to drink on dollar night at Shag Daddy's Beach Bar in North Myrtle Beach.

Sara Jane and I had been celebrating again. We were always

finding something to celebrate, and sometimes, when we couldn't think of anything to cut loose over, we just turned the music up real loud and celebrated ourselves. I remember that Saturday night we were cleaning up the kitchen. General Johnson and the Chairmen of the Board's "Give Me Just a Little More Time" was on the radio; it had become my own personal battle hymn where Winston was concerned.

"Give me just a little more time," Johnson crooned, "and our love will surely grow."

Sara Jane took the other end of my old checkered dish towel and we shagged along with the General as he belted out the chorus, pleading, "'Give me just a little more time, and our love will surely grow. Baby. Please, baby.'" Scooping up my wineglass, I tried to drink and shag at the same time but made a mess.

"Shuffle, ball, change," Sara Jane reminded me when my feet stopped moving, like I knew what that meant. I just watched her feet and tried to make mine do the same.

Sara Jane wanted to call the radio station in Myrtle Beach and request "With This Ring" by the Platters, which was her and Jimmy's song. I wouldn't let her because it was expensive to call long distance back then, so she settled for Clarence Carter's "Too Weak to Fight," which came on right after a commercial for Drink and Drown night at Shag Daddy's and a wet T-shirt contest at another beach bar called Jimmy Mack's.

I knew Sara Jane Farquhar had opened my silverware drawer at least fifty times since we'd started being friends, but she never once saw Emma's little gift I'd hidden all the way in the back. I never really expected Sara Jane to see the dress boxes that were still in the same places Emma had stashed them, but she had been coming to my place almost every day for almost three months and never once saw that little present.

"Sara Jane, you always wash. It's your turn to dry and put away."

She took a clean dishrag out of the drawer by the sink, shagging and twirling around me until she was beside the drain board. She went on and on about Jimmy, stopping just in time to close her eyes and cock her head to the side as she mouthed the chorus "too weak to fight." I talked about school, feeling like Clarence Carter could read my mind. Every time he declared his own weakness for his lover, Sara Jane would pick up a spoon, a salt shaker, or anything else handy that she could use for a microphone and sing right along with him.

I knew Sara Jane liked everything just so and hated to leave the kitchen undone. I'd just enough wine in me to think I couldn't live another day without telling her about all of Emma's things, especially that little box in the drawer behind the soup spoons. I knew what I was doing, sure as the world.

"Oh, just let the dishes drain tonight," she said, which didn't work into my plan at all. "Let's sit outside on the porch and finish our wine. I have something I want to ask you."

"Lazy," I said, flicking dishwater at her off the ends of my fingertips. Clarence gave one last James Brown yowl as Sara Jane scooped up a handful of silverware and opened the drawer real wide, and stopped just short of putting the knives and forks away.

"Zora, why do you have a wrapped present in your silverware drawer?"

"Oh, that. It's not mine."

"Well, who the hell does it belong to?"

"Winston's wife, Emma. She left lots of things here, dresses and such. I think she bought them and hid them from Winston so he wouldn't get mad. I just let everything be. Ooh, I love that song," I said as soon as I heard the first few bars of "Sixty Minute Man." "Would you turn up the radio? My hands are wet."

"Everything?" she asked, ignoring The Dominoes altogether.

We dried our hands on the dishcloth we'd used for dancing. I showed her the dresses in the boxes under the bed and two in the top of my closet. I really made over them because I knew it was eating Sara Jane to know what was in the little box almost as much as it was eating me.

"Oh, my God, you just have to see this cute little angora set. It's blue with little pearl buttons. They look like real pearls." I didn't have the first clue as to what real pearls looked like, but I pulled a box out of the bottom drawer of the bureau and tried to act surprised when she stopped me from opening it.

"Zora, why didn't you open that present?"

"Sara Jane, it's not mine. Besides, it's wrapped and it just wouldn't be right. I've got to tell you, I felt so guilty going through all of Emma's stuff, I just couldn't," I said, like I hadn't taken a complete inventory of Emma's new clothes and tried on every single piece.

"Don't you want to know what's in there?"

"You don't think we should open it, do you?"

"Hell, yes," she said, tearing into it like it was Christmas morning.

The box wasn't taped shut. When she opened it and pushed the powder-blue tissue paper aside, we both gasped.

"My God." Sara Jane whispered, "Do you think that's why he's so sad?"

I couldn't say a word. I blamed it on the wine and ran straight to the bathroom. Every time I retched, I saw the Serendipity box under the bed just like I had that first time I cleaned that toilet. I retched again and couldn't stop.

"Honey," Sara Jane cooed as she held my hair back. "You're so slight. You've got to go easy on that wine."

I sat on the bathroom floor and wiped my mouth with the back of my hand. Before I could say anything, Sara Jane had wrung out a cold cloth and was dabbing my face like Nana did when I was sick.

"You okay?"

"I don't know."

The baby's rattle sat on the table for a long time. It was silver with two big hearts engraved on it. A fancy smaller heart linked the two together. The note card inside the box sent me running for the toilet again. "Our love has created something wonderful. I love you. Always, Emma."

I told Sara Jane I needed some air, but the truth was I couldn't stand to be in the same house with that baby's rattle lying out on the counter. We took our chairs out to the porch where neither one of us said a word for a long time.

"Zora? Do you think he knew?"

"Maybe he did. I don't know."

"If she was pregnant, why did she hide the rattle? Why didn't she just give it to him?"

"I don't know, Sara Jane. Maybe she never got the chance. Maybe she did and that's why he grieves so. Maybe he's grieving for both of them."

Sara Jane and I loved to laugh. Even when we'd had a rotten

day, the two of us could always find something to laugh about. But the whole idea of pregnant Emma and her grief-stricken husband squelched all the romantic fantasies Sara Jane and I had conjured up about Winston and me. And if the earth didn't stop that night, I know the night sounds did. Everything good and sweet about a warm summer night seemed to wonder what in the world was wrong with us.

I couldn't take another minute of silence. "What did you want to ask me earlier?"

"Oh, nothing. It'll keep. You've had enough on you for one night."

"Come on." I tried to smile. "You're my best friend. What is it?"

After a few minutes of me pretending like I wasn't reeling from the thought of Emma carrying Winston's baby, she decided to tell me.

"Well, I was wondering, and you can say no if you want to . . . I wouldn't be mad, I swear. Could me and Jimmy use your apartment?"

"Sara Jane, have you already . . . ?"

"No, we haven't yet, but we're so close. You know he lives two doors down from that Doris Erickson, and she's the biggest gossip in town. I hear she watches her neighbors with binoculars. If we got caught . . . well, I just don't think Mama and Daddy are ready for Jimmy Alvarez just yet. And you know Daddy hates everybody, especially Mexicans. I just—"

"You don't have to say another word." I was amazed at how the thought of Jimmy or making love with Jimmy had changed her. I doubt she had ever cared one bit about her parents' opinion of the other boys she dated.

"Thank you," she whispered with a sly little smile.

I never doubted whether Sara Jane cared for me, but I knew after she went home that night that she truly loved me. Before she left, she put away all the leftovers and the dishes, folded the wrapping paper neatly, and set the closed box back in the silverware drawer. I took it out but didn't open it again. I put it back on the very same shelf where Emma had first hidden it. From then on, I kept my dinner plates someplace else.

11

When I was twelve, Bryda Kay Modean invited me to Bible School at the little Holiness Church down the road from our place. She never told me what to wear and was either too shy or too embarrassed to tell me to change out of my short-shorts and into something more acceptable when she met me halfway between her house and mine. But she did pray, whispering to God, as we walked down that long, dusty road toward the church. I didn't know what she'd gotten me into; I just thought she was awfully religious for a twelve-year-old.

Her long, cotton skirt blew about in the breeze the whole way there, brushing up against my legs, reminding them that they were naked. But I was a lot like Adam and Eve before the fall, and didn't know I was nearly naked in the eyes of the Holiness Church until we got there. There was a whole slew of ankle-length cotton skirts and most every jaw was gaped open at me. Bryda Kay's mama, who wasn't the least bit shy, wanted to send me home straightaway, but the preacher's wife could see that I was about to burst out crying right there in front of everybody. She took me inside the little cinder block building they used for a fellowship hall and tied two long aprons around my waist so that I had a big droopy bow in the front and a big droopy one in the back. The aprons were so long, I couldn't see the least little bit of leg, much less my feet.

The only good parts about Bible School were making crafts and eating snacks. We made brightly colored pot holders on little metal looms to take home and keep. I was so proud of mine because it was the most colorful one of the bunch. The Bible lesson that followed craft time was about Joseph who was nearly beaten to death because nobody liked him the way he was dressed, either. I looked at my pot holder and prayed for the first time in my life that I would make it out of that place alive. Luckily, snack time followed the Bible story and Bible Bingo, because the only thing that kept me there to the end was the promise of cherry Kool-Aid and homemade sugar cookies.

Later on, when Bryda Kay and I parted ways, she said she was real sorry about the way her mama acted. I told her that I was sorry for wearing the short-shorts, thanked her for inviting me, and said good-bye.

"Zora," Bryda Kay hollered just before she rounded the creek in the opposite direction. "I don't think you're going to hell for wearing them shorts. Honest." She smiled and waved, then skipped off down the road like she had saved my soul all by herself.

Mama never cared anything about church, and Nana always said that God is everywhere. After Nana listened to me whimper and carry on about what happened at Bible School that day, she said God was everywhere except the Holiness Church because he had the good sense not to have anything to do with those fool people. While Nana ranted, I pulled at the hem of my shorts with my chin still quivering and swore I'd never set foot in church again.

One day, after school, Sara Jane's mama asked me to go to their church and come to Sunday dinner afterward. I told Mrs. Farquhar I wasn't much of a churchgoer. The only appropriate dress I had, my high-school graduation dress, was packed away in the cedar chest at home, and I knew I couldn't wear Sara Jane's clothes, so I told her mother I didn't have anything to wear. Besides, I'd walked by the First Baptist Church of Davenport a time or two on my way downtown and had never seen so many fancy clothes in my life.

"You can wear one of Emma's dresses," Sara Jane said under her breath.

"Oh, my, that is a problem," Mrs. Farquhar said. She was really sweet and was so thankful I was helping Sara Jane with her schoolwork. But I never expected her to go out and buy me a new outfit. It was pretty, though, pale blue, a church dress, as she called it, with little pumps to match. She was so proud of herself.

"Mrs. Farquhar, I can't accept this. It's too expensive and I—"

"Nonsense. You've put in so much time tutoring Sara Jane. Why, if I had bought you every dress in the store, it wouldn't be enough to thank you properly. Besides, that's what mamas do."

Not my mother. On the way home, I tried not to think about her and the last time's she'd hung up on me. I still loved her in a distance-makes-the-heart-grow-slightly-fonder kind of way; I still cared about her. Mama was such a child, I knew that even with the little bit of time that had passed between us, she most likely still didn't understand why I had to leave her.

I stopped by the Red & White, and bought a tablet and poured my heart out to her in a letter. While part of me felt guilty for writing down words so that when she read them, she couldn't pretend I didn't love her, the other part of me said Mama didn't deserve to know how much she'd hurt me. I was sobbing by the time I signed my name and sealed it up but walked to the post office to mail it right then because if I hadn't, it would have never been mailed.

I met Sara Jane on the steps of the church at 9:45. We had stayed up late the night before, and both of us were just a teensy bit hungover, but Sara Jane promised me we wouldn't be the only ones who had enjoyed Saturday night a little too much. It was a fashion show, just like I knew it would be, with women sashaying down the aisles, showing off their new frocks. Sara Jane said that there were women in that church that had never worn the same dress twice, which made me think that if I started coming regularly, I'd have to wear that same blue dress every Sunday.

As the organist played music, folks talked amongst themselves. Then she played a little louder; everyone was quiet as the choir filed in like a green-robed army. The minister was a solemn, wiry-looking little man with salt-and-pepper hair and Coke bottle–thick glasses. Mrs. Farquhar had raved about him and what a joy for the Lord he had, but he didn't look very joyful to me.

But the music director looked downright euphoric and would make just about anybody who wasn't a Christian want a dose of what he had. He talked before every song, and we sang five or six of them, about what the song meant or what it meant to him personally. When that music began, he waved his arms like nobody's business and shook his head about like he was conducting a great orchestra. Watching him, all I could think about was that I sure would like to give that man a good haircut. He only had about six long, wispy sections of hair that in the beginning were combed in such a way as to try to hide the entire top of his bald head. By the time he was done with the first song his hairs were wild and everywhere, but after each hymn he sat down, took a little black plastic comb out of his pocket, and slicked his hair back across the top of his head.

Mr. Farquhar loved to sing. He had a big, deep voice, and you could hear him over everybody. He also liked to say "Amen" every five seconds or so when he wasn't singing. Mrs. Farquhar would smile and nod and say, "Yes, Lord" so softly you could just barely hear her, because I don't think women were supposed to say "Amen" out loud like her husband did.

When it was time for the sermon, that little wiry man stood up at the podium and preached against everything known to mankind. Some things I knew were bad, like drugs and running around, but others I didn't know. TV was bad. Rock music was bad. He even said beach music was bad. I'd always liked those old songs, and I thought it was funny that the rest of the world had pretty much forgotten The Tams, The Drifters, and the like. But those groups seemed to make a good living playing their sinful music at every single beach town up and down the Carolina coast. And if Jesus himself came down and took a poll of that whole congregation, most all of them would have had to admit they shagged on a regular basis, even if it was just in the privacy of their own homes.

But in the Bible, Job didn't listen to rock music or beach tunes, and the way the preacher tied the whole message into Job's troubles it sounded like he did. I guess the preacher wanted us to believe that all of Job's sins caused his suffering, but it said right there plain as day in the pew Bible that Job was a righteous man.

After the service, everybody shook my hand. Mrs. Cathcart came clear across the other side of that big sanctuary to tell me she was glad to see me at church. Mrs. Farquhar introduced me to several people, telling them I was just like a daughter to her, which I didn't know. Mr. Farquhar said that he didn't want to visit all day like they did most every Sunday because he was hungry, so we slipped out the side door without shaking that preacher's hand, which was fine by me.

Back home, when Nana was living, we used to have a family reunion at our house. The men would set up big tables made out of sawhorses and plywood, and smoke deer meat or wild turkeys, sometimes a whole hog. The women would cover the tables with whatever came out of the garden that summer. Even with all that, I had never seen such a spread like the one on Mrs. Farquhar's dinner table.

There was fried chicken and mashed potatoes, gravy in a little silver boat, and fancy dinner rolls with butter hardened into the shape of sunflowers. Mr. Farquhar loved vegetables, so we had butter beans, corn, crowder peas, sliced tomatoes, and fried okra. The fine linen tablecloth and little napkins were hand-embroidered with Mrs. Farquhar's initials, NGF, and the food that wasn't in china bowls was on engraved silver trays. Mrs. Farquhar got all her ideas from the food section of *Southern Living* magazine, which Sara Jane pointed out was the other Bible at their house.

"Now, Zora," Mrs. Farquhar began as she was serving the dessert. "Sara Jane says you're just like a sister to her, and, if you don't mind me saying so, I believe you're much too young to be off on your own. I just want you to know that I'd be proud if you called me Mama."

If she knew what that word had meant to me over the years, she might have just asked me to call her Nettie, because she was nothing like Mama. She was more like June Cleaver or the TV mom I always wanted.

I loved the way she made ordinary things special and the way she made me feel like I was family without even saying so. But most of all I loved her because her whole life was gathered around that dinner table. This might have suffocated some women, but she looked at her work as beautiful and valuable, from giving her husband a reassuring pat on the hand when he teared up talking about his late mother, to buying a girl like me who didn't have anything a church dress.

"Yes, ma'am," I said.

"Yes, Mama," she echoed.

"Yes, Mama," I said.

Until that Sunday, I guess I never realized how much I missed family, real family, the kind that loves you up good, whether you need it or not. The kind that teases you about silly things you did growing up and makes you feel like you have a place in the world. I loved the Farquhars, but I missed the history I had with my own family.

Sara Jane and her family didn't know about times like when Nana and Aunt Fannie were washing all the little grandkids, trying to get them ready for Santa Claus to come. There were eleven or twelve of us standing in a row like an assembly line with our clean pajamas in one hand and a washcloth in the other. Two by two, we got into the tub. Nana scrubbed us down good; then Aunt Fannie dried us off, dressed us, and put a little dusting powder on the girls.

I was just three years old and wasn't paying the first bit of attention to what I was supposed to do. So when Nana picked me up out of the tub and set me on the floor, I toddled off before Aunt Fannie was done dressing my cousin Carol. I don't remember anything that happened before I sat on the grate of the floor furnace. All I know is, before anybody could get to me, I had a checkerboard burned onto my wet bottom, not bad, mind you, just enough that it looked like somebody drew on my butt with a red marker. Aunt Fannie called me Checkers until I got mouthy at eleven or twelve and told her not to, and to this day, I've never heard the end of it at Adams family reunions.

The next day I woke up with Nana on my mind. I'd dreamed about her. It was a sweet dream, not like the ones I used to have right after I moved into my apartment. She was always angry with me in those dreams. Sometimes she'd just look at me, shake her head, and look away like she did when Mama was falling down drunk and strutting into our house with another man.

When I walked into the beauty school that morning, Mrs. Cathcart took one look at me and asked what was wrong. I told her it was just Monday, but she'd been teaching long enough to know a homesick girl when she saw one. She stood at my station while I finished my first appointment and told me she was sure I'd snap out of it real soon. When we heard the door chimes, both of us looked to see a police officer walking into the foyer. Mrs. Cathcart excused herself from the little pep talk she was giving me and walked toward the sheriff, who was at the reception desk with his hat in his hand.

I couldn't hear what they were saying, but when both of them walked toward me, I was sure Mama was dead or maybe Winston. I fumbled with the curling iron and dropped it twice trying to get it into its little stand, and then I stood up as straight as I could and smoothed my uniform for some reason.

"Zora Adams, this is Sheriff Danforth," Mrs. Cathcart said with the most solemn expression on her face.

"Miss Adams," the man said, and nodded politely, but he didn't smile.

I know I must have looked like a frightened deer. I could feel myself trembling.

"Zora," Mrs. Cathcart said softly, "Ethyl Ladson passed away last night."

"I told the folks at the nursing home I was coming over here to get a haircut," Sheriff Danforth said, "and they told me to ask you if you wouldn't mind too much doing her hair. Actually, the nurse said that Ethyl told her she was going to die that very night. She told the nurse to make you do her hair.

"Well, you know old people. They say all sorts of crazy things all the time. She didn't think anything of it, but when she was closing out her shift, lo and behold, the old woman had passed on just like she said she would. Now, Miss Adams, ain't nobody gonna make you do anything, but the nurse got spooked over the whole thing and figured she'd better do as she was told."

I was so relieved that it wasn't Mama or Winston, I was actually smiling.

"So you'll do it then?" the sheriff said. I'm sure he misread the relief on my face as a sign of agreement.

"Oh." I came to my senses. "I don't know if I can do a dead woman's hair."

"Oh, Zora, this is the highest honor any of us can ever really hope to have," Mrs. Cathcart said, "to be the last thought on a customer's mind right before they pass from this world. An awesome responsibility."

I could tell by the sound of Mrs. Cathcart's voice that she would be crushed if I said no, but I had serious reservations about working on any dead person, much less fiery old Ethyl.

"Sheriff, I'm ready for you," Sissy Carson called.

"Sissy's going to cut my hair," he said. "I'd appreciate if you would just call the funeral home and let them know what you decide."

"Now, Zora, you can do this. I know you can." Mrs. Cathcart started in on me, and she didn't stop until I agreed to go on down to the Garden Rest Funeral Parlor and fix that woman's hair. "I have a little something for you. It'll help you get through this," she said as she led me back to her office.

She took a prescription bottle out of her purse, took four little blue tablets out, and put them in a church-offering envelope she had sitting on her desk.

"What is it?" I asked.

"Just take one of these now, and another one if you have trouble sleeping tonight. It's just a little Valium, dear. Dr. Hobart gave them to me for times such as this."

I nodded and wondered what the other two tablets were for. She handed me a little pointed paper cup she'd filled from the watercooler and watched me take the pill like I was a child. Then she said she'd have Mr. Cathcart drive me over to the funeral home.

"That's okay, Mrs. Cathcart. Sara Jane's home sick today." It was a lie. She'd called me from a hotel at the beach that morning to tell me all about her romantic date while Jimmy was in the shower.

"Won't she be in bed?"

"She'll be glad to give me a ride."

"Well, okay." Mrs. Cathcart sounded unsure about sending me off with Sara Jane. "Don't you be driving now," she called out as I walked to the reception desk to use the phone.

"Promise you won't laugh, Sara Jane?"

"I'm already laughing."

"Remember Ethyl?"

"The old bat at the nursing home?"

"She passed last night and now I'm supposed to do her hair." I had to hold the phone away from my ear she was snorting so loud. "I need a ride, Sara Jane."

"Yeah, but not to a funeral home. Zora, you don't have to do this."

"Mrs. Cathcart talked me into it. I don't have a choice."

"Sure you do, just tell her you changed your mind. Just tell her no."

She was right. I could have marched myself right over to Mrs. Cathcart and told her, living or dead, there was no way I was going to work on Ethyl again. But the truth was, I loved Mrs. Cathcart, and I didn't want to let her down.

"Just come get me. Okay?"

Sara Jane was there in ten minutes with the latest issue of *Bride* magazine and a bunch of other magazines with pictures of happy brides on the cover.

"Is there something you want to tell me?" I asked, leafing through one of the magazines.

"Just looking." Her grin was so big, it was a wonder she could talk. "Are you okay with this?"

"Your sure thing or fixing Ethyl's hair for her date with Satan?"

"Both."

"Sara Jane, I promise you, nobody will be happier for you and Jimmy when he pops the question than me. I just can't believe I'm doing this, but Mrs. Cathcart gave me something to help me get through it."

"A blindfold?" Sara Jane suggested.

I pushed the double doors to the funeral home open and stepped inside. The large foyer was outlined with heavy wooden settees and polished tables, and the old wooden floor creaked just enough to make being there to fix a dead woman's hair even creepier. The dusty scent from the fancy hallway rug or maybe the gaudy brocade fabric on all those couches made my nose sting.

"You must be Miss Adams," the man said in a reverent whisper of a voice. "I'm Bob Platt. The school called and said that you were on your way. Have you ever done this before?" He guided me down a hallway toward the back of the old house.

"No, sir."

"Well, it's not as bad as most people think," he said. "Did you know Miss Ethyl very well?"

"No. I did her hair a couple of times at the nursing home."

"They say she was a terror, this one," he said as he pulled the sheet back.

Now I thought when I saw the corpse I would be repulsed, but I was not. She looked so peaceful, I wanted to touch her to see if she was real.

"Go ahead," he said. "Everybody wants to touch them to see what it's like."

I did. She was cold and hard and her hair was a mess. I don't know if it was the Valium kicking in or the natural annoyance every hairstylist has when they see someone's hair all messed up, but I set my bag down on the little table by the gurney and went to work on Ethyl like it was something I did every day.

She was laid out on a cold metal table with nothing more on than a sheet. Whoever had done her makeup had gone heavy on the blush, but the color of base they used still made her look dead.

"May I?" I nodded toward the tray with every sort of makeup you could imagine.

"My brother's out of town; he's the artist in the family. Me? I'm good at the nuts and bolts of this job, really good with the families, but I've never been good at the cosmetic stuff."

I took a sponge and dabbed some Fawn Beige foundation on Ethyl to make her at least look a little warmer, and blotted over the cheek color until it looked more natural. When I stippled the black circles under her eyes, her skin didn't have any give to it, but the folds of skin in her neck were taut again, which living or dead is always a plus.

"Does she look—" I began.

"Okay? She looks great."

"Does she look too—alive?"

"Well, maybe a little." He took the sponge he'd used to apply

Ethyl's makeup and dabbed below her cheeks so that they looked hollow and gray. "There."

I shrugged and ran my fingers through her hair. It felt the same as I remembered and looked like she'd had a cut and set recently. The curling iron was already hot and I used it to make short, neat rolls. There wasn't much in the way of brushes or combs and the like, so I took a long blue teasing comb out of my purse that had a metal pick on the end of it. I teased the top of her hair just a little, smoothed it over, and picked at the curls until they fell into place.

"You're good," Mr. Platt said. "This old place has lost its shine for my brother; he's not around as much as he ought to be. You know, if you want some side work, I can give you all you want."

"Oh, I can't," I said, still fussing with Ethyl's bangs.

"You don't need a cosmetologist's license to work on the deceased. Anybody can do it."

Even with Sara Jane insisting on paying when we went out and my eating whatever I made Winston every night, I already had gone through half of my kitty. I was broke, but I wasn't desperate.

"No thanks. I just did this for Mrs. Cathcart."

"Well, you're good, real good."

He opened his wallet and gave me a fifty-dollar bill. "There's good money in this business; somebody's always dying."

I told him I was still feeling light-headed, which was true. I'd been there about thirty minutes and had already made ten times more than I'd made in tips the whole time I'd been at beauty school.

"Thank you. I could really use the money." I called Sara Jane.

Mr. Platt took a break and sat with me in the foyer with me while I waited for her.

"I wasn't a hundred percent honest. It's just me now. My brother went on a vacation to the Keys last year, says he's not coming back. Can't say that I blame him. He's working for a charter company taking tourists out on some big boat every day."

"Is that what you want to do? Something besides this?"

"Sometimes, but no. I like the peace and quiet most of the time and helping people deal with their grief. I can't imagine doing anything else, but this can be a lonely business." He was a homely man and single, according to his left hand. He would have looked a lot better with a good haircut. "Since my brother's been gone, I've gotten folks to fill in here and there for hair and makeup. I've even done a few heads myself. They looked all right, I guess. Nobody complained."

Things were quiet for a while, and then he apologized for rambling on. I saw Sara Jane pull up to the curb, and I'd started out the door when I turned around to ask him something.

"Change your mind about the work?"

"No, but thanks for asking me. I was just wondering, did you do an Emma Sawyer two, maybe three years ago?"

"Emma Sawyer," he repeated. "Oh, yeah, I remember her. Pretty woman, well, the picture I saw of her was pretty. She was all tore up when they brought her in here. It was sad. Her mama didn't want her cremated, but her husband, some hippie type at the college here, had it done anyway. Was she a friend of yours?"

"Oh, no. I just—" Sara Jane blew the horn. "I've got to go now. Bye."

I told Sara Jane every little detail about working on Ethyl. She commented how nice it must have been to work on the old woman with her mouth shut. I told her about Bob Platt, that he'd paid me fifty bucks and offered me a job there, which really made her cackle. But I never told her what he said about Emma.

12

~

Mrs. Cathcart moved her mother in with her and Mr. Cathcart about midway though the semester and gave Mother Hannah the title of official greeter for the Davenport School of Beauty. Mother Hannah doled out customers to the students in her own way, using a complicated system based on how much she liked you or how nice you were to her. Her memory wasn't what it used to be, so she carried around a little notepad that she kept in the pocket of the powder-blue smock she wore that brought out the color of her eyes. Every time somebody slighted her or she felt like they didn't show her the proper respect, she'd make a little notation in the book like "Tuesday, August 8, 1983, Gina Franklin smarted off to me for no reason. Stay mad at her for one week."

Sometimes I'd glance up from my patron's hair to find Mother Hannah gazing around the room with an addled look on her face, like she was trying to remember who was supposed to get the next walk-in. I don't know why she didn't write things like that down, but she didn't. Just before the customer got fed up and walked out, she would do "Eenie Meenie Miney Mo" to herself with those long, gnarled fingers and then gave the walk-in to the—very—best—one, and if she was mad at y-o-u, you—were—not—it.

I know about the notebook because Deana Malloy, the girl in the station next to mine, found it on the floor beside one of the hair dryers one day after Mother Hannah had gone home. Deana had a big time reading it out loud until Mrs. Cathcart caught her and gave her a stern talking to about respecting her elders. I don't think Mrs. Cathcart ever told Mother Hannah about the whole incident because if she had, Deana Malloy would never have had a single customer.

Mother Hannah had been a Ziegfeld Girl. I didn't know what that was until she told me her stories about working in vaudeville as a dancer. She loved to talk about her life on the road, but every time she did, Mrs. Cathcart would get real irritated and change the subject. Mother Hannah pretended like the vein in her daughter's forehead wasn't throbbing like there was a swarm of bees underneath her skin and went on about the fancy parties, all the handsome men, and Mr. Ziegfeld himself.

One day Mrs. Cathcart asked me not to talk to her mama anymore about her Ziegfeld days.

I told her I was sorry, that I was just trying to be nice and listen to an old lady who had so many stories to tell. I could see how those stories pained Mrs. Cathcart, so I tried to avoid the subject altogether, but it wasn't easy. I think Mother Hannah kept cornering me because I was the only person who would listen to her.

One day, Mrs. Cathcart was really edgy; she said she was that way a lot because she was going through the change. I think it was because her mama was wearing a brooch she said "Ziggy" had given her.

"Mama, now, I've asked you a hundred times, please, talk about something else."

Mrs. Cathcart's face was bright red from a hot flash. Little beads of sweat ran down her forehead. She dabbed at her face with a lace handkerchief she kept in her pocket, trying to compose herself.

I was minding my own business putting towels in my station because things were kind of slow. I guess there were probably three or four customers in the whole school at the time Mother Hannah strolled over to my station.

"It's a nice day out, isn't it, Mother Hannah?" I said, trying to look busy. "I'd like to be outside, wouldn't you?"

"Zora, did I ever tell you about the time me and Ziggy—"

"Mama," Mrs. Cathcart snapped from halfway across the room before she stormed over to us. "I've asked told you to put that fool-ishness behind you. That was a long, long time ago, Mama. Let it lay."

I looked at Mother Hannah and expected to see her sad and hurt, but if Mrs. Cathcart was having a snappy spell, Mother Hannah was having a defiant one.

"She can't take the truth," she said as she sat down in my chair and checked her look in the mirror like she was still pretty and young. "Absolutely hates it when I talk about her father."

That did it. Mrs. Cathcart jerked the chair around hard so that the old woman faced the mirror. She put her hands on Mother Hannah's shoulders, and lit into her.

"Look at yourself, Mama. You're just an old woman who was a substitute in a chorus line for two nights, Mama. All these years you've romanticized those two lousy nights into a whole career. My God, you never even met Florenz Ziegfeld. You only saw him once, across a crowded theater, so there's *no way* he's my daddy. Buddy Hannah was my daddy, Mama. He was a sweet, decent man who died when I was eleven. You're the one who can't take the truth, Mama. You ran away from home when you were seventeen, and when your daddy found out where you were, he went to New York, tanned your hide, and drug you back to Davenport where you raised six kids on a hog farm. And if I hear you so much as breathe the word Ziggy one more time, I swear I'll . . . I'll . . . Oh, for God's sake, Mama, just let it go."

Every bit of truth that spewed out of Mrs. Cathcart's mouth was like venom. One minute Mother Hannah was a feisty, vivacious Ziegfeld Girl and the next she was a nobody. The old woman stroked the brooch that I later found out she had bought at J.C. Penney and looked at me. She was pitiful.

"Those were the best two nights of my life," she whispered through the tears.

Mother Hannah got up, walked out the front door of the Davenport School of Beauty, and never came back to the school. She died two weeks after that. Mrs. Cathcart grieved so. I know she thought she killed her own mother. I don't know, maybe she did. I guess Mrs. Cathcart just couldn't stand those silly stories another minute any more than her mother could force herself to live and die in the real world.

I felt so bad for Mrs. Cathcart, because I felt the same way about Mama. I knew Mrs. Cathcart's trick of looking anywhere but at the embarrassment in front of her, hoping it would pass. I used to pretend Mama was normal and not a poor replica of Judy Garland. I acted like I didn't want to crawl under the ground and die when she went on and on about how men were drawn to her like yellow jackets drawn to sweet tea. I remembered being red-faced when she showed up drunk in front of the few friends I had, and then I shut those good people out of my life because I was embarrassed. Ever since I could remember, I wanted to snatch my own mother into the real world, but I don't think she could have existed there any more than Mother Hannah.

After the funeral, Mr. Cathcart put that J.C. Penney brooch on my station when he thought no one was looking. I held it in my hand for a moment, thinking about Mother Hannah and all those wild stories she told me before I slipped her dream into my pocket.

"Florenz Ziegfeld." I said it out loud. I said it for her.

Mrs. Cathcart was out a good while after the funeral. Her sister-in-law Doris, who was a licensed cosmetologist, taught our class. Mr. Cathcart handed out the appointments until he found that Swenson girl to do it. Both of them did it fairly, so no one complained.

Sara Jane Farquhar never had to worry about anybody doling out customers to her. She could have been busy from the time the doors opened until they closed if she'd wanted, but she was in love with Jimmy Alvarez, and that took precedence over everything, including school. She had herself a D+ average before Jimmy came into her life, but it just went to hell after that. Still, she had more clients than she could do. More than half of the customers who walked through the doors requested her. What she did for them, she did out of pure natural ability, D+ average or not.

I'm telling you, she could transform the mousiest or the trashiest-looking customer into someone as elegant-looking as her real-life heroine, Jacqueline Kennedy Onassis. Most all of them looked the part, until they opened their mouth to pledge their undying love to Sara Jane, the miracle worker. The rest of us were glad she was there because even Sara Jane could only do so much.

Nearly all the walk-ins who asked for her ended up with one of us. Some of them were happy with their hair, and some of them marched themselves over to that appointment desk to make an appointment with Sara Jane right in front of the poor girl who hadn't done their hair just right. I speak from experience when I say that was just about the most embarrassing thing that could happen.

But Sara Jane was in love, and no matter what anybody said or thought about it, the fact was there was no undoing what she felt. And Jimmy was the hardest worker you ever saw, working seven days a week—that is, before he met Sara Jane. But he was in love, too, so Friday and Saturday nights were their nights, and Monday and Tuesday afternoons and every single rainy day were their days. Sometimes I sat in the sun while the two of them carried on up in my apartment. Sara Jane looked so happy when they floated down those stairs, and I loved the way Jimmy wrapped his arms around her as best he could and gave her one last kiss before he had to leave.

"God, he's good," she said one day, still glowing with afternoon passion.

After Sara Jane and Jimmy started their little rendezvous, I got the best tan I've ever had in my life. "Sara Jane." I smiled as I turned over. "You are so crazy."

"Crazy in love, Zora. Crazy in love," she said as she plopped down in the lounge chair beside me. "How 'bout you?"

Sara Jane hardly ever spent an evening at my place anymore, although whenever her mama called, I told her she'd just stepped out for a minute or two. After a while Mrs. Farquhar quit calling. I guess she figured her daughter was up to something and I was covering for her. But I don't think she really wanted to know what was going on because she never once asked me to have Sara Jane call her back.

Most evenings, I sat on my porch, watching Winston all by myself. Before, when it was Sara Jane and me, we called it "Rear Window," after the Alfred Hitchcock movie. The two of us watched the drinking room show with the same interest Jimmy Stewart had watching his neighbor after he murdered his wife. The only difference was that I watched all by myself now, and instead of burying Emma in the courtyard, Winston was trying to resurrect her in the drinking room.

"Oh, he's about the same," I said when Sara Jane asked. "It's not as much fun as when you're here to give your running commentary."

"I'm sorry. It's just that, well, you know . . ."

"I know," I said, because I did.

Having that kind of unspoken understanding was nice. I loved Sara Jane enough to want to see her happy, even if it didn't include me, and I knew she felt the same way.

"Jimmy's saving up for a ring." Her voice grew higher and higher with every word until the last word was a shrill squeal.

"Oh, Sara Jane," I said, pulling my bathing suit straps back onto my shoulders as I got up to hug her. "I'm so happy for you. When's the wedding?"

"This Christmas. Jimmy doesn't work much during the winter, so he said it'd be the best time for it. We're going to Mexico for the honeymoon and to visit his mama."

"Won't she come for the wedding?"

"He says she won't be too happy if he tells her before the wedding, me not being Mexican and all. He says it would be a whole lot better if he just shows up and says, 'Here she is, Mama.' That way we can have a big wedding here, and I don't have to worry about Daddy embarrassing my in-laws. Jimmy's the one, Zora. He really is the one."

I knew Jimmy was a good man, and I knew Sara Jane loved him more than anything. But I also remembered times at the Sunday dinner table when Mr. Farquhar talked about the "wetbacks" who lived in the migrant camps just outside town, how they would come into the store and buy pounds and pounds of jalapeño peppers.

"Wetbacks ain't got no sense," he'd laugh. "Wonder what're they gone do with all them peppers?"

"Maybe they're going to make jelly," Mrs. Farquhar would say and look at Sara Jane, smiling in such a way that I decided she must know what was going on. "I just love pepper jelly, don't y'all?"

Sara Jane never said a word when Mr. Farquhar got off on the migrant workers. But I noticed she always breathed a heavy sigh of relief when he moved on to another minority. She was certain she was going to marry Jimmy and have his children. She said they wanted lots of them, and it would just kill Jerry Farquhar for his daughter to marry a Mexican. But I was sure when that sweet, tiny culmination of Jimmy and his daughter came into this world, he would forget all that. Mrs. Farquhar would see to it.

Sara Jane had been so excited to share the news about her and Jimmy getting married, it was kind of odd when she was suddenly quiet. I waited for her to say something, but she didn't.

"What's wrong, Sara Jane?"

She poured me some of her special sangria. "I'm not going to pass. I'm going to quit like Daddy did." She looked at me with those sad green eyes and said, "I feel like I'm letting you down."

"No, you didn't let me down. I'm proud of what you've done at school and I'm proud you're getting married and I . . ."

"But you worked so hard with me," she said.

"I know, but I did that because I love you. I didn't want you to go through life being a shampoo girl someplace because you couldn't get your license. Whether it's Jimmy or fixing hair, I want for you what you want for yourself because I love you."

Sara Jane's skills never suffered because of the passion that consumed her. She could still outdo all the girls at school and most any beautician in town, but the truth was, her heart just wasn't in it anymore. She was too busy living out her own sweet romance with a man who loved her more than he loved himself.

13

Every night I tried to tell Winston I loved him the only way I knew how. Since I never had any real contact with the man, I had to make sure that the message was clear, right there on his plate. Sometimes I baked a cobbler using blackberries that grew in the woods behind the garage. I scored tiny new potatoes into red hearts, making V-shaped knife marks on the tops before whittling the bottoms into a point. I learned a lot about fancy food from Sunday dinners at the Farquhars' house and even tied green beans into little bundles with spaghetti-squash bows. Those never made it out of my kitchen because they reminded me of the rattle Emma had left behind.

I was alone again on Saturday night. Sara Jane and Jimmy had gone to the beach for the day. With nothing to do, I spent all day in the kitchen making dinner absolutely perfect. I'd just taken scratch biscuits out of the oven and set them by the window to cool when I noticed Winston in the hammock with one leg on the ground and one slung over the other side. I seriously doubted he could've eaten anything that night. I could tell he was already numb.

Then the thought crossed my mind: What if he never ate any of the meals I made? What if he was too busy drinking to live that he never even noticed the love right there in front of him on his dinner plate?

I shook off the thought and put roast pork and green beans on the plate alongside heartfelt mashed potatoes. I spooned the cobbler into a little coffee cup and covered everything with tinfoil and dashed into the bathroom. I checked my look in the tiny medicine chest mirror while I brushed my teeth. My hair was skillfully mussed; my glossy lips looked wet and inviting like Cover Girl swore they would.

I put on a pair of short-shorts and a white eyelet peasant blouse Mrs. Farquhar had bought me to go with a church skirt. Looking in the mirror, I cocked my head to the side, unhooked my bra and pulled it out of the front of my shirt. There. I twisted up my hair in a sexy little knot, and forgave myself for being braless and desperate.

Winston didn't stir when the screen door slammed shut behind me. The stairs creaked, and my flip-flops slapped the bottoms of my feet, but he didn't stir. I set the plate on the table then and sat down on the picnic bench, watching him sleep. I'd only been close to him once before, the day we shook hands; even then, he kept a distance between himself and the rest of the world that couldn't be measured in feet or inches. I was close enough to reach out and touch him, but content to just watch him sleep.

The wind blew from behind me and I could smell the heavy

scent of a moonflower vine Jimmy had planted beside the garage. It was sweet and sexual and made me want to breathe it in deep, holding it in like a drug. The wind shifted around some more, mingling the smell of Scotch whiskey on his breath with that flower's fragrance.

His breathing was quiet and peaceful. His face looked pained but solemn. I wanted to stroke his hair the way Nana stroked mine when the world was against me. I thought if I could do it just right, his heartache might take to the breeze, mingle with the sweetness of that warm summer evening, and free him from his terrible sadness forever. But I didn't dare.

I watched his chest rise and fall. I lay my hand on my own chest and matched my breathing to each deep, slow breath. Sara Jane had taken his pulse once; I wanted to feel it, too, so my heart could beat in time with his. His skin was pale, slightly olive, his cheeks a little flushed from the whiskey. Twice I reached out and nearly touched him. Twice I pulled away. Finally, I touched a few strands of hair that dangled through the holes in the hammock. They were soft and so precious that I nearly cried.

It was getting dark. I was afraid to stay any longer. I touched his cheek with the back of my hand so slightly; it couldn't have felt like anything more than a whisper. Then I turned to go.

"Thank you," he said.

I froze.

"For the dinner. Dinners."

I stood right by the picnic table and turned to face him in the twilight. I could tell by the look on his face that he didn't know I'd spent the better part of my nights watching him.

"You're welcome." My own voice was so soft I barely heard it myself. I wanted to say something, something meaningful that would cut though the whiskey and stay with him forever.

"Don't stay out too late. It's supposed to rain tonight." I sounded like a stupid weather girl.

"Oh, God." He tried to sit up but smiled this sweet drunken smile, then fell back in the hammock. "I can't get up," he laughed and moaned, like a thirteen-year-old who had just been asked to roll out of bed early on a Saturday morning.

"Can you help me?"

My heart stopped beating. My breath caught in the pit of my stomach where hope and fantasy pretended I was more to him than a girl from the mountains cooking for my keep. I didn't answer him. I went to him, leaned over, and put his arm around my neck. As I pulled him up out of the hammock, his hand brushed against my breast, but I don't think he knew that.

"Just help me get to the door, Zora."

He said my name. The first fat raindrops splattered on us, a preview of the coming storm. I guided him toward the kitchen door. His head drooped so close to my shoulder, I felt his breath on my neck. His scent made me dizzy. When we reached the door, he leaned against the wall with his eyes closed and smiled. My heart stopped again when his hands touched my cheeks and then disappeared into my hair. He fumbled with the clip until it came undone and leaned forward to smell my hair like it was a pretty flower. Smiling, he picked up a handful, held it up to his face, and breathed deeply. Then he disappeared through the door. I could hear him ricocheting off the walls as he walked down the hall and up the stairs to his bedroom.

I wanted to follow him and make him smile again. As I turned to leave, I noticed the Styrofoam plate of food I'd set on the picnic table had a puddle of rain on top of the tinfoil. I didn't think twice about the rules. I didn't care. I picked it up, poured the water off the foil, and went into the kitchen. When I opened the refrigerator door, my heart broke. There were six or seven meals I had prepared. Some had taken hours to fix, and he had just shoved them into the refrigerator and never eaten them. I wanted to die.

I ran out of the kitchen and stopped just shy of the stairs to my apartment. I thought about Daddy Heyward, my second daddy, and how he passed out on our couch every single night he lived with us. I hated Mama for fussing over him like a new puppy whenever he pissed himself or worse, and hated her even more for not knowing how to love somebody who wasn't a drunk.

A gust of wind blew the thick, damp smell of summer rain hard across my face. And there was the scent of the moonflower whose very purpose for existing was to bathe the night air with its own love potion. The combination of the two made the last few minutes I'd spent watching Winston snake around in my mind. I saw glimpses of his hand brushing against my breast and his smile when he touched my hair. I closed my eyes and remembered his earthy scent. He was more than Scotch and a pretty face; I would have bet my life on it. The rain came down hard enough to chase anyone with good sense inside. But I stood there as the downpour washed over me and convinced myself I could have him.

14

I could tell it really bothered Mrs. Cathcart when the crying girl and her fiancé, Harley, came in that morning, holding hands and inviting everybody in the whole school to their wedding. I'm sure she wished the two of them had just gotten married with the same privacy they had when they'd done the deed. But Harley Dimel was nearly forty, and his poor mama had all but given up hope that he'd ever tie the knot. Now that he had him a fertile young thing, Mrs. Dimel figured it was cause enough to celebrate.

She paid for the entire wedding, right down to the bride's dress and the cake, which was good because the Prices didn't have any money to speak of. If they did, I don't think they would have been cleaning the bank for a living. Harley's mama had plenty because she'd put money away in a savings account ever since he was a baby.

Since Nina was already pregnant, the Holiness Church she belonged to refused to marry her and Harley, so the wedding and the reception were held at the VFW Hall. On the big day, Mr. and Mrs. Cathcart and I walked into the hall together. Judging from the look on her face, I don't think Mrs. Cathcart could have wound herself any tighter. It was a simple wedding with the chairs arranged in a little horseshoe and ferns with sprays of daisies in them all around the podium. Half of the chairs were metal with VFW stenciled on the back. The other half were wooden folding chairs from Mr. Platt's funeral parlor.

The organist must have only known two songs, because she played "Cherish" over and over again. But she did know "The Wedding March," and when we all turned around to see Nina coming down the aisle, everybody smiled and laughed. In the entire history of weddings, there has never been such a tear-streaked bride. But there she was with her mascara running down her face and onto her dress. Still beautiful.

After the happy couple left the reception, a bunch of us sat around and talked about graduating in just a few short weeks. We wondered where the time had gone and laughed about our first days of school and how everything was new and scary. Then Jeanetta Smith, who always made fun of Nina, sometimes to her face, started in all loud and drunk.

"Oh, my God, to you remember how you'd hear that sound, almost like a siren far off and it would build and build?"

Jeanetta tried to mimic the sound. Some of the girls thought it was funny and laughed right along with Jeanetta, and the others had a look on their faces like they'd better laugh, if they knew what was good for them if they didn't want her making fun of them.

"And why in the world did that girl even bother with mascara? Do you remember the time—"

I'd seen girls like Jeanetta before and had always tried to be invisible around them. But with Mama flitting around as Judy Garland, I was easy pickings. Those girls just seem have a radar for people like me who silently pray they won't be the butt of their jokes, and they're more than happy to use it. Nina's mother was looking over at our table. I'm sure she wondered what was going on. As loud as Jeanetta was, she probably knew.

"All I can say, Jeanetta Smith, is that you can laugh all you want at Nina Price-Dimel, but she just left the VFW in a limo, with the man of her dreams, and you are still here." I didn't say it ugly. I just finished my drink, got up from the table, gave her a little smile that said, "No harm done," and walked home.

After Nina's wedding, Sara Jane couldn't have waited another day to tell the whole world she loved Jimmy Alvarez. I believe if she had, she would have split at the seams from that intoxicated grin she wore across her pretty mouth. The only problem was that the whole world included her mama and her daddy.

She had fretted for weeks over what they might say, but only because they were almost as important to her as Jimmy was. But the time had come, so she invited Jimmy to church and Sunday dinner, which I told her was a big mistake. I said she should let her folks get used to Jimmy in small doses. However, I did think the idea of a public place was good to prevent the temper tantrum I was sure her daddy would throw.

It was hot that day, real hot. I stood there waiting on the church steps for a while but didn't see them. I thought they'd probably chickened out, but just as I turned to go inside, I caught a glimpse of Jimmy's white truck easing down the street as he looked for a place to park. I could tell when Sara Jane got out of the truck, she was a little miffed about riding in the Toyota, but when he opened her door and she stepped out of the cab, he gave her hand a peck and said something.

Sara Jane laughed the way she always did when he was around. I called it her "Jimmy laugh" because I never heard her laugh like that any other time. She could never stay mad at him for more than two minutes, and truth be told, I'm sure she would rather have come in that pretty red Pontiac Firebird her daddy bought her for her eighteenth birthday. But I think it was important for Jimmy Alvarez to come in his own truck, on his own terms.

"Hey, y'all. I thought you'd never get here."

"Hey, Zora," Jimmy said. "Are you here for the barbecue?"

"Hush, Jimmy." Sara Jane smiled as she took him by the hand.

"They're having barbecued Mexican for dinner at Sara Jane's," he said as he passed through the door and into the church.

As soon as Jimmy entered the sanctuary, he had a reverence about him that I had never seen before. As we walked down the left aisle, Jimmy looked up toward the choir loft and saw the huge cross suspended from the ceiling there and instinctively crossed himself. Several people gasped.

When we sat down, Sara Jane quietly filled Jimmy in on everything he needed to know about a Baptist service. When she told him Baptists never cross themselves, he looked at her like he didn't believe her. I opened my eyes just long enough during the opening prayer to see Jimmy watching the congregation to see if Sara Jane was right. Poor boy, every time we prayed or the preacher read Scripture, I noticed he would squeeze Sara Jane's hand and sit up extra straight, like the urge to cross himself was potentially lethal.

I know Sara Jane's daddy saw Jimmy, but he didn't look our way the entire service. He definitely wasn't his usual smiling-with-the-joy-of-the-Lord worshipful self and didn't sing a note when the congregation sang. Mrs. Farquhar whispered to him every now and then and patted his hand the way she did at the dinner table the first day Sara Jane brought me home with her. She looked over at us and smiled several times, and Sara Jane squeezed my hand because it seemed half the battle was won.

Thank God we had a visiting preacher that day because if Jimmy had had to sit through one of Reverend Lynch's marathon sermons and Sunday dinner, he might have walked out on Sara Jane no matter how much he loved her. During the benediction, right before the preacher ended his prayer, Jimmy crossed himself quickly so no one would see. I shouldn't have been looking, but I was. Sara Jane must have known he did it, too, because she smiled. As soon as the preacher said "Amen," Jimmy let out this huge sigh.

Miss Lucy Mae Brown nearly knocked some poor lady over trying to get to us before we got out of the sanctuary. Just when it looked like we might slip out the side door, she hollered, "Sara Jane. Is that my yard boy you're with?"

Well, most people would have just turned around and told the old biddy where she could go for hollering such a thing in the middle of a crowded church, but Sara Jane didn't.

"Now, Miss Lucy Mae," Sara Jane said with that silky voice of hers, "you know good and well that this is Jimmy Alvarez. He's my beau."

"You don't say," Miss Lucy Mae said with the most amazed look on her face, like Jimmy couldn't do anything but rake leaves and cut grass. "Sir, you are one lucky man to have found such a fine girl, and, if you don't mind me saying so, you are an excellent yard boy."

"No, ma'am," Jimmy said, "I don't mind you saying so. I know I'm a lucky man."

Sara Jane looked at me as we walked to the parking lot and breathed a heavy sigh. "Round one," she said under her breath.

Jimmy's Toyota was just big enough for him and Sara Jane, so I rode to the house with Mr. and Mrs. Farquhar. I would gladly have walked the six or seven miles, but Mrs. Farquhar insisted. The tension in the air of that great big Lincoln made it feel as crowded as a clown car, but nobody was laughing. Mr. Farquhar's face and neck were bright red, and it had been that way ever since Sara Jane sashayed down the church aisle with her fiancé. He looked like he might explode at any moment. I know Mrs. Farquhar was a little miffed, too, because she had been kept in the dark over the whole Jimmy thing, but the two of them were so proper, they were trying not to say anything about it in front of me.

"What did you think about the preacher, Mr. Farquhar?" I asked, to break the silence before the poor man burst right there in the car.

"Not enough bite in his sermon, if you ask me," he said.

"I did miss Preacher Lynch today." There was no doubt that Mrs. Farquhar was trying hard to figure out a way to make peace out of Sunday dinner. Even her voice was different, more soothing than usual, the way you might talk to a frightened animal. I remembered hearing that same tone in Sara Jane's voice when I was sick over the baby's rattle and she was dabbing my face with the cool washrag.

"I can't believe—" he started.

"Jerry," his wife said, for my benefit and for his. "This is not the time or the place."

His breathing was deep and angry. He ran a stop sign, which I don't think he knew, and neither did Mrs. Farquhar, because she was putting all of her energy into keeping him from breaking loose and doing irreparable damage to their family. As he pulled into the driveway and looked at the woman he loved, he surrendered.

"Nettie," he said, "how can she do this to us?"

I don't know what she said because I got out of the car then and met Sara Jane and Jimmy by the curb. I did look back over my shoulder to see Mrs. Farquhar put her arms around her husband and rock him gently. I think she honestly believed that she could love him toward tolerance and acceptance, but, judging from the way he slammed that car door, I had my doubts.

Sara Jane had her little Villager pumps in one hand and Jimmy's hand in the other as they walked across the lawn to meet me. She didn't seem to notice her daddy's display, or if she did, she didn't care. I fully expected her to quiz me as to what her parents said about Jimmy, but she didn't. At first I thought it was because Jimmy was standing right there and she didn't want to hurt his feelings. But Sara Jane had come to a place where she really didn't care one way or the other whether her parents accepted Jimmy, because she did, and that was all that mattered.

"It was Sara Jane's idea to surprise them like this," Jimmy said to me under his breath.

"Hey, y'all," Mrs. Farquhar hollered as she held the screen door open. "Come on in. Dinner's almost ready." Right away, she hugged Jimmy's neck like he was already family. I believe that somehow she must have known that he was the one, just like Sara Jane knew the first time she laid eyes on him.

Mr. Farquhar didn't even bother to get out of his chair to shake Jimmy's hand. He nodded our way but didn't crack a smile as he mumbled something about the Falcons game not being on Channel Three like they were every blame Sunday.

Sara Jane was smart enough not to throw Jimmy into her daddy's den, although I am sure he could have held his own. So the three of us went into the kitchen where Mrs. Farquhar was finishing up dinner. Jimmy entertained us all with stories about Mexico and fussy customers, while I set the table and Sara Jane poured sweet tea in the good crystal glasses. I could tell Mrs. Farquhar was charmed right off.

"How long have you lived in Davenport, Jimmy?" She handed him a glass of sweet tea.

"Not long. I lived with my aunt and uncle; we used to come through here with the migrant camps. I helped them open a landscaping business in Raleigh. Then I started my own company here about six months ago."

Mrs. Farquhar was almost as smitten as Sara Jane. She put her very best bowls and platters on the table so that it looked like the cover of *Southern Living*'s Thanksgiving issue. We stood there behind our chairs, waiting for Mr. Farquhar, who had to be called to dinner three times. Just when it looked like his wife was going to lose her composure, he lumbered into that great big formal dining room with his lucky black Falcons T-shirt on and a look on his face like the big game had already been lost.

I'm sure Sara Jane seated Jimmy to her left so that when we said grace, he wouldn't have to hold her father's hand. I could tell she was anxious about the whole situation because I saw her nearly squeeze Jimmy's in two when her daddy said grace. As soon as Mr. Farquhar said, "Amen," I took one look at Sara Jane and thought it might be a good idea to take cover.

Mrs. Farquhar had outdone herself again, and for a few minutes Mr. Farquhar seemed distracted by all the food. Everybody was passing bowls or platters, dipping this or that onto their plates, everybody except Sara Jane. I saw Jimmy look at her out of the corner of his eye and ever so slightly shake his head, but it didn't do any good. Once Sara Jane set her mind on something, there wasn't much anybody could do. Later on when we rehashed the whole thing over a bottle of wine at my apartment, I told her that at the very least I thought she could have waited until after dinner.

"Mama, Daddy," she drew in a deep breath, then said the words real fast, "me and Jimmy are getting married."

Well, even Mrs. Farquhar was taken aback. Mr. Farquhar dropped the big meat fork on the china platter, and then slammed it down hard on the table. Sara Jane's eyes raced back and forth between her parents like she was waiting to see who was going to fire the first shot, while poor Jimmy just stared quietly at his empty dinner plate. I fully expected all of them to start fussing over Sara Jane's announcement, but nobody said a word.

Then Jimmy looked up from his plate, cleared his throat, and looked Mr. Farquhar straight in the eyes. "Mr. Farquhar, Mrs. Farquhar, I wanted her to wait until dinner was over, but I guess now's as good a time as any. I love Sara Jane." He took her hand in his. "We want to get married. I promise I'll take real good care of her. She'll never want for anything, and—"

Mr. Farquhar laughed out loud.

"What makes you think you can give our Sara Jane the kinds of things she's had all her life? Why, you're just a . . . a yard boy."

"I think what Jerry is trying to say," Mrs. Farquhar said, "is that Sara Jane is our only child. We've spoiled her rotten, always giving her whatever she wants. I, we are just concerned that you might not be able to give her those things, and that it might cause both of you a lot of heartache."

"Well, the yard business is a whole lot better than you think, and—"

"Let me just ask you one thing, boy," Mr. Farquhar said. "Do the two of you have to get married?"

"Yes, sir, we do."

"My God, Nettie, she's pregnant with this . . . this wetback's baby."

"There ain't no baby," Jimmy said. "Me and Sara Jane have to get married because we love each other, that's all. We just love each other."

15

I was running so late I nearly stumbled out the front door of the garage apartment and didn't even notice Winston until I got to the bottom of the steps. He was striding toward me with purpose, a slight smile on his beautiful face. He had something in his hand, a letter. My heart flip-flopped in my chest like crazy over the very notion that finally this man had noticed me. Maybe he couldn't say it out loud, but he was an English professor, for Pete's sake, and he'd written down his feeling for me on paper. The first chapter of our happily every after.

"This was in the mail for you," he said without so much as a *hey* or *how are you.* "If you want your own mailbox, I can have a handyman put one by your door."

"No," I squeaked, "thanks." I don't know what was worse that Monday, Winston's idea of playing Post Office or Mama's letter coming back to me with RETURN TO SENDER written in her scrawl.

I was wounded before I got to school, but when Sara Jane came and got the few things together that were hers before she said her good-byes, that did it. I wasn't the only one affected by Sara Jane's leaving. Anybody could see Mrs. Cathcart's face was full of mixed emotions. She held Sara Jane in her arms like she didn't know whether to laugh or cry, but one thing was for sure, Mrs. Cathcart was going to miss Sara Jane Farquhar.

"Oh, she takes things like this hard," Mr. Cathcart said with a deep sigh as he watched Sara Jane go from station to station. "She wants everybody to finish and get their license, you know. Makes it even harder if they got the smarts Sara Jane has."

"Don't think you're going to get rid of me," she said, as we put our arms around each other. "I've got a wedding to plan, and you've just got to be my maid of honor."

"Oh, Sara Jane," I whispered through tears. "I love you."

She held me at arm's length and looked at me. I don't know why I felt so weak and broken in her gaze, but I did.

"Thank you for getting me as far as you did. I'll never forget that."

It wasn't like she was leaving town or anything; still, her leaving was hard to take. I must have looked peaked because Mr. Cathcart came by after Sara Jane left and told me to go straight home before I infected the whole school with whatever it was that I had. But the truth was that nobody there could catch what I had.

I went home straightaway and contemplated my own heart. I don't know if it was love or destiny or genetics that made me pant for Winston Sawyer, but I had a wanting inside me that could not be satisfied by school or good grades or even a best friend like Sara Jane Farquhar.

When I walked through my front door to my apartment that day, I left it wide open. I slipped out of my uniform and underclothes, got down on my hands and knees, and pulled the box out from under the bed marked Serendipity. Folding back the bronze-colored tissue paper carefully, I gathered up each side of the dress, and let that whisper of silk that had shamed me once before glide across my naked body.

There was no need to look in the full-length mirror I had bought a couple of weeks before. I was beautiful. I stood on my porch so the whole world could see me, including Winston Sawyer. The wind blew my hair about, making me feel light, lighter than air. I closed my eyes, caught hold of the breeze that made the curtains in his drinking room stir, and filled that room with my essence. I felt his touch on the hem of my dress and then on my ankle as he held me fast in wonder. Then his hand slid up my thigh and his lips kissed my belly before the wind picked me up again and levitated me back to my perch.

When I opened my eyes, the fantasy was over, and he was standing at the drinking room window. I have no idea what happened during the time I left my body and invaded the space he had reserved for himself and Emma, but I knew that, for a moment, Winston Sawyer was watching me.

16

Winston started me up every morning, whether he knew it or not, just by cranking up that little MG and giving the motor three short revs before pulling out of the driveway. Normally, I sat bolt upright, peeked through the curtains, and felt desperate that he was leaving me.

But that morning, as I lay there under that flimsy cotton sheet, I was aware of my own special power, something I never even knew I had. I felt like Bo Derek when she jogged down the beach in the movie *10*, or like a comic-book vixen whose superpower was beauty. I got out of bed, ate a little breakfast, and dressed in no particular hurry. The world waits for women like Bo and me. We move at our own pace.

I arrived about eight o'clock, just in time to see Ellen Snellgrove almost die right there in front of the whole beauty school when her mama fell into the foyer. Mrs. Snellgrove crawled over to the brass coatrack and pulled herself up gradually, nearly tipping the rack over twice before she was on her feet. Her bottom half was firmly planted, thanks to the coatrack, but her torso gyrated about, trying to keep pace with the spinning room, I suspect. Being no stranger to stumbling mamas, I went straight to my station and got busy doing anything I could think of to keep from gawking with the rest of the students at Mrs. Snellgrove.

"Mama," Ellen hissed as she went over to her and put her hand on the woman's arm to keep her from spinning.

"Ellen," she said, pushing it away so she could resume.

Ellen looked around the room and saw everybody looking at her, even me, I am ashamed to say. She turned her back to us and grabbed her mama again, only this time she got a better grip.

"What are you doing here, Mama?"

"Get your hands off of me!" she hollered, as she pretended to smooth her blouse, which was buttoned as cockeyed as possible. "I come for my cut and perm."

By this time, Mrs. Cathcart had seen enough. She came over and tapped me on the shoulder, and I followed her over to the foyer. I felt like I was invading the poor girl's nightmare. Ellen looked so ashamed that Mrs. Cathcart was stepping in.

"Mrs. Snellgrove," Mrs. Cathcart began. "This is Zora Adams, one of our best and brightest, and she needs some work on her manicures before the State Board examination. Would you mind terribly if she practices on you?"

The woman looked me up and down.

"And a pedicure, too. There'd be no charge," Mrs. Cathcart added.

"I want my Ellen," she answered, grabbing Ellen and whining in a mocking sort of way.

I tried to look like I'd certainly never witnessed anything that crazy from my own mother, but Ellen never saw my face or anybody else's. She just stared at that terrazzo floor, wishing it would open up and swallow her whole.

"Mrs. Snellgrove, have you ever had a pedicure before?" Mrs. Cathcart managed to loosen the woman's grip on her daughter and steer her toward the manicure station in the back of the school.

As I turned to follow Mrs. Cathcart, I heard Ellen whisper, "Sorry."

I wanted to look at her and smile so that she would know that I'd walked in her shoes, but I couldn't. It was too much like looking at my old self.

"Sorry," I said back.

I don't know why Mrs. Cathcart chose me, because I had a customer waiting for a haircut. I guess she figured if I could handle old Ethyl, I could handle Ellen Snellgrove's mama.

I sat down at the table and asked her twice to slip her shoes and socks off. She didn't. So I bent down and slipped them off for her, and before I could raise up, she propped her legs up on my back and cackled as loud as she could. I rolled my chair to the side and let her feet fall to the floor and pretended like nothing had ever happened.

"Mrs. Snellgrove, would you please put your feet in the tub? It'll feel real nice."

She put her feet in and wiggled her toes around in the bubbly pink solution like a little child. I poured a green solution into two finger bowls and placed her fingers in them. She fussed because the solution wasn't pink, which she said was her favorite color.

"Ellen's mad." She looked at me with a wicked smile.

I didn't say anything. I thought if I didn't contribute to the conversation, there wouldn't be one. I was wrong.

"I hate Ellen," she said, waving her hand around for effect.

I put her hand back in the solution.

"Ellen hates me," she said, loud enough for everybody to hear.

"Shhhh," I said, real soft, the way I had heard mamas quiet their children during church.

"*Don't you shush me.*"

Mrs. Cathcart rushed over to the table. "Nadine Snellgrove." Mrs. Cathcart got right in her face and whispered so loud, anybody could have heard her. "You can either be quiet or leave, because if I hear another word out of you, I'm gonna call the cops."

"Don't let her call the cops. You stop her, you hear? I'll talk pretty; I swear I will."

Mrs. Cathcart walked away in a huff.

"Nobody's calling the cops, Mrs. Snellgrove. You just have to quiet down, that's all."

I put her hands back in the solution. Her fingers jumped about so it looked like the solution was boiling.

"Cops is bad," she said. "They lie. They say I took prescription papers out of Dr. Hess's office. I got back problems, in pain all the time. Pain . . . lots of pain." She wiped her forehead like her fingers weren't dripping wet.

"Ellen doesn't think I'm in pain and her daddy don't, either, but I am."

She buttoned her lip for as long as she could.

"They say I'm a drug addict. Have you ever heard of anything so ridiculous in your whole life?"

I shook my head and worked faster.

"I have all kinds of aches and pains, especially in my back. Got that one when she come along. Clovis says that's not so, but what does he know? He ain't never had a baby."

I'm sure I must have set some kind of record for the fastest manicure and pedicure. "All done," I said with a big smile.

"There's no paint on my fingernails," she whined.

"Your nails are filed and shaped and your cuticles look good. That's the best I can do today, Mrs. Snellgrove, with your hands shaking like that."

"I want paint."

She picked out the ugliest color of orange, and her hands looked awful because she couldn't be still. Her toenails looked better, because her feet were the only part of her body that didn't shake. She paraded out toward Ellen's station barefoot, sashaying and waving her hands about, trying to make everybody laugh, but nobody did. It took her a few minutes to realize Ellen wasn't there.

"I want my cut and perm." She pounded on the back of Ellen's chair with freshly manicured nails.

Mrs. Cathcart marched out from her office, took that woman by the arm, and threw her out the door and into the street, where she proceeded to give Nadine Snellgrove a piece of her mind. Ellen's mama defended herself at first, going nose to nose with Mrs. Cathcart, who I am sure after everything was said and done was appalled that she had participated in such a display. By the time it was over, Mrs. Snellgrove was on her hands and knees crying, right there in the middle of the street with cars honking and people cussing at her. Mrs. Cathcart just walked back inside and left her there.

Nobody asked where Ellen was, although later I found out that Mr. Cathcart had driven her to her daddy's feed store. She didn't come back to school until a few days later.

"Thank you for putting up with my mama," she said. "I couldn't do it anymore. Me and Daddy put her away."

"I'm sorry. I hope she gets better."

"Mama don't get better. She just steps out of the mire so she can take a running jump right back in," she said dryly.

If Ellen had a choice between never being and living with the woman, who regretted the very day she was born, I'm sure she would have chosen to just never be.

"I bet your mama's normal, not crazy like mine," she said as she swept the hair from her last appointment into a dustpan.

I wanted to put my arms around Ellen Snellgrove and tell her she wasn't the only child who wanted to swap out her mother. I know I would have given anything to trade mine for one like Mrs. Farquhar or Mrs. Cathcart. I wanted to tell her about seeing Mama in front of the mirror primping to go out to the roadhouse so that a bunch of drunks would fawn all over her. I wanted to tell her about the time I spent down on my knees praying she'd never come back and then, after she was gone for days, praying she would come home.

But I didn't say anything. I just smiled my Bo Derek smile and acted like I already had a TV mom while that poor girl went right on thinking that she was the only soul in the world who felt the way she did.

17

⌒

Raymond O. Hawkins was the great-great-granddaddy of Mrs. Farquhar, and even though he was long gone, he was honored every year by Mrs. Farquhar's people for being one of the founding fathers of near-perfect barbecue. The Annual Raymond O. Hawkins Barbecue was a big to-do with "connoisseurs" sampling barbecue and the biggest spread of food I'd ever seen.

Since they would have nearly two hundred people milling around their backyard waiting to sample the sacred pig and all the fixings, Sara Jane offered to pick her grandmother up from the nursing home in Myrtle Beach. I saw Sara Jane's car pull up out front and Mama Grayson with her big old Dolly Parton wig, but when Jimmy got out of the backseat, too, I knew there'd be trouble.

Mr. Farquhar dropped his basting mop and stomped toward the house. "Now, Jerry, this is a special day. It comes once a year just like Easter and Christmas. Let's not ruin it," Mrs. Farquhar said. "Please."

He looked helpless and fired up all at the same time, but the poor man could do nothing when she spoke to him like that. I knew it, he knew it, and so did every soul in that room. It wasn't like she was pleading or demanding; she was just letting him know what was important and what was not. I'd seen this before at the Farquhar's house, but I never saw Mr. Farquhar just wheel around like he did and walk away from her. Judging from the look on Mrs. Farquhar's face, I don't think she had, either.

"Mama's in here, Grandma," I heard Sara Jane say.

"Watch your step, Gracie," Jimmy said.

Even Mrs. Farquhar looked a little unnerved when she heard Jimmy call her mama "Gracie," but she rinsed her hands off, wiped them with a dishrag, and met the three of them at the door.

"Mama." Mrs. Farquhar wrapped her arms around her mother and closed her eyes.

"Who are you?" the old woman said, with the most surprised look on her face.

"It's me, Nettie, Mama. I'm your baby girl, remember?"

"Well, Nettie, this is my beau," she said, as she gripped Jimmy by the forearm.

"You're my girl, Gracie," Jimmy teased.

"Don't you be taking my boyfriend now, Grandma," Sara Jane said. "You look so pretty today, though, I don't stand a chance."

Mrs. Farquhar stepped back and surveyed the situation. Her mama, who wasn't quite right, was standing there holding on to Jimmy like they were courting. Sara Jane was teasing her grandmother and looking at Jimmy like she could eat him up.

"It's good to see you, Jimmy," Mrs. Farquhar said, as she surprised us all by hugging him, too. "I like your new beau, Mama."

"Well," Mama Grayson snapped, "don't you be hugging on him, either."

We all laughed, even the churchwomen. Mrs. Farquhar pried her mama's hand off of Jimmy's arm and told her she was taking her to the bathroom to freshen up a bit. Sara Jane introduced Jimmy to everybody in the kitchen, and I guess he must have melted every heart there with the kindness he showed Mama Grayson, because all of them were polite to him in a very real sort of way.

"I'm gonna go speak to your daddy," Jimmy said, and the whole room went silent again.

Sara Jane didn't say a word. She just raised her eyebrows like she wasn't too sure he should do that just now. But Jimmy looked so strong inside and out, he wasn't about to let anything deter him from becoming a part of that family, not even Sara Jane's daddy.

She came over to where I was slicing onions and gave me a hug, but the whole time she had her eyes on the backyard.

"Your mama already spoke to your daddy," I whispered. "She told him to behave himself in not so many words. I don't know, though, he just walked off in a huff."

We stood at the window and watched Jimmy walk across the yard to the tables where the men had just set the pigs on large wooden slabs. He extended his hand to Mr. Farquhar, who didn't offer his at first. But the preacher was standing right beside him, and he shook Jimmy's hand, so I guess Mr. Farquhar felt like he had to.

"Jimmy brought his books to show Daddy," Sara Jane said, keeping her eye on Jimmy.

"What'd you say, honey?" Mrs. Farquhar said, as she ushered her mama into the kitchen.

"I was just telling Zora that Jimmy brought his books to show Daddy. He's got a good business, Mama."

"I'm sure your father will be impressed," Mrs. Farquhar said, "whether he likes it or not."

"Where's my Jimmy?" Mama Grayson called out real loud.

"He's right out back, Mama. I'll take you to see him," Mrs. Farquhar said.

"He's such a sweet man. Has the prettiest brown eyes." Mama Grayson smiled.

"Such a sweet man," Mrs. Farquhar echoed.

There were so many people at the barbecue that Sara Jane's daddy could avoid Jimmy all day and half the night without making himself look bad. But poor Jimmy was so anxious to get to know his future father-in-law he didn't get the message. I was glad that some of the guests had begun to leave because judging from the look on Mr. Farquhar's face, I don't think he could have taken being shadowed for another minute. Everybody offered to help clean up the aftermath, but Mrs. Farquhar was adamant that the cleanup was as much a part of the family tradition as the barbecue itself.

Sara Jane said this was all new to her, but I suspected Mrs. Farquhar was exhausted from feeding two hundred guests and watching her husband stew all day. At any rate, nobody put up a fight when they were told to go on home and not worry about cleaning up.

Sara Jane was tired. Jimmy told her to sit down and prop her feet up, but she refused, which made Jimmy work all the harder so there would be less for her to do. Every once in a while I would see Sara Jane's mother speak to her daddy without turning her head toward him and looking at him. She didn't seem happy. Mama Grayson sat in a big rust-colored Barcalounger the men brought outside for her, sound asleep.

It took almost two hours of hard work to get the yard back to normal. The rental company would come and take the tent down Monday, according to Mrs. Farquhar, and there were only two things left to do—wake Mama Grayson up and take her home, and carry the Barcalounger back inside the house.

"Mr. Farquhar, I'll help you get this chair inside," Jimmy said when he came back from loading bags of garbage onto the Red & White grocery truck parked out front.

"Sara Jane and I'll get it. You go on home now," he said without even so much as a thank-you for all Jimmy's hard work.

Sara Jane and I were standing there with Mama Grayson while she stretched her legs a bit. Sara Jane just looked at her daddy and walked off. If she had not left me there holding Mama Grayson's arm, I would have left, too, because I didn't want any part of what was coming.

"Well, sir, I'd like to finish up here and maybe if you got a minute—"

"I don't have a minute," Mr. Farquhar said dryly. "You get now. Go on home."

"Show him your books, honey." Mama Grayson sounded like Jimmy really was her boyfriend. "Jerry, hush up and listen to Jimmy."

Nobody ever looked at Mama Grayson like she was a senile old woman. She was loved and revered by everyone, but just then her son-in-law cut his eye around at her like she'd better not say another word if she knew what was good for her.

"Books," he said with a laugh, "you say you brought your books?"

Now even Jimmy's patience was wearing thin, and rightfully so, but he didn't let up. "Yes, sir. I thought we could sit down and you could take a look and see—"

"See nothing."

"See that I can take good care of Sara Jane."

Mr. Farquhar's face was full of meanness from holding back all the ugly words he wanted to say. He reared his head back and laughed at Jimmy again. That was when he first noticed his beloved wife and daughter standing beside Mama Grayson and me with their hands on their hips in disgust, and their feet set apart like they were ready for a fight.

We stood there and watched Jimmy and Mr. Farquhar walk out to Sara Jane's car.

Mrs. Farquhar closed her eyes several times, I am sure to pray. I think we all did except for Mama Grayson, who was getting a little miffed at Jimmy for leaving her alone. Sara Jane looked at me, but neither of us said a word. Jimmy and Mr. Farquhar must have stood under that streetlight for an hour. It was too late to drive all the way to North Myrtle Beach to the nursing home, so we all went back inside and put Mama Grayson to bed.

Sara Jane and her mama took turns standing at the picture window watching the two men by the curb. Nobody could tell how things were going, but Sara Jane made the comment that things must be going all right because her daddy was still out there. Finally the two men walked into the house.

"Sara Jane," Mr. Farquhar said gruffly, "Jimmy here has something to say, and you better listen and listen good."

The color drained from her face. She grabbed my hand. I felt her trembling all over.

Jimmy looked her straight in the eyes. He pulled a little black velvet box out of his pocket, got down on one knee, and offered himself to her for the rest of his life. Sara Jane looked at her daddy, who was so taken by the moment he couldn't speak. He just looked at her and nodded his head, then held his own beloved wife and cried.

18

I remember Daddy buying Mama a new dress he couldn't afford. It wasn't fancy, but pretty, light, flowy cotton with little flowers on it. She stood there holding it up to her, squealing like a little girl at Christmastime, as she twirled about in front of the full-length mirror. It was the prettiest thing I'd ever seen. He bought it to take her to Rock City for their anniversary. I guess that was about a month or two before he died. They'd never been anywhere before, and with those SEE ROCK CITY billboards all over the mountains, I guess he thought he'd take her there to see what all the fuss was about. I remember asking, then begging him to take me along. Nana set me down and told me that this was their time. That night, I sneaked into Mama's room while everybody sat on the front porch. I twirled around in that dress myself, wishing it were my time for such things.

That's how I felt about Sara Jane and Jimmy getting married. I was truly happy for them and considered it a bona fide miracle that the Farquhars had given them their blessing. Between the run-in with Ellen's mama and my own wanting, I wasn't feeling so all-powerful anymore. I was back at that blamed window every day whenever I heard Winston's car coming or going, wondering if my time would ever come.

I didn't go to church that Sunday. I phoned Mrs. Farquhar, who fussed at me for not calling her "Mama" again, and told her I wasn't feeling well and that I wouldn't be there for dinner, either. She was happiest when she was planning things, especially events that involved fancy food, so she was thrilled over the prospect of a big wedding.

"You rest, Zora dear," she said. "I know you're tired; you worked yourself to death yesterday. But you take care of yourself, you hear, and clear your calendar for next weekend, because me and you and Sara Jane are going to Atlanta to find the perfect wedding gown."

"Atlanta?"

"Now, hush. You sound just like Jerry." She laughed. "I told him we can't just go down to the Bridal Barn in Davenport or that trashy little Chéz I Do over in Myrtle Beach and pick out a dress. We have to have the most perfect, which Jerry says means the most expensive, bridal gown in all the land."

"I'd be honored to go."

"Oh, just the thought of shopping with my girls makes me so happy. Now, how are you feeling?" She went on, quizzing me about my symptoms, like one of those TV mothers, before she said good-bye, and I loved her for that.

I lazed around, and didn't really do anything other than cook Sunday dinner for Winston, who wasn't home. I fried chicken, opened a can of corn, and made a box of instant mashed potatoes for the first time in my life. I'd gotten caught up in Sara Jane's theory that love is just like it is in her romance books; it was easy for her to believe that because life had worked out that way for her. That night, my offering to Winston reflected my new view of reality.

It was nice that day, cool fall weather but bright and sunny. I put a sweatshirt on, took my own dinner down to the picnic table, and sat right across from his plate. I also brought a bottle of red wine and one of the wineglasses that Sara Jane and I borrowed from a little bar in North Myrtle Beach. Still stuffed from yesterday, I just picked at my chicken, but the wine was good and sweet, and I felt, I don't know, grown up there having drinks and dinner by myself.

After a while, I pushed the plate aside, balled my knees up to my chest, and pulled my sweatshirt over them like I did on cold winter mornings back home. I sipped my wine, watching the birds flying south, and then there were some that were going the opposite way. I wondered if they knew this or if somehow they would miraculously end up where they were supposed to be before it was too late and winter had set in.

I'd had just enough wine in me not to move when Winston's little MG drove up into the yard. It was dusk. He politely turned the headlights off when he saw me sitting there.

"A picnic," he said, standing there looking at me. I couldn't tell whether he was drunk or sober. I didn't know which I was, either.

"It is a picnic table."

He smiled, sat down, and took the tinfoil off of the plate. "You don't have to do this, you know," he said, as he started to eat.

"You don't seem to mind," I said, as I filled my glass a little too full.

He picked up the glass, took one sip, and winced over my choice of wine. Before I could say anything, he went into the house. He came back with an expensive-looking bottle of red wine and a real corkscrew.

I screwed the top back on my bottle. "Imagine that," I said as he poured my wine onto the ground and filled the glass half full with his. I swirled it around and sniffed it like I had seen Robert Wagner do on that TV show *Hart to Hart*. Taking a dainty little sip like I was Stefanie Powers, I nodded in approval. I can't describe the taste: It was so many flavors from the earth, but then I couldn't pronounce the name, either, because it was something French, and I didn't want to embarrass myself during my TV moment.

He took the glass out of my hand and took a sip.

"This is good," he said, turning the glass up. "Very nice."

If I'd been sober, I would've been worrying about silly things like what my hair looked like or what I was wearing, but my head was light, and I felt bold. He sat across the table from me and refilled our glass. It didn't take more than the very idea of our lips touching the same glass to arouse me. More than once we reached for it at the same time. Our hands brushed against each other. If the table had not separated us, I would've touched him and aroused him, too.

"Didn't you help me into the house," he asked as he poured the last of the good stuff into the glass, "a couple of weeks ago?"

I opened my mouth to say something; he put his fingers over my lips. Closing my eyes, I nodded as his fingertips slid down my chin and the length of my neck.

He drained his glass again. "Your hair, it smelled like rain." If he had asked me to get down on all fours and bark like a dog just then, I swear to God, I would have done it.

His plate was clean; the wine was gone, so there was no excuse for him to stay. The silence was awkward because we weren't drunk enough to crawl across the table and melt together. I stood up first to say good night. I wanted him to see me walk away, and if he couldn't come after me, I wanted him to want me.

I didn't have to look back over my shoulder to know that he was watching. As I climbed up those stairs to my little perch, I had the power again. The door was wide open so that only the screen separated us. I took my clothes off, not where he could see, but somehow I knew he was still watching my place. I touched myself for a while the way I wanted him to touch me, then reached for an old cotton shirt to sleep in. Watching each button slide through the hole, I was nearly breathless by the time I got to the last one.

I walked to the front door to close and lock it and saw him standing there, looking up at my apartment with my empty wineglass still in his hand. I guess he was wrestling with thoughts of me and Emma, of coming up the stairs and opening my front door without knocking. I closed the door, went to bed, and slept better than I had in a long time.

I woke up before the alarm normally went off, which was good, because I had forgotten to set the clock for seven. Mrs. Cathcart was holding a class meeting before the school opened, which she did from time to time. The meetings were usually about business that pertained to the school itself and school policies, but from the way she reminded each of us to be on time, we all knew that this one was important.

Mr. Cathcart had five brothers—a printer, a caterer, a food broker, a manager at the Davenport Country Club, and a bum. Mr. Cathcart called his baby brother a bum, but in truth, he was the disc jockey at the only radio station in town, and made his living spinning easy listening hits on the morning shift and as a DJ at weddings and parties. All of them came in handy for Mrs. Cathcart's annual Davenport School of Beauty Winter Graduation Dinner and Dance.

Now, if you asked any other cosmetologist about her graduation, she would probably look at you like you were crazy. Most stylists just take their State Board exam and then start their first job without the least little bit of fanfare. This would have been unthinkable for Mrs. Cathcart. Everything from birthdays to Arbor Day was a big event for her.

She handed each of us a fancy envelope, hugging us and telling us how proud she was. I ran my finger under the wax seal and pulled out the card inside. It looked like a wedding invitation except it had a picture of a pink pair of scissors cutting a lock of black hair.

You and an escort are cordially
Invited to attend the annual
Davenport School of Beauty
Winter Graduation Dinner and Dance

Saturday, December 1, 1983
The Davenport Country Club
Dinner is served promptly at six o'clock in the evening
Dancing to follow in the Grand Ballroom

"Your parents may purchase tickets for twelve dollars apiece or twenty per couple," Mrs. Cathcart said. "It's a grand affair, and it fills up right quick, so you need to let me know as soon as possible how many tickets you will need. Again, I'm so proud of each and every one of you, and I'll . . ." she paused, "miss you next term. I'll truly miss you all," she said. Then she went into her office and closed the door where she had herself a good cry.

"She's like a mama about letting y'all go," Mr. Cathcart said. I think he loved the way she made so much of things other people might look at as small and insignificant as much as I did.

When Mrs. Cathcart finally came out of her office, her eyes were red and swollen, but her hair and makeup were absolutely perfect. She acted like nothing had happened and spent most of the day encouraging us to start interviewing for a job after graduation. She said we could work as shampoo girls on our days off from the school at one of the shops in town to get our foot in the door and see how we liked the place. I asked her about a couple of salons. I could tell she didn't like some of them, but she never said anything bad because the owners were probably alumni of the school.

"Will your mother be coming to the dinner, Zora?" she asked.

"I don't know. I haven't heard from her in a while."

"You haven't heard from her?"

Mrs. Cathcart took one look at the appointment book and saw

that my customer was ten minutes late. If she'd stopped to read the embarrassment on my face, she would've never hauled me into her office and closed the door. I knew what was coming, sure as the world, but I never talked about Mama to anybody, not even Sara Jane.

"Where is your mother?" she asked me, like I was a lost child.

"I don't know. I've called a couple of times since school started, but she hasn't answered."

"Do you want me to help you find her?"

"No, ma'am. Mama's probably not your idea of a mother, and to tell you the truth, she was never my idea of one, either. It's just her and me. She doesn't have much to do with her family or my daddy's family. I'll go home, maybe for Thanksgiving. Maybe."

She hugged me one last time and opened the door. Everybody looked to see if my face was stained with tears, but it wasn't. I had choked back tears so many times living with Mama that I'd choked them out.

One of the beauty-supply salesmen came into the school later that morning and mentioned that Ronnie's Two was looking for a shampoo girl. Ronnie's was a shop in a little storybook cottage at the end of Main Street that was owned by Ronnie Nussman. He was Mrs. Cathcart's sister's boy, though Mrs. Cathcart never mentioned him, and he was not an alumnus of the Davenport School of Beauty. Ronnie went to school in Atlanta and opened the shop with his cousin, Fontaine Durrier, who was also Mrs. Cathcart's nephew, though she didn't claim him, either.

Fontaine and Ronnie had more boyfriends than anybody in town. I guess they were the only two men around back then who weren't shy about being that way. It didn't bother me any. I figured it was their business what they did between the sheets. The majority of the townspeople gossiped and raised their eyebrows at those two, but they certainly weren't opposed to letting them style their hair. I think this is because Fontaine and Ronnie were called to fix hair, just like Mrs. Cathcart said we were.

I phoned Ronnie shortly after the beauty-supply man left, right after Mrs. Cathcart went to the bank. I knew she wouldn't think too much of it. She had given us a list of alumni that were hiring, but none of them appealed to me. Ronnie was real sweet over the phone. He told me to come on by, that he was just dying to meet me.

When I walked through the door, Ronnie came sashaying over, carrying on about me like I was a little doll.

"Fontaine, would you look at this princess. Isn't she precious, and that color. You can't get that out of a bottle. Just look at this hair, hair for days."

Fontaine didn't have much hair. He raised his eyebrows and looked at me like, *here he goes again.* As he styled a woman's hair, she was baring her soul to him. I heard something about a divorce settlement and a lying son of a bitch over the blow dryer. I don't think Fontaine was listening, but you couldn't have convinced his customer.

"She gave up her therapist for him. He sees her every week and it still costs her less than that headshrinker over in North Myrtle Beach," Ronnie whispered. "Now, Zora, tell me all about yourself."

"There's not much to tell." I told him I was looking for a job and I'd be available for full-time employment December 15.

"Where are you from, Zora?" he said. "I want to know about you."

"Well, I'm from Cleveland. South Carolina. It's a little tiny town in the mountains, about forty-five miles from Asheville. My daddy passed on a long time ago. It's just me," I said, hoping I wouldn't have to rehash everything about Mama twice in one day.

"Oh, you poor thing." Ronnie looked like he might cry. He held my hand and told me all about his family and his new boyfriend, George, a construction worker who did mostly roofing and traveled a good bit. Before I left, I think I knew everything there was to know about him because he was so open about his life.

He said the job was mine if I wanted it, at a dollar-fifty more an hour than the beauty-supply salesman told me the job paid. I told him I'd have to think about it.

I opened the door to the shop, tripping the little chimes that hung from the ceiling. "Bye now," he called after me like he might tell me to dress warm or make sure I got enough to eat. "Bye," I called back, thinking how odd it was that Mrs. Farquhar wanted to mother me, Mrs. Cathcart wanted to mother me, even Ronnie Nussman wanted to mother me. Everybody wanted to mother me except for my own mama.

19

✦

Sara Jane came around about nine o'clock and surprised me with flowers. It was just a little spray of daisies and red carnations in a coffee cup that said, "I love you." I had never gotten flowers from a flower shop before, so when I held them up to my face to smell them I was surprised that flowers from a florist don't smell good, if they even smell at all.

"They're beautiful." I set them in the middle of the kitchen table and opened the card. "For my very best friend and maid of honor. You are so loved. Always, Sara Jane."

"Sara Jane Alvarez," I added, as we both squealed in excitement. She glanced down toward the drinking room.

"He's still at it, I see," she said, as Winston filled his glass. "He's looked up here a time or two. Oh, my God. Did you see that? I swear he looked right up here."

"It's such a pretty night out; he's probably looking at the stars,"

I said, feeling a little guilty that Sara Jane shared every little intimate detail of her life with me, and I couldn't tell her about drinking wine with Winston. It was my nature to let the world go on and on about itself, to keep things inside. I learned to be that way after Nana died, and I was left to take care of Mama by myself.

"There's not one single star out tonight," she said, with her hands on her hips."And he's looking up here, surer than shit."

"I've noticed that, too," I said, which was true. "I've talked to him a couple of times, but nothing comes of it. To be honest, I've just about given up on the man."

I know sometimes she seemed hurt that I couldn't share even a little bit of myself with her. But what would I say, that my mama had all but disowned me, that Winston Sawyer had spoken to me and smelled my hair?

Sara Jane didn't stay long. She had to meet Jimmy at Connie Harmon's house, because Connie was throwing a big engagement party for the two of them. She said there'd be lots of parties, and her mama had already bought both of us three new dresses to wear. I kissed her and thanked her. And I remember thinking how funny it seemed to make so much over a wedding. But Mrs. Farquhar's friends were just like her when it came to entertaining, and they were all going to try to outdo each other before Sara Jane made it to the altar.

After she left, I sat on my couch listening to the fall breeze blow the leaves about outside. The air was crisp, like mountain air. I heard the screen door to his kitchen bounce a time or two against the jamb and thought it was the wind. I heard footsteps walking across the gravel, stopping twice for a few seconds, and then slowly coming up the stairs.

He was there at my door but didn't knock, just opened it, and stood there looking at me. Neither of us said a word. I went to him hesitantly and stood as close as two people can without touching. I felt his breath and smelled the sweetness of Kentucky bourbon. He closed his eyes and laid his head on my shoulder and let me press my lips against the sweet spot on his neck as we stood there breathing, barely touching.

I wasn't scared or nervous. I was full of wanting as he lifted my chin and kissed me and would have melted into a little puddle right there on the floor if I hadn't kissed him back. Then he scooped me up the way the heroes did on the cover of the Gussie Foyette books and set me down on my bed.

The bedroom light was out, but the light from the kitchen was generous. I undressed the only man I'd ever worshiped while he undressed me. I remember gasping out loud at his beauty. He laid me down on the bed and stroked my body; his eyes were closed like he was playing a fine instrument.

He let me touch him and know him and without saying a word, we made love. The music our bodies played lasted for a long time. Exhausted, he closed his eyes several times, like he was glad he was with me, and then he would look away, like maybe he shouldn't have walked up the stairs in the first place.

I think he felt obligated to lie close to me and stroke my hair. I could feel him wanting to leave.

"Stay," I whispered.

He kissed me like he meant it, dressed, and left me there in the dark. I could smell him on the pillow, the faint scent of some cologne Emma probably bought for him. I hugged that pillow tightly to me and prayed he would come back. About an hour later, I got out of bed to lock the front door and noticed that the lights were out in his house, even in the drinking room. I went back to bed and fell asleep pretending Winston Sawyer was still in my little bed.

The first thing on my mind when I woke up the next morning was that trip to Atlanta for the whole weekend. I didn't want to go. I was afraid of what might happen if I left Winston there alone. Would he come to his senses? Would I ever see him again? But I had to go for Sara Jane and her mama, because they had been so good to me. Anyway, I had two days to either work up the nerve to go or make up an excuse to stay.

I hoped Winston would answer those questions for me that night. Out of some crazy superstition, I made sure everything about the apartment was exactly how it had been the night before. I sat in the same spot on the couch and listened to his footsteps come up the stairs. He never knocked. Maybe because it really was his place, or maybe it was too much like asking for permission. He came into the room and I went to him. He didn't smell like liquor.

There was a little breeze that blew through the room carrying the strains of a scratchy old blues tune he had put on the stereo in the drinking room. He held me close, shuffling his feet about ever so slightly in time to the music. I guess songs must have been real short way back then, or maybe they just seemed that way because my heart stopped every time the music did, but he kept right on dancing. I didn't know if it was the music or not that sent him up those stairs to dance with me. Whatever it was, I closed my eyes and rested my head on his shoulder, and prayed he'd never stop.

I pulled away, just enough to see his face. He smiled at me and pressed little angel kisses on my lips before the music started again; our feet moved in time to the slow, soulful sound. I don't claim to know what he was thinking during that time. All I know is that I was entranced by Winston Sawyer and his music, and I couldn't have stopped dancing even if I wanted to.

I ran my fingers through his long, beautiful hair and pressed my fingertips on the back of his head so that his lips moved closer to mine. He kissed me the way he had made love to me the night before, wholly and wantonly. As we opened our eyes, still high from the electricity that had passed between us, I saw something there, like he had suddenly come to his senses.

I had seen that look sometimes on the face of Mama's men, especially the married ones. "Stay and have a little drink with me," I whispered as I rubbed his hand across my cheek and then down my neck until it rested on my breast. He looked at me and nodded his head because he could see that I knew just what he needed. He needed a drink as much as I needed him.

When I handed Winston a bourbon and water, he looked at me funny. I just smiled and dabbed my finger in his glass before putting it in my mouth like it was chocolate cake batter or something good. I knew he drank Scotch straight up or sometimes on the rocks, and when he was out of Scotch he drank bourbon, and when he was out of bourbon, he drank gin and tonic. But I remembered the sweetness of it on his breath that first night we made love, and I think he did, too, because he pulled me close to him, sipped that drink, and asked for another.

I fetched it quick and then laid my head on his chest to feel the rhythm of his breathing and set mine in time with his.

"Don't you want a drink?" he said, as he kissed my hair.

I shook my head. His touch, his smell, his sad blue eyes intoxicated me so that I was already drunk.

After three or four bourbons, Winston was less inhibited and didn't seem to be thinking about leaving anymore. Mind you, he wasn't falling-down drunk, the way he was the night I helped him into the house, but I know the liquor erased any ideas he had about leaving.

He stood up, and from where I sat, he looked like a prince reaching his hand out to me, leading me to happily ever after. I took his hand, and we walked together to my bedroom.

So many things were different than the first night we made love and Winston went home straightaway. They gave me hope and made what was going on between the two of us seem right. He didn't seem to mind my inexperience in lovemaking because I was eager to learn. He showed me what to do to please him, and I liked the power that came in knowing that I could make him breathless, too.

Still, he never said much of anything, and I didn't, either. We spoke with our eyes and our hands and our bodies; we spoke in a language of wanting and contentment. Whenever I opened my mouth to say something, he always pressed his fingers across my lips and kissed me so that my head was light and airy.

After a long while, he whispered, "I have to go."

"Why?" I whispered back.

He waited for a moment, thinking, I suppose. There was no reason why he shouldn't stay. He didn't have anyplace to go other than to bed, alone.

"Don't go." They were the first words I'd spoken above a whisper since he came up the stairs to my little place. He looked at me. I saw that he needed to stay, to lie beside me and feel alive. He settled back down on the bed, put his arm around my waist, and was soon asleep.

20

I woke up the next morning and saw Winston picking his clothes up off of the floor. I rolled over on my back, trying to breathe: in, out, in, out, real slow so he couldn't see the panic bouncing around inside my body, lighting me up like a pinball machine. He slipped his pants on and smiled an awkward smile akin to that "what am I doing here?" look that had passed across his face a few hours before. I smiled back and pulled the covers up to my chin. It was an awkward time. He would give me a little half smile, and I would return the look. Then there was that seductive silence left over from the night before that made it seem like there was a gaping hole in the middle of the room.

He sat down on the bed, tied his shoes, and didn't look at me until the alarm clock went off and startled both of us. He looked at me and laughed. "I'll see you," he said, as he gave me a quick kiss on my forehead.

"Tonight?"

He didn't answer. I wasn't sure he heard me, but I was afraid to ask again. He started out the bedroom door.

"Winston," I called.

He looked back into the room, like he was surprised that I'd said his name.

"I'm going with a friend to Atlanta this weekend."

"Okay," he said, like I had just asked him to take the trash out.

"Well, I won't be here," I was sounding more stupid by the minute, "to cook for you."

"Okay," he said again, like it didn't matter one way or the other, and walked out the door.

I fretted over him so that I was miserable at work the entire day. Everybody asked me what was wrong. I just told them I didn't feel right, and that was the truth. My ten o'clock perm took me forever to roll up, and as soon as I put that smelly wave solution on her hair, I set the timer for thirty minutes and headed to the break room.

I bought a Coke and some Lance peanuts, pouring the peanuts into the bottle the way Sara Jane had shown me. I sat there wishing I could be more like her because I was sure Sara Jane wouldn't have felt as helpless and stupid as I did that morning.

"You got man troubles, girl." This was not a question. It was a statement.

Sissy Carson sat down next to me. She propped her feet up in the chair beside me and let out a long, breathy sigh.

"No, I'm just tired."

"No, I'm tired. You got man troubles," she said, matter-of-factly.

I remembered one time when Sara Jane's preacher had talked about the sign of the beast on the evil one's followers during the last days of the world. Not that Winston was the devil or anything, but I remember wiping my forehead with the back of my hand, swearing again that I was fine. But at twenty-six, Sissy was probably the oldest and the wisest of us all. I was sure that somehow she saw the sign on my forehead and knew I belonged to Winston.

"You're too damn private, Zora. You can't keep everything inside of you. It'll kill you just like it did Ed."

Like Mama, Sissy had married at fourteen. She lost three babies and quit trying because she said the losing part hurt too much. By the time she turned twenty, her first husband divorced her for being barren. He married her sister, and they'd had six kids, so far. Sissy dated a good bit, which some of the girls said meant she slept around a lot, and had a succession of men, of which Ed was one. She had man troubles so much so that she was considered to be an authority on the subject.

"I'm fine, really," I said, because if I couldn't bare my soul to Sara Jane Farquhar, I certainly wasn't going to tell Sissy Carson anything.

"Suit yourself," she said as she rubbed the sole of her foot. "Damn it if I don't got me another needle hair."

"Needle hair?"

"Those little hairs that get in your shoes and work their way into your feet. Them blond ones are the worst. You can't see 'em to pick 'em, and you got to pick 'em out with a needle and a pair of tweezers or you'll go lame."

"I don't know anything about needle hairs," I said.

"Well, something's worked its way under your skin, Zora Adams. Come on now, you can tell ol' Sissy. What's his name?"

I heard the timer go off at my station and excused myself without telling her my problems, and she looked at me like I had just refused free money.

The perm didn't take for the woman. When I told her there was no charge and that I'd try again in a couple of weeks, she said it was okay, that she'd never had one take, and she'd been trying on and off for twenty years. At that point, I should have just thrown up my hands and given up, because the rest of the day was slow, three haircuts and an upsweep.

Looking at the magazine picture that the upsweep lady brought in, it was every bit of ten years old. At first I didn't think I could do it. But when I was done, her hair looked all right, and she was pretty happy with it. She tipped me a dollar and said she'd tell all her friends about me. It took me so long to fix her hair; I hoped she would just keep it to herself.

I was tired by the time I got home and just grilled a couple of pork chops on the hibachi. Two baked potatoes and a little tossed salad made a nice dinner, but then there was the dilemma as to whether I should put Winston's dinner on the picnic table, which might make it look like I was trying to keep him at a distance. If I set two places at my little table, it might look like I was expecting too much. I decided to wait until I saw him drive into the driveway. Then I would poke my head out my door and casually ask him if he was ready for dinner.

I took my place on the couch and fell asleep, around nine o'clock. Just after midnight, I woke up and looked out the window.

The MG was not in the driveway, the house was dark, and the food was cold. I couldn't have eaten anyway because I was all stirred up inside. I was sure something horrible must have happened to him, so I left my door unlocked, hoping that if he was okay, he would come upstairs and let me console him, but he didn't.

I woke up the next morning with that same sick feeling in the pit of my stomach. Every light in the gingerbread house was on, a sure sign that Winston had come home drunk and had gone back to his own bed. What did that mean?

I couldn't go to Atlanta, there was too much at stake. But I thought about Sara Jane and her mother and knew I had to go. I rushed around throwing things in that worn-out old American Tourister suitcase and was brushing my teeth when Sara Jane tooted the horn at eight o'clock sharp.

I grabbed my bag and slipped the key into the door to make it look like I was locking the place up and then turned the doorknob to make sure it wasn't just in case Winston didn't have a key. As I started down the steps for the car, Mrs. Farquhar got out, hugged me, and insisted that I ride in the front.

"Zora, doesn't that teacher live there? Isn't he the one whose wife died a couple of years ago?"

"Yes, ma'am."

I wanted to stand on the hood of the car and declare my love for the man who'd made love to me the night before, not the stranger that I woke up with that morning. Mrs. Farquhar would have been mortified, but Sara Jane would have jumped up there with me and celebrated because she knew how much I wanted Winston and that I believed that wanting was love.

"I can count on one hand the number of times I've seen that man around town," Mrs. Farquhar said. "He never comes into the store. Poor thing. You know he has to eat."

"Mama, you sound like the man hasn't eaten in two years."

"Well, Sara Jane, as far as I know, he hasn't."

We all laughed, which must have been a cue for Mrs. Farquhar to start telling her stories. She told us all about her fancy engagement parties and her wedding, and how she nearly had to elope with Mr. Farquhar because her daddy thought he was a nobody. She told us about the groomsman who passed out during the ceremony right before the vows were exchanged. Everybody thought it was because the church was so hot, which was partly true. The fact that he had been taking a nip or two didn't help matters, either.

"And at a Baptist wedding. Have you ever heard of such a thing in all your born days?" she asked.

Neither of them hushed the whole way to Atlanta, which made me think that nobody would ever share their family history if it weren't for long car trips. Not that I had any firsthand knowledge of this. We didn't have a car to go anywhere to speak of, and nobody wanted to rehash our family history, except for Nana, who only told the good parts on the porch late at night.

When we pulled up in front of the downtown Hyatt, I tried to act like it wasn't my first time staying at a hotel. The place looked like a palace, or at the very least, a mansion. But it was surprising to me that our rooms were so plain compared to how fancy the lobby was. After we unpacked, I looked inside the smallest refrigerator I'd ever seen and saw Coca-Colas and a dozen tiny liquor bottles. I ran my hand across the bedspread and pictured Winston with a bourbon and water, stretched across the king-size bed, wanting me. Not Sara Jane sprawled out on her side of the bed going over our itinerary.

We ate at The Varsity, which is the most famous hot dog joint in the whole world. From the name, I thought it might be an expensive restaurant, but the food was good, and Mrs. Farquhar declared that everybody who set foot in Atlanta had to eat there before they left town.

When we got back to the hotel, she announced from her adjoining room that she was going to bed early because she wanted to be at Rich's Department Store when the doors opened. All greased up with pink Merle Norman cold cream and dressed for bed, she hugged and kissed us good night and told us to go on to sleep even though the store didn't open until ten o'clock.

"Good night, girls." She turned out the light. "Get some rest now, because we're going to scour the entire city until we find the perfect wedding gown for my bride-to-be."

"Good night, Mama. Love you," Sara Jane said.

"Good night, Mama," I said without being reminded.

I could barely see Sara Jane, but I could feel her lying there in the dark, trying to figure out whatever it was she had to say to me. A couple of minutes passed. The only sound in the room was the hum of the heater and an occasional car horn from the city street below.

"You all right?" she asked.

I wasn't all right. I had lured Winston Sawyer up to my place with a few biscuit crumbs, and short of locking him up, I didn't have the first idea of what to do with him. Even worse I had no idea what I was going to do without him.

"I'm fine."

"Zora . . . Jimmy has a friend." She paused. "Look, I know you have the hots for Winston Sawyer, but this guy is real nice and good-looking, too."

I still didn't say anything.

"Anyway, if you decide you want to meet him, we'd love to fix you up."

"Thanks."

We were quiet for longer than we had ever been since we met. "You know I love you, Zora, and I want you to be happy. But I've got to ask you, what are you holding out for?"

"I don't know," I said, and it was the truth. "I'm thinking of changing my hair."

Sara Jane was quiet. Everybody at school, including her before she quit, used to mess with their hair all the time when they didn't have any customers. They cut and colored and fixed each other's hair like they were fixing their lives. Except me. I'd thought about it before, but after the night Winston picked up a handful of my hair and breathed it in, I was afraid that if I changed it, the spell would be broken.

Now I wanted something different out of Winston. A few highlights and a trim couldn't hurt.

"Don't cut it," Sara Jane said definitively. Even in the dark I could feel her smiling, hopeful. "We can do foils, just a few tiny streaks of ash blond. Like a reverse frosting, but it'll look natural. Just leave it to me."

21

~

As we stood in front of Rich's in downtown Atlanta, watching the store manager on the other side of the door walking toward us, a wicked wind swirled around the building. The cold, damp air cut through us as we huddled together, watching that man who didn't seem to be the least bit hurried. He fumbled a big bunch of keys about, trying to find the right one, and dropped them once just for spite, according to the lady behind Mrs. Farquhar.

When the door opened, a handful of bargain hunters pushed past us and were already gliding up the escalator to the second floor before we got to the cosmetics counter.

"A woman's wedding gown should transform her," Mrs. Farquhar announced, as she took off her leather gloves and stepped onto the escalator.

"Into what?"

"Royalty, my dear Sara Jane. Royalty."

"You are too much, Mama." Sara Jane looked at me and rolled her eyes, but I could tell she liked the fact that her mama wanted to turn her into a princess. I guess any girl would have wanted that, even me.

"You think I'm kidding, but you will know when you slip into that perfect dress. Before the buttons are buttoned and the veil is on, you will know it is as right for you as the man you are marrying. It's the exact same feeling."

I tried not to gawk over the store, but it was hard. Rich's was the most incredible place I had ever seen, and Mrs. Farquhar said it was the place to shop, short of going to New York City. I couldn't imagine a finer store anywhere.

The Bridal Room was set in a corner of the store with a mannequin bride and six fancy bridesmaids at the entrance. Another sleek mannequin in a black sequined gown was perched on top of a baby grand with her head turned toward the plastic wedding party. There were several artificial bouquets in a big wicker basket at the base of a pedestal, and just about every issue of *Bride* magazine from the past few years was in another basket beside a half dozen chairs upholstered in pink satin.

"Good morning," a woman with big hair drawled as she adjusted the chain attached to her eyeglasses. "And how are y'all this morning?"

"We're fine, thank you, just fine," Mrs. Farquhar said. "We're from out of town and we've come in search of the perfect wedding dress."

"Well, congratulations. I can tell you, you came to the right place. We do all the really big weddings in Atlanta, you know, and, of course, those darling debutantes wouldn't think of going anywhere else to order their dresses. Let me see your ring, honey," she said as she reached for Sara Jane's left hand. You could tell she wasn't impressed. "Where are y'all from, now?"

"Davenport, South Carolina." Mrs. Farquhar beamed. "Right close to Myrtle Beach."

"Oh," she said, as she tried to steer Sara Jane over toward a rack of samples that were on sale. "We just put these on clearance this morning. And let me tell you there are some nice dresses here, half off of what you see on the ticket, and if you see a little mark on 'em or a split seam, we'll knock a little more off the sale price."

Mrs. Farquhar looked peeved by the big-city saleslady who had written the three of us off as country bumpkins. But before she could say anything, a smartly dressed older woman walked into the department with her skinny, redheaded daughter who looked absolutely miserable, and Darnel, as her name tag said, left us to ourselves. I couldn't help but notice the way she made over that ugly girl and brought out dress after dress for her. Darnel did everything but kiss the girl's bony butt and that huge diamond ring on the girl's finger.

Mrs. Farquhar saw a young saleslady walk through the department and stopped her.

"Excuse me, Miss. Could you please help us?"

"Yes, ma'am, I'll try. I don't usually work in this department. This is Darnel's domain, but it looks like she's busy. What can I do for you all?"

"We are looking for the perfect wedding dress," Mrs. Farquhar began again.

The woman didn't ask to see Sara Jane's ring or talk snooty to us. She showed us all kinds of dresses before excusing herself to check on something in the stockroom. None of the dresses she showed us were fitting right; none of them were making Sara Jane feel like a princess.

"This is going to be a long day," Sara Jane said, as she sat down in a big pile of white fluff.

Darnel walked by us a couple of times but was too busy nipping at the heels of that miserable redhead to notice us. It made me wonder why Mercedes, as her mama called her, was even there. I don't think it was for love.

A little boy came zooming through the department into the dressing room looking for his mother, who also happened to be the mother of the redhead. He had too much energy for all of us, especially Darnel, who looked nervous as he raced about. But she was determined to make a big sale, even if she had to bite her tongue until she got it.

"When I get married, my girlfriend is going to wear a frog suit," the little boy hollered as he dove under the skirt of his sister's dress and hid.

"Damn it, Alexis," Mercedes cussed her own mama. "*Do* something about him."

"Of course, dear," the woman said, like that ugly girl really was a princess.

It took her a while to drag Jeffrey out from under all that taffeta and crinoline with his sister still on the pedestal, and by this time I'm sure poor Darnel had to be thinking the country bumpkins from Davenport were looking pretty good. Alexis pulled the little boy onto her lap and wrapped her long, slender arms around him in lieu of a straitjacket.

"Now, Jeffrey, you must settle down."

"I'm gonna wear a frog suit to 'Cedes's wedding and say 'ribbit' when it's time for her and the poop-head to say I do. Then I'll be all practiced up for when I get married."

"Jeffrey," Alexis said with the most serious look on her face. "Now, what did I tell you about weddings? Don't you remember? Whose day is it first?"

The boy thought for a minute. "The bride's."

"That's right." She was delighted but still holding him tight. "And then whose day is it?"

"The bride's mother." He was figuring out how things work real fast, because he was losing the excitement that had propelled him like a motor.

"And then whose day is it?" she asked.

"If he's lucky, the groom's." The little boy was nearly sedate.

"Good boy," she said and kissed him on the forehead.

Sara Jane was in the dressing room waiting to take her turn on the pedestal while her mother and I watched the Mercedes and Jeffrey Show. All of us were peeved that Darnel was letting that ugly girl hog the pink-carpeted platform, especially Mrs. Farquhar. When Mercedes was done, Sara Jane came out in a pretty little off-shoulder gown.

"Honey, can you step down and let Miss Myers up there a minute?" Darnel asked after Sara Jane had been on the pedestal for about three seconds. Sara Jane didn't like that dress anyway, but she looked at Darnel like she had better think twice before she made that request again.

"Tell me . . . Margie," Mrs. Farquhar said to the woman who had been so helpful to us. "Do you work on commission?"

"Yes. Yes ma'am, I do," she said with a puzzled look.

"Good, because I think I see the perfect dress right there." Mrs. Farquhar pointed to a particular gown behind glass doors that was locked up tight with the other gowns in the Designer section.

"Yes ma'am, I'll go get the key," Margie said, excited over the prospect of making a big sale. "Darnel, I need the keys to the glass closet."

"Margie, I was helping these folks earlier. I'll get it for them; you can go on back to Lingerie now."

Darnel left the redheaded girl there standing alone on the platform with no one to ooh and aah over her, because her mama was off chasing Jeffrey again. She opened the case and pulled the dress out and showed Mrs. Farquhar the price tag. "Three thousand dollars," she announced, looking for the sticker shock in Mrs. Farquhar's eyes.

Mrs. Farquhar took the dress out of her arms and handed it to Margie. "Can you help Sara Jane into this one, please? I think it'll do just fine."

When Sara Jane came out of the dressing room, I knew exactly what Mrs. Farquhar meant about knowing when you've found the perfect dress. I have never seen anything so beautiful in my life. It wasn't just the dress or my beautiful friend; it was the two of them together that left no doubt that this was indeed the dress.

The ugly redheaded girl announced to her mother, so that God and everybody could hear, that there couldn't possibly be anything for her in Atlanta. On their way out, the girl's mother was trying to appease her by promising to take her to New York or Paris if need be to find the right dress. Darnel watched them go and then watched us like we were going to steal something.

Margie took the long train out of its special bag and gave it a gentle shake; the beaded white illusion with inset lace flowed down the pedestal steps out the entrance of the department. "It's cathedral length, honey," Margie whispered as she pinned the veil on Sara Jane's head and looked like she might just cry over such a beautiful sight. "It's perfect."

22

With the perfect dress ordered and paid for, we were high as kites and decided to set out for a mall everybody in town was talking about. Lenox Square made the downtown Rich's look cheap and plain, like those dresses on the sale rack in the Bridal Room. Mrs. Farquhar was so excited over the prospect of shopping in stores like Saks and Neiman Marcus that she talked in hushed tones when we passed through their doors, like they were holy places.

I paid too much for a plain little bangle that was just costume jewelry, but it came in the prettiest little gold foil box that said "Saks Fifth Avenue" in raised letters across the top. The saleslady put it in a fancy paper sack that I kept for the longest time, even though I lost the bracelet a couple of weeks later at one of Sara Jane's parties.

Mrs. Farquhar bought a tiny box of Godiva chocolates with four pieces inside, one for me, one for her, and two for the bride. I didn't know anything about fancy chocolates, but that little candy was the best thing I had ever put in my mouth. I looked on the bottom of a two-pound box and nearly fell over when I saw that the box of chocolates cost more than the entire outfit I was wearing.

Mrs. Farquhar shopped, and Sara Jane and I gawked at the rich people and the rich prices of most everything there. I decided there were two kinds of shoppers at that mall—folks who looked like they belonged there and folks like us who came to gawk. We didn't mind being gawkers, and I know if Mrs. Farquhar had not spent a small fortune on Sara Jane's dress that day, she would've blended right in with those rich people.

"Sara Jane, let's look at a few dresses for your trousseau," Mrs. Farquhar called, holding up a silk dress that looked similar to the one under my bed back home.

"I know you're probably sick of this by now, but I can't say no to her when she shops like this. Do you want to look around? Maybe meet us back here in an hour or so and we'll have lunch?"

"Sure." Not knowing if I'd ever see such a place again in my lifetime, I wanted to explore the mall. I had what was left of the fifty dollars I'd earned styling Ethyl's hair; I hadn't intended to spend it, but when you're with somebody who shops like the Farquhars do, you're so caught up in the moment it's easy not to worry about if you're going to have enough to eat later on. You just shop.

The least expensive place in the mall was Rich's, which wasn't as big as the downtown store but tried to be every bit as grand as the other Lenox Square stores. Luckily, the prices were the same. Somehow, I ended up in the Lingerie Department with $37.50

burning a hole in my pocketbook, staring at a pretty little short thing on a mannequin.

"Do you like it?" The saleslady smiled and winked at me. "It would make a good early Christmas present for some happy man. You give him that, and no telling what you'll get."

She laughed, making me blush.

"What is it?"

"It's a teddy. It's short and sweet and guaranteed to work wonders."

While I was gawking at the mannequin, she'd pulled one from the rack that was just my size and was dangling it in front of me the way Mama had dangled her "Cabaret" outfit, only this time I was enticed.

"There's no harm in trying it on." I nodded like a zombie as she led me to the dressing room. "It comes with silk panties."

I slipped into the teddy and wondered what in the world I'd need the panties for. The hem of the thing came just above my bare bottom. My long legs were tanned and lean. One of the spaghetti straps slid off of my shoulder sending chills down my thighs at the thought of Winston's fingers pulling the straps down, his breath on the lace edge of the neckline as he pushed it out of his way. The price tag caught my eye. Fifty-five dollars.

"It's on sale," the woman hovering outside the dressing room door called. "I know it looks like a dream on you."

I could make $37.50 go a long way back in Davenport. "How much on sale?"

"It's worth ten times what it costs and it's forty percent off."

I did the math and looked at myself again. Minutes later, I

stuffed $4.50 in my pocket, then hid the flimsy thing in the bottom of my purse.

We ate lunch at a fancy restaurant and celebrated our "good shopping luck," as Mrs. Farquhar called it, with a slice of grasshopper cheesecake. Now, I must admit I was put off by the name, but it was every bit as good as that Godiva chocolate and was so rich, I slept most of the way home. Mrs. Farquhar slept, too, with her prize for the day, a little sample of the wedding gown fabric, in her hand. I woke up a couple of times to check on Sara Jane, because I knew she wanted to hurry up and get home so that she could tell Jimmy she had found the dress.

"Are you getting tired?"

"I'm fine, Zora." She smiled. "Go on back to sleep. We'll be home before you know it."

When I woke up, she was pulling into my driveway. I wiped my mouth with the back of my hand and smiled at Mrs. Farquhar, who was still fast asleep.

"She's worn out," Sara Jane whispered. "It's more the excitement of the hunt than the actual shopping that does it to her."

"Thanks for inviting me. I had a ball."

"Don't forget your purchase." She handed me the Saks bag with the bracelet in it.

I was glad it was dark and she couldn't see the shame on my face. I told myself it came from keeping things from someone who loved me and was always as open as can be, but it had more to do with my motive for buying that little piece of lacy silk and the woman's guarantee it would work wonders.

"I love you, Sara Jane." I slung my pocketbook over my shoulder and heard the bag crinkle inside. "Have fun with Jimmy tonight."

She put the car in gear. "Zora, you know this isn't going anywhere. Think about what I said about Jimmy's friend, okay?"

"We—" I wanted to say I loved him and we'd made love. I wanted to tell her I'd bought something to charm Winston with and hoped I'd be trying on a wedding dress one day. "We had fun, didn't we?"

She nodded and I closed the door as quietly as possible. Sara Jane waved and pulled out of the driveway. The day had been so full that other than buying the teddy, I truly hadn't thought much about Winston, or Jimmy's friend, or any man for that matter.

As I climbed the stairs, I wondered if it had something to do with what Mrs. Farquhar called "Retail Amnesia," meaning that just looking at or actually buying something new makes you forget your troubles. I thought about Emma, wondering what she could have possibly been trying to forget when she lived with Winston. Before, I'd always thought she was just a lot like Mrs. Farquhar and just loved to shop.

I walked into my little place and noticed the magazine I'd left on the couch was gone. Two glasses and a cereal bowl were in the sink. I pushed my bedroom door open, the bed was unmade.

"I meant to straighten up this morning," he said, from the old chair in the corner of my bedroom.

I looked at him and didn't say anything.

He walked over to the bed and pulled the spread up like he was trying to make the bed. "I had a bad night and just wanted to stay here. I hope that's okay?"

I nodded, not really knowing what that meant. Then he looked at me and somehow I knew that it had something to do with Emma. Whether it was her birthday or their anniversary or the day she died, it had crushed him so that he had taken refuge here.

I walked around the bed to where he stood and kissed him on the cheek. "I'll fix us some dinner."

He followed me into the kitchen. There on the counter was a small accordion-like wine rack filled with nine bottles of wine and two good crystal glasses.

"Do you want some wine?" he asked.

He never said he bought those things for me, but I knew he did. He opened a bottle of Beaujolais and spent the next few minutes trying to teach me how to pronounce the word properly. We drank that fine French wine with bacon and eggs, and toast with peach preserves Mrs. Farquhar had given me that summer.

"I missed you," he said, while I was cleaning up the dishes.

My heart stopped. "I missed you, too," I whispered.

He turned the little radio on until he found some music so we could hold each other close and dance. It seemed like I had never left at all, and this was the way things should be. While the man on the radio was announcing the next song or selling something to the other listeners, we kissed and nuzzled each other, waiting for the music to begin again.

We danced for a long time without stopping, not even for a drink. After a while, we wandered into the bedroom, and I went into the bathroom to change into the short little sexy thing I'd bought in Atlanta. When I came out, he smiled at me, and I remember thinking this must be what it's like to love and be loved.

The next morning, the phone rang and woke us up. I reached across Winston and answered it.

"Zora?" Mrs. Farquhar said. "We sure missed you at church this morning. Aren't you feeling well, darling?"

"I'm fine," I said. "I guess I just overslept."

"I'm so worn out from our trip, I didn't cook. Jerry and Jimmy went out to pick up some barbecue. We'll hold dinner for you, if you like."

"Oh, no ma'am, y'all go ahead. I'll be fine. I'm just going to hang around here for a while. Maybe clean up a little bit."

"Well, you rest up, but if you change your mind, do come on by."

He never asked who was on the phone, just spooned up close to me and kissed the back of my neck. He pulled the sheet back and watched his fingers travel over my body. He loved to do that, and sometimes it seemed like he did it for hours.

I lay there thinking about when I was a child and the times I trespassed in the pasture of some rich guy's mountain home, losing myself amongst his horses. One of the mares, Jezebel, so her fancy halter said, quivered when any male got near her, even the geldings. It was funny to watch her eyes widen as she called to them. The other mares made a game of running hard from their lovers, but she ached for them like I ached for Winston.

I wish he hadn't known this about me the way the other horses knew it about Jezebel. I wish he had to talk to me, had to seduce me with words, because I think that maybe things might have been different.

I didn't realize that he'd dozed off and I startled him when I asked if he wanted some breakfast. He stretched and yawned. "I'll cook for you," he said, which felt strange because I've never been good at letting somebody else do for me. He got in my kitchen and messed up every single dish and pan I had as he panfried two little beef filets with some garlic, then dumped a whole carton of sliced mushrooms over them and put the lid on. He cut the ends off of green beans and steamed them in a pot that he jammed my colander into, then wrapped two potatoes in tinfoil before throwing them in the oven. The thermostat was set way too high, but I didn't say anything, even when the bottoms of the potatoes were crusty and hard.

"Beaujolais or Pinot Noir?" he asked as he set the table.

Even though he'd schooled me on pronouncing the names of fancy wines, I felt better pointing at the bottle. He opened the wine, poured a tad in the glass, and swirled it around. After taking a tiny sip, he nodded in approval.

"Good choice," he said.

He had obviously gone to the grocery store while I was gone because he made me a salad with some kind of dressing that he made from scratch.

"Thank you," I said as he put the bowl in front of me. If he could cook like this, what in the world did he need me for?

The entire meal was great, and if we'd had a little sliver of that grasshopper cheesecake like I had in Atlanta, it would've been perfect. I was so charmed by this man and the fact that he had done something sweet for me, I never noticed the absence of conversation. We enjoyed our food in silence like we did our time in bed, and that seemed so natural at the time.

The wine was going straight to my head. I sat across from him at my little table and slid my foot up his thigh until it rested between his legs. He put his napkin in his plate and began to massage my foot, then gradually slid his hand up my thigh.

He pushed back from the table and came to where I was sitting, and pushed the spaghetti straps off of my shoulders. I closed my eyes and let him enjoy making me crazy for him. I should've learned something from those mares and the way they brought their lovers to their knees with the chase. But my mind was awash with lust and red wine and something else that I had to say before I burst.

"I love you," I whispered.

He looked at me like I had said something in a language he didn't understand and hugged me close. It wasn't the way lovers hold each other; it was more how a brother or a sister might hold you. He said nothing.

I knew I had to get Winston into bed, to please him more than ever because that was the only way I could keep him. So that's where we stayed the rest of the day, drinking, sleeping, and touching in silence.

23

I don't know why I crept about the apartment so quietly, because Winston was still drunk from the night before. I dressed and ate a little biscuit left over from Thursday's dinner, looking in on him every so often and then one last time before I left. His face was so peaceful, vulnerable, almost innocent.

The morning was crisp and beautiful, like apple season in the mountains. Leaves rustled about as I tiptoed down the steps of the garage apartment and stepped into a world of live oaks awash with color. Not the brilliant reds and oranges of the hardwoods back home, but deep greens and rich browns. Still pretty.

I walked like a little girl playing dress-up in her mother's clothes, grown-up and giddy at the same time. I loved playing house with Winston. It agreed with me, having my man, loving him to the point that I was grateful to be alive just so I could feel this way. I spoke to everyone I passed by. I could tell by the way an old woman smiled and nodded back at me that she knew what I was feeling, that she had felt that way herself at one time.

If I hadn't been tethered to the ground by graduating and getting a job, I would have floated right up to that sweet November sky and made a place there for me and Winston forever. Instead, I glided through the door of the beauty school, hung my jacket up on the rack, and turned around to find Sissy Carson right in my face with an annoying know-it-all smirk.

"Who is he?" she asked.

"What?"

"I've seen that look too many times on my own face. Come on and tell now. Who is he?"

I smiled and pushed past her to sign in at the appointment desk. It galled her so that she followed me around while I got a permanent out of the storage closet for my first appointment and restocked my station with perm rods and clean hairbrushes.

"You know they're all shit. Every single one of them."

I gave her a look and waved to Ellie Jeffords, who was checking in for her appointment with me. Ellie used to be the poster child for happiness, but in the past few weeks she seemed to be renting it rather than owning it. She came in four times last month and always wanted to do something different to her hair, not in the way that she just wanted a change of style; it was more like she was trying to change something else, something that even an ordained cosmetologist couldn't fix.

She was married to Ned Jeffords, a good-looking young attorney who worked for his daddy's law office in town. She came into the school with the longest, silkiest chestnut hair that you ever did see, clear down to her waist, and said she wanted it cut, short like a pixie. Now I never cut anybody's hair from real long to short, so I talked her into cutting it right about to her shoulder blades. Two days later, she was back, wanting to go even shorter and talking about a perm. I told her I didn't think a perm was such a good idea because her hair was great just the way it was, but that I would cut it to her shoulders if she wanted.

When I was done, I handed her the mirror and watched her look at herself. The haircut framed her gorgeous face. She was beyond beautiful, but I don't think she saw that. She said I did a good job and that it didn't have anything to do with me before she made an appointment for the very next week for another haircut and a perm.

"If you don't want to do the perm, I'll go somewhere else, Zora." She didn't say it mean like, just sort of matter-of-factly.

Ellie's wanting to mess with her hair like that didn't make any sense to me. But I promised I'd do the perm and told her I thought she looked perfect the way she was. She just smiled at me. It was then that I saw between the lines and knew for sure that this woman was miserable.

"I know you don't want to do this, Zora," she said as she sat down in my chair that morning.

"What does your husband say?"

"Ned? He's so busy studying for the bar exam and chasing after his daddy's coattails, he doesn't say much. But his mama . . ."

I noticed her hands begin to shake, and she had the same look on her face that someone does when they really need a drink.

"Do you spend a lot of time with Mrs. Jeffords?"

She nodded as I began to section off her hair to wrap it for the perm.

"She's horrified I come here. Says a woman in my position in the community should never go to a beauty school, but my mama always came here. She brought all seven of us. Sometimes we got good haircuts and sometimes Mrs. Cathcart gave us an extra cookie because the girl messed up our hair. If this place was good enough for Mama . . ." Her voice trailed off.

I got her hair rolled up and put the solution on. I sat down on a little stool in my station and set the timer. She hadn't said much for a few minutes. I thought maybe she didn't want to talk, which was fine by me and one of the ten important telltales Mrs. Cathcart taught us about meeting our patrons' needs. But she looked too fragile to be left alone, even for twenty minutes.

"We met in high school," she began. "I don't know why Ned was attracted to me. It didn't make any sense. Mama said I was his Indian chief."

"His what?"

"You know, rich man, poor man, beggar man, thief, doctor, lawyer, Indian chief." I nodded. "Ned was voted Most Everything that was good—popular, humorous, most likely to succeed. Somewhere in all that he chose me."

"Ellie, you're beautiful, inside and out. Why wouldn't he choose you?"

"I don't know. For a long time I thought he did it to make his folks mad, but that wasn't it. Ned says he fell in love with me the first time he saw me at high school. I had gone to the same school with him since we were in the sixth grade, but I guess he didn't notice me then. He doesn't see me much now, either, but when he does, he's so . . . sweet."

"That's good."

"Yeah, he keeps telling me that once he feels comfortable, like he's got a handle on things and as soon as he passes the bar, he'll spend more time with me, but how can that be? His daddy says that once he passes the bar, I'll never see him. He said that to me like he was proud of it. I think they hope that I'll just get fed up and leave Ned, but that would break his heart, and I could never do that."

The timer went off. I rinsed her hair out, put the neutralizer on, and let it sit for a while. Mr. Cathcart asked me to answer the phone for a few minutes because the receptionist was out, and his hearing aid battery was out. He asked us all to take turns that day, and I wished that he had asked me later, because I sure hated to leave Ellie just then.

When I heard the timer go off, I asked somebody to take my place at the desk while I rinsed Ellie's hair and blew it dry. No matter what she did with herself, she was still gorgeous. She ran her hands through the soft curls and asked me to pencil her in for the same time next week to go blond.

I wanted to tell that her hair was perfect just the way it was, that the color was so true I could never have gotten it out of a bottle, but I knew it was no use. I wrote her name down in the appointment book and gave her a little reminder card, even though she said there was no need.

"Do you have any plans for the rest of the day?" I thought I might ask her out to lunch. She sure looked like she needed a friend.

"Yes," she said plainly. "I'm going to get pregnant."

"Oh, well," I said. "I was just going to see if you wanted to go to lunch this afternoon, but it sounds like you're pretty busy."

She thanked me for the invite and for doing such a good job with her hair and left. Sissy Carson had been waiting all day to get another dig in on me, and I saw her watching Ellie the whole time she was sitting in my booth, whispering to the old biddy she was working on. She strolled over to me with that same smug look she'd had since that morning.

"She doesn't belong here," she said matter-of-factly. "And what in the hell is she doing to herself? Her pretty hair's gonna be all burned up with perms and color."

I still didn't say anything, just went about my business. But I thought about Ellie all day and how the Jeffords had done her. I'd heard all kinds of talk about what they'd said, about her being white trash, how they'd threatened to disown Ned if he married her. Even worse, after they accepted the wedding, they'd paid for the whole affair and didn't invite a soul that Ellie knew or loved. Life was terrible for her, and I guess Ellie thought that since Ned was their only child, her life might be better if she had a baby.

At first, it puzzled me as to why Ellie Jeffords was forever trying to change the way she looked. But after a while, I realized she believed that if she looked different, her world might just be different, that somehow in all of that she would find happiness. I know that sounds crazy, but since I realized this about Ellie, I've seen it in other women who come to my station and look in that big mirror the same way. They want something different, a change. They want to be happy.

24

"Hey, girl. Look what I have. Got your color." Sara Jane opened the screen door and dangled a bag from the beauty-supply house my way. "We can get right on it, soon as you're done cooking."

Winston had sort of moved in. The last thing I wanted were the kind of highlights that came out of a bottle. I wiped the flour off of my hands with an old dishrag and gave her a big hug while I tried to think of a way to tell her I'd rather die than color my hair.

"Oh I'm just making cubed steak, fixing a little gravy. What are you up to?"

"Well," she tossed the bag on the couch, "aside from making you even more beautiful, I'll tell you if you pour me a drink."

She raised her eyebrows when I uncorked a bottle of the good stuff Winston and I hadn't finished the night before. She didn't say anything about the fancy crystal glasses, either.

"Mama said Connie Harmon hadn't heard whether or not you were coming to the party Saturday night."

"Oh gosh, Sara Jane. I thought I sent that RSVP card to her." I shuffled through some papers that were on my counter and found the envelope with the fancy little reply card inside. "I am so sorry. Of course I was planning to go. I just don't know what has gotten into me lately," I said, which wasn't true at all.

"It's no big deal." She was looking around the place like something was different but she wasn't sure what it was. "Connie . . . does all kinds of stuff . . . silly stuff for the wedding party . . . especially the maid of honor and her date."

"Oh."

I could feel my face turning red because I didn't know what to say. It turned out that I didn't have to say anything. Somehow, during our conversation, Winston happened to start up the stairs. I guess as he neared the top, he must have heard Sara Jane talking, and he went right back down the steps and into his own house.

She stood there with her hands on her hips, smiling at me. It wasn't the kind of smile that comes when someone lets the cat out of the bag. It was more sheer disbelief that I had kept such a thing from her. I wanted to crawl under the floor and stay there until she got over whatever it was she was feeling. Instead, I just shrugged my shoulders and kept my eyes on the floor like the guilty soul that I was.

"I parked on the street around front. I guess he didn't see my car."

There was a long silence between us. Some grease popped out of the frying pan and landed on my arm. I didn't even flinch, I let it sear my skin. I deserved it. She waited for me to say something, to tell her what was going on, but I didn't. Then she surprised me by turning around to leave.

"Don't go."

She stopped in the doorway, holding the screen door wide open. Her back was to me, but I could tell she was crying, not boo-hooing, as Nana would call it, just silent tears of disappointment in her best friend.

"I'm sorry, Sara Jane. I know you've told me everything about you and Jimmy, but I don't know any other way than to keep things to myself. Please come back. Sit down and talk to me. Please."

She took another step out the door.

"Sara Jane, I don't know what to do. It's not at all like I thought it would be." I was crying now. "I need you."

I didn't have to say another word. It was like calling in the U.S. Cavalry or Superman, but instead of wearing a big *S* across her chest, she wore a smile that told me she'd help sort everything out.

"You know I love you." She sat down on the couch.

I took the cubed steak up, pushed the frying pan off of the hot eye, and wiped away my own tears as I sat down beside her.

"I don't know what we are," I began. "Sometimes it almost seems like we're married. Sometimes it seems like he's a complete stranger."

She nodded her head and listened, coaxing the words out of me by just being there. I had always thought that if things ever progressed with Winston the way I hoped they would, the two of us would be squealing and jumping up and down like we did for her and Jimmy, but it wasn't that way.

"Well, honey, is this what you wanted?" she asked softly. "Are you happy?"

"Sometimes." I raised my eyes and looked at her like I had done something wrong. "I told him I loved him."

"And?"

"And nothing. Well, he hugged me and didn't say anything . . . had a couple more drinks, and we ended up in bed."

I saw her wince. She held me close.

"You deserve better than this," she said. "You're sweet and beautiful. You're a prize, that's what you are. I see it in you. So does Jimmy and Mama and Daddy, and if Winston can't see that, well, damn his soul."

Sometimes I believe Winston really was damned from the beginning, but I know I didn't come into the world that way. I never needed a man just to be. I was strong and proud, nothing at all like I was the first time I saw Winston.

"What else do you do," she said, "besides eat and sleep together?"

I shook my head.

"He hasn't taken you anyplace?"

"No," I whispered. For a moment, it was like somebody had washed the windowpanes, and I could see Winston and me for what we were.

"Ask him to Connie's party."

"What?"

"Ask him to the party. If he has any feelings for you at all, he'll go, or at least try to go. If he doesn't, well, we'll worry about that if it happens."

I hugged her again and told her how much I loved her. She asked me which of the new dresses I was going to wear. She suggested I wear my hair up if I wore the crepe strapless one but didn't mention coloring my hair. She knew enough about the way that works to know that the change was up to me. We went into my bedroom, and I stuffed the teddy under some clothes on the floor in my closet and tried things on while she fiddled with my hair, laughing and carrying on like we always had.

Sara Jane left about an hour later. I was trying to resurrect dinner from the mess I'd made when I heard him coming up the stairs. I wanted to look him squarely in the eyes as he walked through that door in such a way that he knew I meant business, that if he wasn't going to play house the right way, he could just take his wine rack and crystal glasses and go home.

"I didn't know you had company," he said, as he opened the door.

Then he smiled at me and my knees buckled. He came over to where I was making gravy, wrapped his arms around me, and kissed the nape of my neck. He took my hand in his and dabbed my finger in the mashed potatoes, then put it in his mouth, licking, and sucking every bit of it off. We went straight to bed with no supper.

He was exhausted and fell asleep easily. I tossed and turned until I finally just gave up. I tried to clean the kitchen without waking him. The fan on the little space heater in my bedroom made a good bit of noise, and I was sure I could get the kitchen straight in a minute or two without waking him up. I put the potatoes and gravy in the refrigerator and threw the corn in the trash. The meat was like rubber, so I threw it away, too. I was wiping down the counter when I turned around and saw him standing there.

"Couldn't sleep?"

I shook my head. The whole time I was cleaning, I'd been thinking that he'd only said my name once and never took me places. He never asked me what I liked and didn't, unless it pertained to sex. He didn't know my middle name or what my favorite color was, and he couldn't tell you my birthday if you held a gun to his head.

"What's wrong?" He tried to nuzzle me.

I scooted away from him and just stood there with my back to him.

"Did I do something wrong?"

I shook my head.

"Come here." He reached for me and pulled me close.

I looked into his beautiful face and wanted to die right there. After he kissed me, he shuffled his feet about slowly like he was dancing to the music we first heard together. I stayed still.

"Tell me what you want," he whispered in my ear, sending chills down the nape of my neck.

I didn't say anything at first. It took me a while before I realized that I was dancing to his music without even knowing it. He closed his eyes and kissed me, but I didn't kiss him back.

"There's a party," I said, and stopped shuffling my feet. I looked up at him. "Saturday."

"I'm not much on parties." I swear he blushed, which melted me completely. "You want to go?"

I nodded but didn't look at him. Then he lifted my chin up and looked me in the eyes. "We'll go then. Together."

*

Connie Harmon's house sprawled over the lot that overlooked the fourteenth tee at the Davenport Country Club in an intimidating sort of way. She said it was because number fourteen was just the teeniest little par three, that the house wasn't really that big. But it was eleven thousand square feet according to some glossy blond country-club woman I overheard gossiping in the kitchen, who acted like it was hers and was far more interested in showing it off than Connie was.

I don't know why Connie had that big house, with her husband dead and her children grown, but after I met Connie, I discovered that whatever she did, she did in a big way. Lots of the women from her country-club life sniped over such an extravagant engagement party, but I believe Connie made that party the event that it was because she loved Sara Jane.

Now Connie was the only one of Mrs. Farquhar's friends who was a drinker. None of her parties were dry because she argued that even Jesus liked to have a little drink when he partied. And even though Nettie Farquhar was a dyed-in-the-wool Baptist, she never once fussed over Connie's ways because they were more like sisters than friends.

Connie was the maid of honor in Mrs. Farquhar's wedding and a couple of years later moved in and took care of her day and night when Sara Jane's mama had trouble carrying the twins she eventually lost. When Sara Jane was four, Mrs. Farquhar's only sister shot and killed herself. The whole tragedy left Nettie Farquhar so devastated, she couldn't get out of bed for months. During all that,

Connie took Sara Jane to her house, spoiled her rotten, and loved Sara Jane every bit as much as she loved her own children.

"Zora Adams," Connie bellowed as we walked through the door. "Who's this marvelous-looking man you've got on your arm? Are you single, darling?" She extended her hand to Winston, who kissed it obediently and smiled. "Because I sure am."

"Mrs. Harmon, this is Winston Sawyer."

I watched her as she sifted through her mind for that name. Then her face lit up, and she took Winston's arm and linked it through mine.

"Well, now, it's a pleasure, a real pleasure," she said. "But I'm here to tell you, Mr. Sawyer—Do you mind if I call you Winston?—you've got yourself the sweetest, most gorgeous single young thing in the whole county. But a beauty like Zora won't stay that way for long, I assure you."

I blushed, and she let out a laugh.

"Y'all come on in and get yourself a drink. Sara Jane's in the living room, and Jerry's got Jimmy over there bragging about that yard business of his to a bunch of old men, which just goes to show that miracles really do happen." Connie pointed us in the direction of the bar, excusing herself to answer the doorbell.

"She's sweet, but she's like a whirlwind," I said to Winston, who looked a little rattled by Connie's ways. He nodded and ordered a Dewar's, straight. I drank Coke, as I knew Sara Jane would because we never drank in front of her mama and daddy.

I found Sara Jane and could tell she was surprised to see Winston. She looked like a movie star in a cream-colored satin dress with her mother's diamond necklace and dangly earrings. I kissed her cheek, told her how beautiful she looked, and then introduced the two of them. She behaved herself and didn't ask him his intentions, which I knew she was dying to do.

"Where's Jimmy?" I said.

"Over there with Daddy." She smiled, pointing to the balcony that overlooked the swimming pool. "I almost wish that he still hated Jimmy. Daddy's turned him into his deer-hunting buddy, his fishing buddy, and his football buddy. It's like Jimmy's the son he never had, but I kind of liked it when I had Jimmy all to myself."

"I can't believe it," I said, as I watched Mr. Farquhar slap Jimmy on the back as they both burst out laughing at a joke somebody had told.

"I almost came by the other night, when they went to the high-school football game together, but Mama made me work on the wedding invitations."

I turned to say something to Winston, to explain the whole situation and what a miracle it really was that Mr. Farquhar had actually consented to the wedding, but he was gone. I found him at the bar with a funny look on his face.

"You okay?"

He looked down at his glass and shook his head.

"What's wrong?"

He threw back the drink, then nodded for the bartender to pour him another. The bartender looked at me like I was the one who could give him permission for such a thing.

"Dewar's," Winston said clearly. "Straight."

Although we'd only been at the party a little less than an hour, there's no telling how many drinks he'd already had. The bartender looked at me again, shrugged his shoulders, and refilled the glass, but he didn't look happy about it.

"And this is Zora Adams," I heard Mrs. Farquhar say from behind as she put her hand on my arm. "Jerry and I love her to bits and we've all but adopted her."

"Zora, this is Mrs. Grace Timmerman from my bridge club. Her husband, Bob, runs the paper mill here in Davenport."

"Pleased to meet you, Mrs. Timmerman."

"Well, aren't you a lovely young thing. You're Sara Jane's maid of honor, aren't you, dear?"

"Yes, ma'am . . ." I was going to introduce them to Winston, but when I turned around, he was gone. "Oh, uh, it's a real nice party . . . isn't it?"

"Well, sure it is," Mrs. Timmerman said. "Connie Harmon doesn't do anything halfway. You are coming to my party for Sara Jane now, aren't you?"

"Next Saturday?" I said, and she nodded. "Yes, ma'am. I'm looking forward to it."

Ladies like that love to chitchat, and by the time they were done chitchatting with me, Winston had been gone about fifteen minutes. I walked through the house looking for him, trying not to appear desperate, searching the balcony and the patio downstairs before making my way back up to the great room.

"Where's Winston?" Sara Jane said, as she motioned for Jimmy to leave those old men and come to her. I watched him slip away and walk toward her with a look on his face that said he was hopelessly in love.

"I don't know," I said, as Jimmy wrapped his arms around his girl. Sara Jane laughed and said something to him under her breath that I didn't understand.

"How are you doing, Zora?" Jimmy said, leaning over to kiss me on the cheek. He got that from the Farquhars, who are always hugging and kissing folks.

I gave him a little peck back. "Fine. I haven't seen you in a long time. But I hear if things don't work out with Sara Jane, you're getting engaged to her daddy."

"Well," Jimmy said with a grin, "he may not be good-looking, but he never complains about me watching too much football." Sara Jane elbowed him in the ribs, and Jimmy wrapped his arms around her again. "Is this not the most beautiful woman you've ever seen in your life?"

"Absolutely," I said as I watched them slip into a room that looked like an office and close the doors.

"Now everybody wants to be swept off their feet by good lovin' like that, don't you think?" Connie Harmon said from behind. "I know I do."

"This is such a nice party, Mrs. Harmon. Thanks for having me."

"Well, honey, I couldn't help but notice that nice-lookin' man you came with easin' out that side door over there, with a fifth of my good Scotch."

I could feel my face was flushed and stung like I was going to burst into tears. She put her arm around me and we walked toward the door.

"Now, if I had a man as delicious as that, I'd be hot on his trail before he could stray too far. And as far as you and the Scotch are concerned, I look at it this way—the man does have good taste, now doesn't he?" She kissed me on the cheek, and then gently pushed me out the door.

It was windy and so cold my teeth were bumping together. I wrapped my arms around myself, rubbing my bare shoulders, wishing I hadn't forgotten my wrap. My feet were wet from walking the golf course, looking for Winston. I was too embarrassed and ashamed that he'd left to call out his name. But there was something presumptuous expecting him to come running toward me; there was also the possibility that, if I called him, he might just run the other way.

It was maybe an hour or more before I found him sitting in the middle of a green with the Scotch in one hand and the flagstick in the other. He raised his head and smiled at me, then must have remembered why he was there and dropped his head like somebody had snipped the imaginary string that had lifted it up in the first place.

"Why did you leave?"

He didn't look at me, just shrugged his shoulders and started to take another drink.

"Come on, I'll drive you home," I said, pulling him up like I did that night he was in the hammock. He handed me the half-empty bottle and I threw it as far as I could before pointing toward the lights of the party. He could walk pretty well, but stumbled from time to time. I opened the car door, helped him in, and told him to stay put while I went inside to say good-bye.

I saw Sara Jane across the room talking to a bunch of ladies gathered around her. I waved good-bye. She cocked her head to the side like she didn't understand and then smiled and waved me on. I looked around for Connie Harmon and saw Mr. and Mrs. Farquhar along the way. I told them that Winston didn't feel well, which was true. They said they were sorry they didn't get to talk to him much, and they told me how pretty I looked and how much they loved me being a part of their family.

"You found him," Connie said as I walked into the kitchen.

I nodded. "It really was a wonderful party. Thanks for everything and . . . I'm sorry about the Scotch."

She hugged me, giving me a little extra squeeze. "Don't mention it, darling, don't mention it at all," she said as she put her arm around my shoulder and walked me toward the kitchen door. "Now, Zora, I bet there's more to that man than just good looks, and it appears that you have the dubious pleasure of finding out exactly what that is . . . or what it isn't." She kissed me on the cheek, and then wiped the print of her lipstick away like I was a little girl. "Just make sure he's worth the effort."

25

When I woke up the next morning, Winston was watching me sleep. I smiled at him, then remembered Connie's party and turned away. I picked up the alarm clock and looked at the time—eight o'clock. Setting the clock down hard on the nightstand, I rolled out of bed without so much as a single word.

"Where are you going?"

"To the bathroom," I said without looking at him. "I'm going to get a shower and go to church with Sara Jane, probably eat dinner over there."

"You're mad," he said, without any indication as to whether or not he cared.

"I'm going to church."

The water felt good and hot. I thought about those old musicals that came on Saturday afternoons on Channel Twelve and wondered if it really was possible to wash a man right out of my hair the way that pretty blond lady did in *South Pacific*. Just in case it was true, I shampooed twice.

When I got out of the shower Winston had written SORRY on a paper napkin and was gone. The note made me think about what Connie said the night before at the party, and I wondered if Winston really wasn't worth the effort.

For the first time in a long time, I primped for myself, drying my hair, making sure my makeup was perfect and that my nails matched my dress. I looked at myself in the mirror and caught a glimpse of the girl who left the mountains just a few short months ago. It was like seeing an old friend.

As I strutted down Main Street, two boys pulled alongside of me and drove real slow. One of them was kind of cute. They eyed me until the car behind them blew his horn for them to move on. They said something flirty and peeled out before I went into the church.

"You're looking spry this morning," Sara Jane said as the choir filed in and we rose to sing the first hymn. I just grinned and sang "Onward Christian Soldiers" right along with the rest of the sinners.

Somebody different was sitting in old Reverend Lynch's place in the pulpit that morning. He smiled a lot while the choir director introduced him and his guitar.

Connor Morris stood up, and thanked the choir director while he adjusted the microphone, and picked up a guitar that was leaning against the pulpit. I'd never heard anything other than the piano and the organ played in that church, and I noticed some folks didn't look real happy as he began to play. But when he opened his mouth to sing, all was forgiven because he sang with such sweetness and conviction that lots of folks had tears in their eyes. When it was over, an old man in the very back of the church started clapping, which Sara Jane said nobody ever did. Before too long the whole congregation was clapping, and folks were saying, "Amen," even some of the women.

We sang a few more hymns and we sang them differently, like Brother Connor had given us permission to praise the Lord. I think everybody there was enthralled with that man, including me. I don't know if it was because he was so handsome, tanned, and blond or because he was Spirit filled, but I couldn't have taken my eyes off of him even if I had wanted to. Sara Jane and Jimmy paid attention, which they never did, because they usually had church all by themselves.

Connor Morris preached about love, real love. He said that it knew no bounds, that it was limitless and undying.

"Love is patient." He paused for a moment and looked around the congregation. "Love is kind. Love does not envy or boast; it is not proud." As he continued reading, I started thinking about Mama and how the only thing she ever did that was even close to being mother-like was read to me out of that old red-and-white Childcraft fairy-tale book. It was part of a forty-eight-volume set that came with some old World Book Encyclopedias that my daddy bought one time when I was in the first grade, to celebrate my learning how to read. Mama loved those stories as much as I did, and whenever I was sick, she would read her favorite story, a version of "Rumpelstiltskin" called "Tom Tit Tot." Even though the two of us could recite the whole story by heart, she always read it with an excitement in her voice, like she was reading it for the very first time.

Mama never could sit still for very long without nodding off, so she usually fell asleep after the first couple of pages. If I felt real bad, I'd just go right on to sleep, too, but sometimes I'd slip out of bed, take the book out of her lap, and finish the story myself.

She always seemed to stop just short of the part when the king promises to marry the girl if she can spin a whole roomful of straw into gold. The poor girl tries and tries but can't turn straw into gold, and nothing, short of making a deal with the devil, will get the job done. Now, I'm not saying here that Winston was the devil. What I am saying is that I sure could relate to that girl because no matter how much time Winston and I spent in bed, I could never turn what we had into love.

Listening to the preacher go on about perfect love, it was easy to see the difference, easy to step out into the aisle when the first note of the altar call sounded. Something had stirred inside me; it felt like God and yet it was a part of me. I stood in a long line of sinners who wanted perfect love, too. Finally, after I don't know how many verses of "Just As I Am," Connor bent over and I confessed my sins to him. I didn't get more than three or four words out before I started sobbing and trembling in the presence of the Lord.

Connor Morris took his hand and turned my face up so that I could see his. I have marveled to this day over that man's eyes and how intense they were, but not in an anxious sort of way. He smiled at me and told me that Jesus would wash me whiter than snow if I wanted to be baptized. He asked me if I wanted to be a new creature. I couldn't speak. I could only nod my head and cry, because I did want to be a new creature.

Fifteen of us were baptized right then and there. The teenage boy who went before me lost his footing when he was immersed in the water and started kicking wildly, which made the children in the congregation laugh out loud. Several of them were most likely pinched for it because some were crying when I stepped into the warm water.

A little girl who was the first person baptized that day came out of the pool just glowing. "That water was so warm, I peed."

Her mother grabbed her by the arm and marched her toward the changing room fussing all the way. "You better thank your lucky stars you accepted Jesus, young lady. Otherwise you'd get a good spanking for doing such a thing."

I walked toward Connor, my coarse cotton baptismal gown puffed way up on top of the water. I kept pushing it down around me with one hand and almost forgot to give Connor the handkerchief the lady helping us in and out of the baptismal pool had given me.

"What is your Christian name?" he said so the whole congregation could hear. I didn't say anything. "Your whole name," he whispered.

"Zora May Adams."

"Zora, I'm going to put this handkerchief over your nose and lean you back," he whispered. "Just hold on to my forearm, relax, and take a good deep breath. You'll be fine." I nodded and looked into his eyes that were sweet and brown. "Zora May Adams, I baptize you in the name of the Father, and the Son, and the Holy Ghost."

As he said those words, he tipped me back in that warm water. I guess I was nervous because I forgot to breathe before he dunked me.

"Raised to walk in newness of life. Amen," he said as he brought me up, coughing and sputtering, full of redemption.

"Amen," the congregation echoed.

The lady who had given me the handkerchief started to tear up when the first sinner was baptized and made a point to hug each one of us as we came out of the pool dripping wet. She handed out towels, too, and looked like she needed one herself because, by the time I came out, she was as soaked to the bone as the rest of the new creatures.

Normally, the church office mails out a letter with all of the necessities for the big day including a change of clothes and an extra pair of underwear, which is underlined twice. I know this because I saw Jimmy's letter before he was baptized. I didn't know you were supposed to keep your clothes on underneath the gown, so while everybody else was wringing wet, the only thing I had on under my gown was my bra and panties. I stuffed them in a little plastic bag the handkerchief lady had given me after the service and avoided shaking the preacher's hand because it just didn't feel right without underwear.

When I saw Sara Jane and Jimmy, they hugged me, and Mrs. Farquhar and Mr. Farquhar were so happy they cried. We went home to their place for Sunday dinner, and Mr. Farquhar told me about when he was baptized in the river near his homeplace. He remembered everything about that day and described it in such a way that I wished I had been baptized in a river, too.

After dinner, Sara Jane and Jimmy dropped me at my apartment. I told her that I was ready to meet Jimmy's friend, maybe even go to one of the engagement parties with him.

I climbed the steps to my apartment and didn't give Winston

Sawyer a second thought. When I opened the door, I was ready to ask him to leave if he was there and reclaim my own place and my own self. But then I saw a table set for two and a dozen roses arranged in a pretty glass vase.

He walked out of the bedroom with a big box behind his back. "You're home," he said, kissing me lightly on the lips and lingering close just long enough to weaken me considerably. "I'm sorry about last night," he said, kissing me again while I tried to recall my name. "I have something for you." He handed me a dress box that was wrapped in pretty blue paper. "Go ahead, open it."

I did hesitate, but not long enough to really count. He watched my face and knew I had forgiven him before the bow hit the floor.

"I was in the coffee shop across the street from the store the day you tried it on," he said. "I knew you wanted it. You looked so beautiful. Do you remember?"

Of course I remembered. I'd tried on that indigo beaded gown at one of Emma's fancy little dress shops downtown. I don't know why I even bothered to go in there. I knew I'd never be able to afford that pretty thing in the window. But I just had to try it. The woman said she didn't usually do layaways but it looked so good on me, she said she'd make an exception. As nice as she was, I knew it'd take me a year to pay for it, so I said no.

"The woman who owns the store has a kid that was in one of my classes last semester. I got her to go down to the store this morning so I could have it for you when you came back. I wanted you to have something nice to wear to your graduation dinner."

I ran my fingers over the beads that were not the loud, flashy kind. They were the exact same color as the dress, and they made the dress look like something out of *Vogue*. I could tell he wanted me to rush into the bathroom and try it on, but I didn't. The new creature inside me was battling the old creature.

"I saw the invitation on the refrigerator. I want to take you," he said, as he reached for my hand and held it in his and kissed it, making sure he was truly forgiven. "To the dance."

I was in and out of that dress in a matter of seconds.

26

⌒

"Baby, is that you?"

I didn't say anything at first. I thought about my letter she had scrawled RETURN TO SENDER on and how sick I felt when it came back to me. I wanted to slam the receiver down hard so she could see how it felt, but I didn't. "Baby?" she said again like I hadn't heard her the first time.

Mama wanted something all right and wanted it pretty bad because she'd never called me baby before.

"Mama."

"Hey, there. How you been?" she asked like we were picking up not where we left off but from a long, long time ago when things were just okay between us.

"Fine."

There was a long silence. I could hear the alarm clock ticking away the seconds. I lay down on the bed and twirled the phone cord around with my fingers, first one way, then another as she went on about a grease fire at my uncle Heath's fish camp and how Simpsonville had gotten their own Dairy Queen.

"So how's school?"

"Fine."

More silence.

"Dody Haskins shot and killed Miss Bertha's dog last week and caused a big stink with everybody taking one side or another. I'm telling you, it was a real mess. I told Cindy Bates that I . . ."

"Mama?"

"What, honey?"

"You sent my letter back."

No answer.

"When I tried to call, you hung up on me."

Still no answer.

"And now you just call me up and start talking like we do this every day?"

"Zora May," her voice was shaking. "I ain't had a drink in six weeks and no man neither since Butch left."

I'd hated her for so long that it was hard to hear her talk like that and harder still to think of things changing. "I'm sober," she said again, which set my heart to hopscotching across fine lines that had the mama I'd always wanted on one side and the mama I hated on the other. "And Butch, well, he's gone," she said like I hadn't heard her the first time.

I didn't know who in the hell Butch was, probably just some man she'd taken up with since I left. I thought about the others that came around our house and how she lived for them, the way she ate up their attention like it was good and sweet even when it wasn't. I remember watching her make over them like they were the end all and wondering why she couldn't do that for me, not even once.

"What do you want, Mama?"

"I want you to come home." She choked up a little bit. "I know we got things we got to get straight, things I got to make right, and I'm wanting to do that, Zora May, I am. Your uncle Heath's going to loan me this truck so I can come down there, on your day off, and we could have a little bite to eat, talk things out. I'm different now. Better. I know Nana'd be proud. I know I didn't give her much to be proud of when she was living, and you know your daddy . . ."

She said his name and broke down completely. It had been ten years since he died, but sometimes the wound was still fresh and deep.

"Mama, don't cry. Listen, I'm off Wednesday afternoon, you can come then."

"I got a surprise for you," she said with that little hitch she gets in her voice whenever she cries.

"You don't have to bring me anything, I'll see you Wednesday."

"Okay. Zora May, I know I said Nana'd be proud of me, but I know for sure she'd be proud of you going to school."

I couldn't breathe. I felt like someone was standing on my chest and if I heard another word about Daddy or Nana or the new and improved Mama, I was going to die. "I have to go now. Bye."

"Bye, baby."

I hung up the phone and felt awash with guilt because I knew Nana would never be proud of what was going on between Winston and me. I remember her shaking her head over every stray man Mama brought home, but Nana never said a word because she knew our souls were crushed the day Daddy died, especially Mama's. I think in a way Nana felt sorry for Mama because she was so desperate to find a man to take my daddy's place.

Mrs. Cathcart didn't say anything when I was late for work that day. Mama had messed with my mind and my heart so that nothing went right that morning. I mixed the wrong color three times in a row and was ready to just give up. Then my customer said she'd wasn't real sure she'd look good as a blonde and that she thought it was the Lord's way of saying so. So I gave her a cut and set, and she tipped me two dollars.

I stayed pretty busy most of the day. It must have been a school holiday or something because we had so many little kids come in for haircuts. The only bright spot of the day was when Nina came in and brought the wedding pictures, which were beautiful, but some of the girls thought she brought them by just to rub their noses in her wedded bliss.

"How are you feeling?" I asked as I leafed through the photos.

"Good, real good. You'd think nobody'd ever had a baby before by the way they treat me. I can't lift a finger around Harley or his mama. They've been so good to me."

"I think it's a boy," I said, because Nana had always said if you carry them low and out front, it's sure to be a boy, and Nina was definitely out front.

"I don't care, long as it's okay. They say I'm due the end of February, so we'll find out soon enough, I reckon."

Nina didn't stay long. I watched her as she went from booth to booth showing her pictures and talking to the girls. Somebody asked if she was going to work after the baby came. She said she couldn't imagine leaving that baby all day even if her mama kept it.

I loved the way Nina stroked her big belly and giggled when that tiny baby tossed about inside her, and the way she glowed like a new bride and a new mother should. Seeing Nina made me think a lot about my own mama, thoughts neither Daddy nor Nana ever allowed me to think about because they loved me so good. The one question I kept coming back to over and over again was, why didn't Mama ever love me that way?

27

It was two o'clock on Wednesday afternoon when I came home from school to find Mama sitting there on the steps to the apartment. She'd always fussed over herself so that she never looked anywhere near her age, but that day she looked plain, dressed in an old pair of jeans and a white cotton blouse with the shirttail out. Her thick chestnut hair was pulled back in a simple knot and she didn't have a speck of makeup on.

She got up, dusted off her fanny, and then wiped her hands on her pants leg like she might shake my hand. Before either of us could say anything, we had our arms wrapped around each other, and I held her while she cried. Her hair smelled like baby shampoo instead of honky-tonk smoke. My heart beat a little faster because somewhere in me the tiniest fiber of hope for her to be a real mother was still alive.

She held me at arm's length and looked at me with clear eyes like I was something precious.

"I ain't Judy Garland," she said laughing and crying at the same time.

"I know, Mama."

"I can't even sing." She wiped away tears and stood up straight so that she was almost as tall as me. "Ain't had a drink in almost seven weeks, and no men friends, either."

"That's real good, Mama."

"I'm so glad you said I could come," she said, wiping her eyes with her sleeve. "It took me hitting bottom, honey, but I'm here, I'm here with you now."

I don't know why I didn't cry. Maybe it was because I wasn't sure I could believe what I was seeing, Mama there all penitent, wanting to make things right between us. I put my arm around her slight frame and we walked up the stairs together side by side. She'd take one step and then another, looking at me like it was hard for her to believe, too.

"Oh, this is pretty," she said like she had to say something nice. "You got your sitting area and kitchen, and then your little bed and bath. Yeah, this is right pretty," she said, running her hand along my kitchen counter. She stopped when she got to the wine rack and two crystal glasses that sat next to it and looked at me and smiled.

"It's not much, but it's been nice to have this place so that I don't have to work a second job and go to school. A lot of the girls have to do that. Two of them had to drop out," I said, putting my jacket and purse on one of the hooks by the front door. "I'm going to change out of this uniform, Mama, so just make yourself at home."

She didn't sit down. I heard her walking around my little place over and over again like she was afraid to settle in one spot. When I came out of the bedroom, she was pulling a good-size box out of her big shoulder bag and was trying to straighten out the bow that was mashed.

"Oh. You want your surprise now? I wrapped it. Go on, now. Open it."

"Mama, I told you not to get me anything."

I tore off the bow and took the tape off from one end of the box and then the other. It was just an old pasteboard thing that said McKerrin Drugs on the side, but when I opened it and pulled back the tissue paper, I was a little child again. "Where did you find her?" I pulled my rag doll out of the box and held her close.

She smelled earthy, like she had been in a cedar chest for a long time. Me and my daddy and her were best friends when I was little.

"You used to set her up by that old oak tree out back by the shed and have tea parties, didn't you? What was her name? It was Myrna, that's right, ain't it? That's what you called her, Myrna. Like Myrna Loy."

"Where did you find her?"

Mama's chin quivered and she looked away. "I'm trying to make amends, honey. It was bad for me to take and hide her right after your daddy passed. That was real bad of me and I'm sorry."

She stood up and began to pace the room again. "And look at you drinking now. I reckon you're past eighteen." She ran her hand across the top of the wine rack like she could use a drink herself.

"Imagine that, and fancy wine, too. Maybe it'll do more for you than it did for me, 'cause drinking never done me no good. Took me a while to figure that out, though. You got a man friend?"

She gave a little laugh when she saw me blush. "'Course you do. Pretty thing like you. By the time I was your age, you were five, going on six. Couldn't have no more kids after you come along. Didn't need none, though. Had you, and your daddy."

I told her I needed to start dinner and explained a little about my arrangement with the owner of the apartment. She said she wanted to help and that she'd learned how to make biscuits since I left, that it took her two five-pound bags of flour to get them right, but now she could make them as good as Nana's.

She rolled up her sleeves and got busy proving it while I fried some chicken and creamed some potatoes. After Mama finished up the biscuits, she took the strings off of some pole beans and talked about home. She didn't say what she was doing now, she just went on and on about how pretty the fall had been and how the apples were gone but that it had been a good crop that year for the farmers.

"You thought about coming home?" She pulled biscuits out of the oven that looked like a picture. "You'll be graduating soon. I know I'd like it if you was there with me."

"I don't know, Mama. I talked with a fella about a job here."

"Is he your boyfriend?"

"No, Ronnie owns the nicest beauty shop in town. He's real nice, and I have friends here now, too."

"Oh, you always kept to yourself at home. Didn't have many friends."

My head snapped back like I'd been slapped; she didn't have a

207

clue as to why I was embarrassed to bring people over to our house. "Are you still at the shirt factory?"

"Hell, no," she said with that sideways grin I always loved to see whenever she teased my daddy. "I was supposed to get the next supervisor job that come up, and they passed me by and give it to that Mason girl. Berton Rollins took me in the back room because he seen I was all mad, crying. Said not to worry, that he could fix things for me with the higher-ups. Felt me up right there but never did what he said he was gonna do, so I quit there. I'm working for one of them rich ladies that used to come up the mountain during the summer, but she's retired now. Stays on up there all year long."

"What do you do for her?"

She put her hand over her mouth and with a sly look on her face, she told me that she cooked and cleaned for the woman, which was right funny for two reasons. One, Mama never cooked much of anything the whole time I lived at home, and she sure never cleaned.

"She's from Chicago. Don't have good sense. You should see how much she pays me for just one week, more than I ever made at the shirt factory, and in cash, too."

She caught me up on everybody back home while we fixed our plates and didn't take one bite until she saw the look on my face when I tried those biscuits. She was right. Nana would have been proud.

"I got to leave out before dark," she said as she took the last bite from her plate. "This was real nice, wasn't it? We'll have to do it again real soon." She looked at me, trying not to tear up. "You know I come to say something. Do you think we could let the kitchen sit for a while and just talk?"

We went over to my little couch and sat side by side. Mama sat on her hands and stared at the floor. Every so often, she looked at me and smiled like she was trying to get up the nerve to say whatever it was she needed to say. As much as I used to wish terrible things for her, it was hard to see her so uncomfortable. I picked up Myrna, straightened her yarn hair, and waited.

"Well, I guess I told you more than once I hadn't had a drink in a long time. I got to thank getting let go from the shirt factory for that," she said, looking up at me to see if I remembered she said she'd quit. "I didn't drink none when I was growing up and not much at all when your daddy was living. Then Heyward come along and . . . Leon, and I was as much of a sot as they were. Looking back, I know I stayed that way because they sure looked better when I was drinking, especially Heyward. Sometimes I just shake my head and wonder if there's anything up there when I think of laying with that man."

"He was a sorry-ass drunk," I laughed. "But he was a nice sorry-ass drunk. I remember thinking you'd be upset when he died."

"Hell, no. I made you get one end of that old couch he pissed all over, I got the other, and we put it on the trash pile out back. It made a right good fire, remember?"

"And we bought a new one the very next day." I wiped a tear away.

"And Leon, well . . ." Neither of us was laughing anymore. "But what I come here to say—about your daddy—"

I felt the color drain out of my face. A wave of nausea shot through me. I was nine again, sitting on the little bench in our backyard listening to Mama and Daddy fighting. I couldn't make out what they were saying because their words were jumbled up together in all the shouting. When they stopped, dead silence filled the whole mountain. Not so much as a cicada uttered a sound.

Daddy stormed off. I ran after him. He stopped and scooped me up in his arms. He held me so tight I could hardly breathe. Then he put me back down and told me to mind him and stay put. The dry grass from the drought crunched under his feet. His shoulders jerked up and down as he walked away. He was crying hard.

"Nothing's been right in my life since your daddy died, nothing. Now, I used to think it's because I keep picking the wrong man. I thought I was trying to fill that big hole your daddy left inside of me when he passed, but that ain't so." She was crying hard. "I loved my Boyd, oh how I loved your daddy, Boyd."

I broke down and held her while she sobbed from the pain of trying to right the past. I stroked her hair like Nana would have and kept hoping what was happening between us would suddenly feel right but it never did. I was still mothering for both of us.

"Anyhow, I come to set things right. To say what I done and make my 'mends."

There was a hole inside me worn deep from trying to decipher the horrible argument I'd overhead. I always thought if I understood what really happened that last time I saw my daddy, then somehow his dying would be easier to take. But as I looked into my mother's eyes, suddenly I didn't want to know what really happened that day when, as one of the boys I went to school with put it, my daddy hugged a train. I shook my head, but the words wouldn't come out. *Stop. Don't say it. Let it lay.*

"He could never pay me enough attention, nobody could. I was mad at him. I told him you wasn't his. That I'd laid with his cousin, but it wasn't true. He didn't have to do what he did, he could have looked in your eyes and known it wasn't true.

"I ain't lying no more." She shook her head violently and took a tissue out of the box. She blew her nose and tried to smile. "I think you always knew he done it because of me. I know I've always been such a mess because I couldn't admit that, but I'm better now. I come to say I'm sorry for all the bad things I done. And I'm sorry for being so weak, for never taking care of you any better than I did." She touched my hand and I jerked away from her like a hot stove.

"Thanksgiving's in a couple of weeks. Come on home and we'll cook up a storm." Her voice sounded warm and soft like a kindergarten teacher's on the first day of school. "I'll take you into town and help you find a job fixing hair. If that don't work out, I know they're hiring at the shirt factory."

As much as I hated Mama, somewhere inside me there was still a powerful yearning for her to be the way a mother ought to be. I thought that feeling had died a long time ago, but there it was doing battle with the awful truth she'd just spoken. Then I thought about Winston and how going home might not be such a bad idea. If I left, he might straighten up and fly right just like Mama did.

"I'll think about it," I said, and she nearly knocked me over hugging me. When she finally let go, she said that she really needed to get on back because she didn't like to be on those mountain roads late at night. That was news to me, but it was good news. She went in the bathroom to freshen up, and I started clearing the table.

I heard the car door slam and Winston hurrying up the stairs. He threw his briefcase down by the door, came over to the kitchen counter, and poured himself a full glass of Scotch.

"Your friend here?" he asked after draining the glass.

"No. It's my mother. Are you all right?"

He didn't seem to notice I'd been crying. He let the last few drops of his drink drain onto his tongue and poured himself another.

"What's wrong?"

"John fucking Ridgeway," he said, like I knew who he was talking about, "almighty head of the English department. He's always on my case."

I was smart enough to know that we had so little in common, if Winston and I ever started talking, the illusion of what we had together would be gone. He knew this, too, but was too upset to play our game. Early on, if I forgot the rules, he'd press his fingers against my lips and look at me with those deep blue eyes that hypnotized me into thinking we didn't need words. So I went to him, put my arms around his middle, and nuzzled his neck.

"He likes to pick out a student every semester to pick on—no, to fail. This time, he picked a student I had last year. Bright girl. He failed her every test. Gave the tests back for the kids to look at in class and then took them up for good so that nobody could compare answers. She tried talking to him. That didn't work, so she came to me." His glass was empty again. He wrapped his arms around me. His breathing was slower now; the Scotch had begun to kick in. He looked at me, suddenly remembered the rules, and kissed me until he heard Mama fumbling with the lock on the bathroom door.

I guess she must have heard Winston's voice and knew there was a man about. She came out of the bathroom with her hair down. She'd either pinched her cheeks or used some of my blush in the medicine cabinet. The collar of her blouse was flipped up and it was unbuttoned real low, and she had tied her shirttail tight around her flat, milky white belly.

She introduced herself to Winston, eyeing him so that I was too embarrassed to look at either one of them. She flashed him a smile, gave me a little peck on the cheek, and said good-bye without another word about Thanksgiving.

28

Miss Cunningham called me the Monday before Thanksgiving to see if I needed a ride home. She said she was flying to New York for the holiday but would be glad to come get me after school on Tuesday. I almost said yes just to save myself the $37.50 for the bus ticket, but I was afraid she might take one look at me and know I'd been doing more for Winston than cooking his dinner.

She told me Deana Malloy scored 1560 on her SATs, which was quite a feat for a small-town school like ours. I listened to the excitement in her voice as she talked about the different colleges Deana was looking at and smiled to myself, happy that Miss Cunningham was finally sending one of her own away to college.

"How's Winston?" she said, after we had talked about everything but him.

"He's good." There was a long silence. "He eats good."

"That's great, Zorie; I'm so glad you're there to look in on him.

Hey, listen, I've got to get those midterms graded before tomorrow. Call me sometime, okay?"

"Happy Thanksgiving, Miss Cunningham."

I waited a minute or two, swallowed hard, and dialed the number at home. Before the call had a chance to go through, I hung up and got some laundry together. Anything, even scrubbing the toilet and wiping down the baseboards in the apartment, looked good compared to calling Mama. A couple of hours later, the apartment was spotless, and I knew if I fretted another minute over calling her, I'd probably have taken the clean dishes out of the cupboard and washed them all over again.

"The number you have reached is not in service at this time," the recording said. "If you need assistance, please hang up and dial the operator."

At first I thought I dialed the wrong number, but after two more tries, I knew it wasn't a mistake. Well, now I was really worried and set about calling every relative I could think of, but nobody was home. As a last resort, I called Aunt Fannie, Uncle Heath's wife, and held the phone about a foot from my ear.

"Hello."

"Aunt Fannie, this is Zora," I hollered back because she's almost deaf.

"My Lord, child, I haven't heard from you in a good spell."

"I know. Aunt Fannie, I tried to call Mama to tell her I was coming home, but the phone's been cut off. I just know something's wrong because she's expecting me to come home for the holiday. Do you think she's all right?"

"Honey, your mama ain't been right since your daddy died and she didn't do too good after you left." Aunt Fannie let out a deep sigh. "Couldn't nobody help her. But she got better and we was all glad 'til about a week ago when she took to the roadhouse. Got a job waiting tables. You know your uncle Heath's went over there more than once and tried to straighten her out, but after a while he just give up."

Aunt Fannie said that her daughter, Tina, wanted to have Mama committed. Tina was committed when she was just twenty, and she always suggested that whenever there was a problem. I don't know why because it never helped her much.

"She met some truck driver. He come through here with his own rig, a pretty one, too, had pictures of wild horses on the side. Heath said that man looked like one of them ZZ Top fellows with one of them long, stringy beards, and Lord if he didn't have her name painted above his on the door there. Well, they say she took one look at that and jumped in the truck. They headed down the mountain 'cause he had a load to haul clean to Texas. Your mama ain't got no luck but bad with men. I 'spect she'll be calling any day now for us to get her back home soon as this don't work out. Maybe she'll call you."

I thanked her for telling me, but it was a hollow kind of thanks that set my head to spinning with all kinds of blame because I hadn't packed up and gone the very night she begged me to come home. I was so busy wallowing around in guilt that I didn't hear Winston come in, and I wasn't sure how long he'd been listening to the conversation. He didn't ask me any questions, just lay down on the bed and held me.

He pushed my hair to the side and kissed me. "Let's go away for the holiday."

I turned around and looked at him. I didn't smile or melt like

I might have if he'd said it a minute or two earlier. All I could think about was the fact that I'd never been away from home for a holiday in my life.

"I don't know," I said, "I—"

He put his fingers over my mouth. I kissed them and took his hand and pressed it against the side of my face.

"We'll drive up to The Homestead in Virginia. It's a nice place; you'll love it. You can wear your new dress to Thanksgiving dinner."

"Okay," I said, not able to turn loose of the sadness then. But I loved him for trying to make me feel better and loved him even more because we were finally going someplace special like a real couple.

In the back of my mind, I truly believed Mama would call. She'd ask me if I wanted sweet-potato pie or pumpkin pie, because they were all the same to her. Every year, Nana would just shake her head at the thought of Mama even asking such a question and set about peeling the sweet potatoes.

Mama hardly ever cooked, but when she was a little girl, she learned to make a real good pineapple upside-down cake and had made it every year since for Christmas and Thanksgiving. I missed the way our house smelled during the holidays, like baked goods and smoked ham. I ached for these things so that I closed my eyes and went right to sleep.

When I woke up that morning, his suitcase was packed and sitting by my front door. I knew good and well Winston went into his place for clean clothes and liquor. Sometimes I wondered if it bothered him to go into his house or if he just got what he needed without giving it much thought. He looked up from his newspaper, took a sip of coffee, and smiled at me. "Good morning."

"Good morning. Mmmm, coffee," I said as I kissed him on the cheek like we were making a commercial. He poured me a cup out of a little carafe, something else he brought over from his place. "What time is it?"

"About seven."

I finished my coffee, jumped in the shower, and was packed and ready to go before eight. He jammed my suitcase into that tiny trunk and hitched his to the luggage rack with a couple of wiry red bungee cords. Then we got in the car together and left as if we did that every morning.

By the time we reached the foothills, some of the spell of playing house had worn off. I felt strange, like something important was missing. These mountains looked the same as my mountains, but I knew they were different and it made me ache for home. Winston pulled off the road at places marked Scenic Overlook. We got out of the car three or four different times along the way and stood by the guardrail, looking out over God's country.

He hugged and kissed me in front of God and everybody. He slid his hands up under my sweater and didn't stop when a car whizzed by. He always had a way when he kissed me of nearly taking my breath away, along with my good sense, so I didn't flinch, either, even when a big semi drove by. I guess folks up that way were used to seeing lovers like us stopped alongside the road, because they didn't slow down or honk their horn.

Another big semi passed by and I wondered if Winston brought Emma here, too. Had he stopped along the way to touch her breasts and kiss her the way he had me? The higher we went into the mountains, the more he wanted me. He stopped one last time but I'd been thinking too much, so when he started to kiss me I turned my head, which wasn't at all good because he could always find that little sweet spot at the base of my neck. His breath was hot, and he whispered in my ear.

"I want you."

I kissed him, then slipped out of his arms and ran to the car, which excited him all the more. He drove so fast; the next thirty miles were a blur. I knew how crazy that was in the mountains, but by that time I didn't care. I was a bundle of wanting him, but most of all, wanting to check into that fancy hotel as Mr. and Mrs. Winston Sawyer.

I could tell he got a kick out of the look on my face when we drove up to the place. I'd never seen anything like it before, massive, redbrick, intimidating. I'd seen some rich folks' chalets back home, places they came to a few days out of the year, if they came at all. The Atlanta Hilton was elegant, and Connie Harmon's house was, too, but they all paled in comparison to The Homestead.

We parked by the front door, and the bellboy looked disgusted when he saw the MG, knowing there couldn't be enough bags for us to need assistance. Winston slipped his suitcase off the rack, got mine out of the trunk, and handed the valet the keys. We walked into the lobby and right up to the desk.

"Can I help you?" The woman behind the desk eyed Winston like I wasn't even there.

"Sawyer, Winston Sawyer," he said.

"Let's see," she said, flipping through some papers. "Winston Sawyer and—guest," she said as she smiled at me.

She looked him over more than once as he signed whatever it was she put before him. I knew he was a good-looking man, but I thought it was right tacky of her to make over him like that. He took the key from her and put his arm around me as we walked down the hall together. Looking back over my shoulder, I flashed her a little smile, but she didn't smile back.

He opened the door to our suite and let me walk in first. It looked like something out of one of those decorating magazines I like to leaf through at the Red & White and made me feel like I ought to tiptoe with bare feet—clean bare feet. And all of those pretty lamps and knickknacks, well, they were just to look at, way too nice to touch. I was so in awe of the place that I didn't even notice Winston on the phone.

"Room 307," he said, and then he hung up the phone and looked at me. "I ordered some champagne." He kissed me. "I think there's a Jacuzzi in the bathroom. Why don't you go start the water?"

There was pristine white tile everywhere in the bathroom and crystal light fixtures with dangly prisms that made rainbows on the walls and the ceilings. A great alabaster tub with a swan for a spigot was sunk into the floor like a little swimming pool. Not knowing any better, I turned the Jacuzzi on before the jets were covered and water went all over the place. When I screamed, Winston came running.

We laughed and sopped up the water together and Winston added some extra towels to our room service order. By the time he got back from answering the door, the floor was almost dry. He put the clean towels on the little bench by the shower and that pretty silver bucket beside the tub and opened the bottle. There was a loud pop as the champagne poured out of the bottle like it had a mind of its own. He filled two glasses full and handed one to me.

He saw the look on my face after I tasted it. "Ever had champagne before?"

I shook my head and took pretend sips of the stuff because it didn't appeal to me at all. He'd take a drink and undress me a little bit. Then he would have another drink and take off a little bit more until all my clothes were on the floor. By the time I stepped into the hot, steamy water, he'd had two glasses of champagne and finished mine. Champagne really got him going. He did a sexy little striptease while he finished off the first bottle, then he opened up another one and turned on the Jacuzzi. God, that water felt good, like the hot spring back home only better.

I finished the half glass he'd poured for me, and he finished the bottle. Somewhere in between all that we made love twice, sometimes splashing more water on the floor than the Jacuzzi had. I don't know how long we stayed in that tub before Winston said it was time to get out and dress for tea. He did that for me, I know, because he was pretty tight by then and would have chosen happy hour over tea any day.

I didn't know what to think about going to tea because the only tea parties I'd ever been to were the ones me and Daddy had with Myrna at home in the backyard. We would laugh and sing songs. He'd always fill his teacup full of liquor when he thought I wasn't looking. I loved that strong, sweet smell back then.

Now I felt silly, drinking hot tea out of little tiny china cups, and the spoons they gave us looked like they belonged in a dollhouse. I watched the other women there sitting like they had a cane pole up their backs, sipping and nibbling cookies and fancy little sandwiches. No matter how fancy this was, no matter how many times Winston looked at me to see if I was impressed, I still felt silly.

I was glad when we changed into some comfortable clothes after teatime and went for a walk. We hiked a good ways from the hotel and sat on a ridge where we could see the world, the way I used to see it up on the mountain.

"Are you cold?" he said.

"No." I smiled. "I'm from the mountains. I don't get cold too easily. This place reminds me of where I come from. That stream down there looks just like the one at home—the pass between Turtle Dove and Hitchcock Mountains. I never thought I'd miss that sight like I do. It's so flat in Davenport."

"It is beautiful here," he said, and looked out on the same horizon like he was missing something, too. Neither of us said anything as we watched the sunset color the November sky. "We'd better get back. We have to dress for dinner."

We ate in the grandest dining room, where Thomas Jefferson himself once dined. I remember wishing I had a whole case of champagne when I first met Winston, because after he finished another bottle during dinner, his tongue was loosed and he began to tell me all kinds of things. For sure, liquor made him dark and mysterious, wine made him want to take me straight to bed, but champagne made him horny and downright talkative.

"The first time I had champagne," he began, filling his own glass to overflowing, "I was eleven. My parents had a New Year's Eve party and the stuff was everywhere. There was even some kind of champagne fountain. My cousins and I went around the room finishing off glasses the guests had left sitting around. A couple of times the glasses were full, and we'd laugh whenever the guests stumbled around looking for their drinks. Everybody was so drunk, including the grown-ups, that nobody noticed us at the fountain, pounding down the stuff.

"The four of us got really drunk, and right as the ball dropped on TV, I threw up on the living room floor." He laughed. "My mother said she would never forgive me for that, but she did, of course."

Winston had never told me anything about himself. Although I'd wondered about things like where he grew up and what his job was like, I didn't dare ask. So when he shared a little bit of his own history with me, I was taken aback. Then I thought about my own mother, who, no matter what she said, I knew had never forgiven me for leaving her. "My mother got mad when I left home. It's not the kind of mad you were talking about. I mean really mad. I thought maybe you figured out that something had happened with me and her when you met her that day she came to the apartment."

When we spoke it was always about general stuff like coffee and sex, so he never really knew how to talk about things like this with me. He nodded and pretended to be interested. When the waiter went by, he ordered another cognac and asked for the check. I helped him back to our room and undressed him because I knew he'd fall asleep the minute his head hit the pillow. I took my clothes off and nuzzled up beside him.

"I love you," I whispered as I lay behind him. "I love you so much. I think—"

He rolled over and pulled me close to him and breathed a heavy sigh.

"Love you," he said.

29

It's easy to look back now and see things the way they were, the fact that on any given day, Winston started drinking anywhere between noon and four. He'd eat a late supper and then drink steadily until he passed out. Somewhere in all that, he managed to make Sara Jane's notion of "whiskey dick" an old wives' tale before he reached for a bottle of Scotch or bourbon, or whatever was handy, and finished himself off for the night.

I've often wondered how he could go to bed drunk like he did, night after night, only to wake up the next morning, horny as a goat, never feeling a lick of pain. I remember seeing my daddy suffer most mornings so that the only cure for him was a little hair of the dog, but Winston wasn't like that at all. He was up every morning and out the door to work like he'd had nothing but a little sweet tea with dinner the night before.

Maybe if his body had chastised him more, he might not have

taken to drinking. But he did, and drinking had become a part of who he was. Waking up with him pressed up against me, I never liked the sour smell of alcohol that came off his skin. The way he rested his chin on the crown of my head, he'd breathed on my hair all night so that it smelled like the bottom of a whiskey barrel. I didn't mind it so much on that particular morning, because I was still high off of the words he mumbled in his sleep the night before. I lay there with his arm draped across my waist replaying them over and over again in my mind, putting an "I" in front of the garbled "love you."

He woke up around seven, we showered together and went downstairs to a dining room that was full of people who must have come to "America's premier mountain resort" to graze from buffet to buffet. I thought it was crazy for folks to eat like they were, it being Thanksgiving Day and all. I told Winston I thought I'd just have some juice and a piece of toast, but I don't think he heard me, because he ordered an omelet for himself and a toasted pecan Belgian waffle one of the cooks recommended for me.

Those two fellows got to work on our order, dipping and flipping and sautéing all kinds of good things. The short, jet-black-skinned fellow handed me a pretty china plate with the biggest waffle I'd ever seen. He ladled some hot syrup over the top, plopped on a scoop of butter, and sent me on down the line where a tall, good-looking man with pretty skin the color of coffee with a good bit of cream was making three omelets at a time. He piled a big southwestern one onto Winston's plate and moved on to the next person.

After breakfast, we walked down to the barn where the stableman had two horses ready to go. Winston's horse was a fine black

Tennessee Walker, and the man said the bay mare he saddled for me was, too. I don't think she was a Walker because she was a rough ride. Winston's horse, Jim, had the smooth gait of a merry-go-round horse.

"Have you ridden much?" the man asked as he showed me where to sign the liability waiver. I shook my head, and he looked at Winston like he had been told different.

"Her name's Ariel. She's a good girl. She won't get away from you if you pay attention. She does get a little excited when you start back to the barn, but they all do."

"We'll be fine," Winston said as he mounted his ride.

The man helped me up on Ariel's back and tightened my saddle a little more. "They're all good trail horses. If you get lost, just give them their head. They know the way back. You'd better watch her on the steep trails," he told Winston, and I knew he wasn't talking about Ariel. He looked like he wanted to say something else but didn't; he patted Jim's neck and walked off toward his little hole-in-the-wall office, most likely to pray for me.

We started out past a bunch of folks dressed in fancy red coats on horseback. Between them they must have had twenty-five dogs that barked and yelped like they thought they were going to die.

"They're fox hunters," Winston said over the noise.

It seemed unfair, that little fox being outnumbered like he was and all those serious hunters looking like they were going to war.

I wondered if any of them had even seen a mountain fox close-up before. A little vixen came into the yard one summer day, just as tame as you please, like she was coming to supper with the rest of daddy's hunting dogs. With her acting the way she was, I knew she was rabid and yelled for Daddy. He was sleeping his toddy off in that old recliner on the front porch and fell all over himself, hollering at me to stay put while he got his gun.

She was so sweet that it seemed wrong to kill her, but it had to be done. The rabies had made her just crazy enough so that she wasn't afraid of people anymore, and if Daddy hadn't killed her right then, she would have been foaming at the mouth in a couple of days. She was a pretty thing, though, and smart, too. Even with the rabies, you could see that in her eyes.

A horn sounded, jerking me back from my daydream. The dogs barked even louder as they led the riders toward the woods. They all galloped at full tilt, which made Ariel wheel around and take off with them. I pulled back on the reins as hard as I could but she still cantered, which sure seemed more like an all-out run to me. Winston had to catch us and hold her bridle until the excitement passed. He leaned over in his saddle and talked to her in low, hushed tones that made her ears twitch back and forth with excitement.

That was the nicest time I ever spent with Winston, riding all day like we did, only stopping to eat a sack lunch from the saddle-bags. Sometimes, if the trail was wide enough, we rode side by side and held hands. We rode as far as the trail went and got off to stretch a bit. Winston was different around horses. I guess he must have been around them a lot growing up, but he never said so.

I lay on the brown meadow grass that was soft and thick, and watched him tend to them before he lay down beside me.

"Last night," I whispered, "what you said . . ."

He smiled and laid my head on his chest. "Champagne makes me crazy, throw in a little cognac and . . . I can't imagine what I said."

"Well, you said you loved me."

He didn't move, but I could feel his heart beating fast, and his breath was crazy like he was failing a lie detector test. I didn't say anything. I let the silence make him talk.

"You know I care about you. That's why I brought you here," he said. "I like what we have, I like being with you and having you there when I wake up in the morning, but right now, that's all I can give."

I should have sifted through all those words and noticed that he never mentioned the word "love," but I didn't because we fooled around a little bit. We didn't do it right there in the meadow. We just did enough to make everything, even with the absence of love, seem romantic. The ride back to the stable was easier than when we started out. It helped that Winston was in front of me so that Ariel stayed behind Jim. Both were anxious to get back to the paddock, so when we reached the clearing by the barn, the horses cantered a little bit and would have run if we hadn't held them back. Ariel went right to her spot at the hitching post and waited while I slid off of her back. I thanked the stableman, who looked relieved I'd come back in one piece. Winston kissed me on the forehead and told me I rode well for not having ridden much. He put his arm around me as we headed back toward the hotel.

On the way up the mountain, between stops at the scenic overlooks, Winston had told me about the history of the resort that was built around a hot spring and the legend of the Indian brave who they say discovered it. He said there was an important gathering of tribes, and each tribe was supposed to send one representative. One young brave was eager to get to the gathering, so he ran and ran until he collapsed in exhaustion in the springs. The soothing waters revived him and gave him extraordinary powers, so that when he reached the tribal conference, he spoke so eloquently that he was chosen to lead all the tribes. There were other legends, but that's the one I remember the most.

I was sore from all that riding, so we went swimming in one of those hot springs The Homestead is famous for. I was amazed at how good I felt when I got out, so good that I think the legend of the Indian brave must have been a true story. I went back to the room, ran a hot bath, and soaked for a little while until Winston came and joined me. It was around six o'clock, I think. He'd been sober all day, but he must have gotten into the mini bar. I could smell Scotch on him, but he wasn't drunk yet.

It was odd dressing for dinner at night, but I kind of liked it. Winston looked so good in his coat and tie, and I loved the way he made over me in my new dress as we walked down to the Grand Dining Room and waited to be seated. We walked to our table, and the maître d' smiled at me and told me how lovely I looked, and he wasn't just saying it. Everybody was looking at us because we were so beautiful.

Winston ordered a Scotch for himself, champagne for me.

"I really don't like champagne much."

He looked totally surprised and ordered a bottle of Cabernet instead.

"For my red girl," he said, as he approved the wine before I tasted it.

A string quartet played songs I'd never heard before, classical, but beautiful. For the first time since I'd set foot though the door of The Homestead, I felt like I was part of the grandeur and not just a poor mountain girl pretending to be somebody. Winston reached across the table and held my hand. He looked at me, not so much with wanting, but with a look in his eyes that said he was comfortable with me. I ate my dinner almost giddy about the changes I was seeing in him.

"Winston Sawyer?" I heard a man behind me say. "My God, man, it is you. Sloshed, of course, but then I've come to expect that of you."

Winston's smile disappeared; he nodded at the man.

"And who might you be?" the stranger said to me, like he was better than everybody there.

"Zora May Adams," I said, extending my hand like a grande dame who'd had too much to drink.

I'd never listened to myself before that night, never thought that I sounded like some hick from the holler, until then. But as soon as I said my name, Winston winced. He knew what was coming.

"Zora May Adams? Oh, well, dear, let's not leave out the May. It gives your name such a mountain-esque ring, don't you think?" The man laughed at me and then turned his attention to Winston. "Tell me now, did you find this one wandering the woods, or is this an Eliza Doolittle experiment from one of your classes?" He put his hand under my chin and I pulled away. "Really, Winston, I know your drinking is a disgrace to yourself and the department, but I can tell you, no matter how much Scotch you drink, this one will never be a fair lady."

He might as well have punched me in the stomach. I trembled with anger and hurt. My stomach pulsed hard, keeping time with my racing heart. I was going to throw up. Winston just sat there, with a smart-ass look, and snagged the waiter for another drink.

"Zora, this is John Ridgeway, God of the English Department."

He reminded the waiter for a second time in less than a minute that he needed another drink. "Fuck you, John. Mind your own goddamn business."

He nursed his new drink like nobody else was there, including me. John Ridgeway turned away, and walked out of the dining room toward the elevator.

"Asshole," Winston said. Then he looked at me and tried to reach for my hand. "I'm sorry, did you want another drink?"

I know Winston saw me leave but didn't come after me. He probably couldn't have even if he had wanted to. I took the elevator to our floor, packed my things, splashed some cold water on my face, and carried my bag down to the lobby.

I scribbled a note on a piece of paper and then wadded it up. Winston deserved nothing, not even an explanation.

"Ma'am, it's late. This is no time to be on mountain roads."

"Just throw this away for me."

"Ma'am, please don't leave." He took the note and tossed it into the trash can. "It's really not a good idea for folks to go out in the mountains this late at night."

"I am mountain folk." I said it and walked out into the night.

30

Thank God I had the presence of mind to change clothes and put on some good walking shoes before I left because I wouldn't have gotten very far in high heels and a sequined dress. I must have been a sight, walking down that country road crying like I was, with my suitcase in one hand, the contents of the mini bar stuffed in a shoe box. The closer I got to the main road, the harder I cried. When I finally reached the highway that hugged the side of the mountain, I threw those tiny liquor bottles as far and as hard as I could. Most of them went tumbling down the mountainside; the rest scattered in pieces across the pavement.

I remember the moon being nearly full, and I could see a little house in the distance. It wasn't my home, but then it was, not the same exact home I had left, but a mountain home. I couldn't tell how far away it was or exactly how to get there. All I knew was that I felt like I was going to die if I didn't get to that house.

I started walking faster toward the light and would have run all the way if it weren't for that blame suitcase. It took about an hour before I finally stumbled up the steps. There was a commotion inside as the porch lights suddenly came on and a hard-looking old woman opened the door.

"My Lord, child."

I couldn't say a word. I just fell into a heap on her porch and cried so hard, I almost passed out. She hollered for her husband to help get me inside, but the words were muffled. I was inside of a cocoon; the whole world was far-off and distant to me as they wrapped me in blankets and smothered me with mountain love.

Still, I couldn't speak. All I could do was cry. She must have recognized me as one of her kind because she held me close and rocked me in her arms. Her husband made some warm milk and handed it to her to give to me. She held the cup up to my mouth, making me take little sips when I could.

"Drink it now, child. It'll help you sleep." Then she pressed her lips together and looked like she didn't want to ask the question that was on her mind. "Did somebody hurt you?"

Well, that was all it took, and I went to sobbing again.

"Should we call the sheriff?"

When I shook my head, she knew it wasn't that kind of hurt. They stayed up with me until I finally stopped crying.

"Rachel, I'm going on to bed. Are you going to be all right with her?"

The old woman reached out, touched her husband's hand, and smiled at him in such a way that it made my heart ache.

"I been sick with the flu," he said. "Ought not to be around nobody with this old fever. I didn't think about it when I was help-ing you inside, sure hope you don't get this mess."

I nodded, and she smiled at him like a young thing and waved him on to bed.

"Do you want to call somebody?" She pulled the telephone over to where I was sitting.

"It's long distance. I can pay you."

"I don't care, and you ain't paying nobody nothing."

She dialed the number, and when I heard the person on the other end, I started to cry again. As the woman took the phone from me, I could hear the worry in the voice coming from the receiver. "Hello? Hello?"

"Ma'am, this is Rachel Blevens. I'm calling from Ashwood, Virginia. I got your girl here. She's hurting bad."

"Sara Jane?" I heard her cry out.

I shook my head.

"No ma'am, your other girl."

"Zora?" she said, loud enough for me to hear.

The woman looked at me, and I nodded.

"Yes ma'am. She's all tore up about something and showed up at my doorstep. Me and my husband been caring for her."

They talked back and forth, but I couldn't tell you what was said because by that time I was so exhausted, I could hardly hold my head up. I lay back down on the little settee and was soon asleep.

There is so much in this world I'll never know, that I'll never understand, but one thing I know for certain, there is a bond of sisterhood and friendship that overrides all things. It came to me before sunup the next morning as a ready-made rescue with tears and hugs that drew me in, almost suffocating me with its warmth and safety. It came with a knock at the door, after I'd been asleep for a good while. The woman peeked out the little window and opened the door. Sara Jane and her mama came into the room like a whirlwind, with their coats over their bathrobes. They had not even stopped to dress.

We all stood there huddled up, crying, although they had no idea as to exactly why. They were crying for me because I hurt so badly, because they loved me and would never let me bear the pain I felt alone. The sisterhood had driven two hundred and twenty-five miles to my rescue in no time flat, and not even the Rapture itself could have kept them from getting to me.

"Thank you for taking care of my girl," Mrs. Farquhar said.

"I told you she could stay the night. This sweet one's no trouble. Ed's harder to nurse with that old flu than this pretty young thing."

"I just couldn't stand the thought of her hurting and me and Sara Jane not being with her. Thank you for letting us come at this late hour."

"It's near three o'clock. We don't have but one other bed and the settee; you all are welcome to it."

"Thank you, but we'll head home. We stopped at a quick shop on the way here, and Sara Jane went in her bathrobe, of all things. She got us both a huge cup of coffee, so we have enough caffeine in us to last us all the way back to Davenport. But thank you so much. You'll have stars in your crown when you all get to heaven for taking care of my girl."

Sara Jane wrapped me in her coat and was standing there in her bathrobe. She put her arm around me. "I love you," she whispered. "We're here now; everything's going to be all right."

We got into the car, which was still warm. It felt good. They didn't ask me what happened right off. Mrs. Farquhar and I sat in the back and she laid my head in her lap and let me sleep. I guess we were about an hour from Davenport when I woke up. I was ashamed for all of the trouble I'd caused them, which made me close my eyes and start crying again.

"Now hush, child," she said. "I love you so. You're mine, just like Sara Jane. There was just some terrible mistake somewhere along the way and it took a long time for you to come to me. But you're here now, where you belong, and I swear I'd rather die than to see you suffer like this."

"Did he hurt you?" Sara Jane said as she looked up in the rear-view mirror for my reaction to the question. "If he laid a hand on you, I swear Jimmy will beat the shit out of him."

"It wasn't like that," I said. "There was this man . . . and he said . . . I don't know, awful things . . . and Winston just sat there, drinking . . . and drinking . . . not saying anything to him . . . Oh, God, he doesn't love me."

"Jimmy ought to beat the shit out of him anyway."

"Zora," Mrs. Farquhar cooed, "your family loves you so. Please don't give this sorry excuse for a man another thought."

"But—" I began.

"But nothing," she said. "Everything's going to be all right. We'll make it so."

I shook my head and turned my face away. "But I think I'm pregnant."

*

Sara Jane and her mama didn't take me to my little apartment. They took me home with them. I stayed in the guest bedroom with a homemade quilt Sara Jane's great-grandma had made for my bedspread and pillows Mrs. Farquhar had embroidered with little fall leaves. They brought me meals on a silver bed tray, and I ate food that a sick person might eat, like grits and dry toast, chicken broth, and Jell-O. For some reason, they gave me lots of ginger ale to drink. I reckon I was so sick inside my heart over the whole mess with Winston, they thought this kind of food would be good for me. And then there was the baby.

I'd missed my period two weeks ago, but didn't give it much thought because it was a lot like Mama—painful, just showing up whenever it had a mind to. I didn't even let myself wonder if I was pregnant, and if I had, I would never have told anybody. Nana always said it was bad luck 'til a woman was through her first three months. I can't say I was surprised; as often as Winston and I did it, I was bound to get pregnant. We never used anything and he never asked me if I was on birth control, so I figured it was all right by him.

I wasn't real sure how I felt about a baby. I wasn't thrilled, but I wasn't upset. I thought my feelings would be determined by Winston's reaction, which isn't the way things should be at all. Maybe in some sad way, I thought the baby might make up for the baby he lost with Emma, and the three of us would all just live happily ever after.

Mrs. Farquhar had her family doctor come by the house and

check me. He told me he hadn't made a house call in ten years and hadn't done obstetrics in twenty, but that he could never say no to Nettie Farquhar. He was nice, talked a lot, tried to make me feel comfortable while he examined me. I answered his questions in a voice just above a whisper and never looked at his face.

I could have just used the home pregnancy test Mrs. Farquhar put on the dresser; there was no reason for him to come. The way Sara Jane and her mama fussed over my broken heart made me feel like I needed a doctor, but doctors don't heal that kind of hurt.

"Well, Zora, you're healthy, there's no doubt about that, and you're pregnant, too, there's no doubt about that, either." He took his specs off and rubbed the bridge of his nose, then folded his hand under his elbow and looked at me. "I know you're not married, and you know, these days you don't have to have a baby if you don't want to."

Now I thought that was the craziest thing I'd ever heard. It wasn't the baby's fault that I made my bed with a man who could never be a daddy. Even though I wasn't real crazy about having this baby alone, the thought of doing away with it never crossed my mind. I was just pregnant, and hadn't given any real thought about life nine months down the road.

Mrs. Farquhar was in the room the whole time he examined me. When I didn't answer his question, she sat down on the bed and stroked my hair. "Zora, honey, how do you feel about this baby?"

"I don't know," I whispered where only she could hear, "but I'm not doing away with it if that's what he means."

"Don," she said, "Zora's fine?"

He nodded.

"She wants this baby."

"She's a young girl. I only brought it up because I thought I should. No offense intended."

"None taken," Mrs. Farquhar said, and she thanked him for coming and walked him to the front door. She returned a few minutes later with more ginger ale and a giddy look on her face. "We're gonna have a baby."

She hugged me, and I think she was relieved that I didn't know any other way than to let the life inside me just be. I puffed up a little and started to cry. I did that a lot in the beginning, just like the crying girl. Everybody blamed it on hormones, but a part of me grieved for what Nina and Harley had and how happy they were about their baby.

"My daddy died when I was nine, and I know what it's like growing up without a daddy . . . it's just . . . awful."

"This baby," Mrs. Farquhar said as she crawled in bed beside me and put her arm around me, "will have family, real family, who will love him as much as a body can possibly be loved. Or her. This child will be so loved because you are loved."

She sat there with me and told me about her pregnancy with Sara Jane. She also told me about when she lost the twins and how important it was for me to take good care of myself. About that time, Sara Jane came in with some lunch, solid food—turkey noodle soup made from the Thanksgiving carcass and a grilled cheese sandwich.

Mrs. Farquhar had missed the Day-After-Thanksgiving sales on my account. She told Sara Jane and me that she was going to run to the mall for just a little while, which meant she'd be gone for at least three or four hours.

After she left, Sara Jane and I talked about everything except Winston. She told me the bridesmaids' dresses had come in, and that her dress would come from Atlanta just five days before the wedding.

"Mama's counting on you moving in with them."

I hadn't given any thought as to where I would go or what I would do. "Sara Jane, I can't do that. You all have done everything for me. I just can't."

"She really believes that you and the baby are going to live here," she paused. "Come on, Zora. You need a place to stay, and Mama and Daddy will need you after the wedding. You know how she loves to do for us. It'll break her heart if you say no."

I knew I had to do something. I couldn't just lie there anymore like I was sick. I had to get up and make some decisions for my baby and me.

"All right," I said. "But I'm gonna work and pay my own way. The State Board's next week, and I can probably still get that job at Ronnie's if I want it."

"Do you want me and Jimmy to go to the apartment and get your things?"

"No, I will. It might take me a while, but I'll go. I've got enough clothes to last three or four days in my suitcase."

"Mama took your things out of your suitcase to wash them. I saw the dress," she said, looking like she wasn't sure she should have mentioned it. "I know it must have been beautiful before you ripped it up. What do you want me to do with it?"

"Burn it."

31

"So you're just leaving, is that it?"

I hadn't heard him come up the stairs. He was standing in the doorway; I turned my back to him.

"Don't go."

I shoved the wine rack and crystal glasses hard up against the wall and taped up everything that was mine in the pasteboard box.

"I know something happened that night with John because he's trying to kick me out of the English department. But I don't know what happened with you."

He was behind me, close enough that I could feel the warmth of his body. But I felt nothing.

"Look at me, Zora." I turned to face him. "Talk to me."

"I hate you. Get out of my way."

"Zora."

"Damn it, stop saying my name."

"Why?"

"Because you never say it."

"That's not true."

He put his arms around me. My stomach pulsed hard. I couldn't breathe. My heart beat like a washing machine; the sound had migrated from my center to my head, pounding in my ears.

"Get out of my way."

"Talk to me."

I wretched in the kitchen sink and wiped my mouth with the back of my hand.

"Get out of my way."

"My God, what did I do?"

"Nothing."

"I don't remember." He touched my face. "Whatever it was, I'm sorry."

"You did nothing. You always do nothing. It's too late."

"Why?"

"If you cared anything about me, you wouldn't have let that man talk to me the way he did. If you cared, you would have come after me."

"I'm sorry."

"I was so stupid to think I could ever be anything other than a distraction so you don't have to think about Emma."

"Emma? This doesn't have anything to do with Emma. I was just—"

"Drunk. I know your kind because my mama brought home men like you all the time. You know how to drink and screw real fine, but you don't know the first thing about how to love."

"Please. Don't go."

"Get out of my way."

"I know you're pregnant," he blurted out. "The man at the desk didn't throw the note away."

I wanted to kill him. I closed my eyes and tried to hold the words inside.

"Well then, you know that I have to leave. That's what Emma did. She left your sorry ass so you could drink yourself to death."

"What are you talking about?"

"Emma was pregnant, just like me. She was leaving you. Wasn't she? Because you're a drunk."

"Shut up. You don't know that . . ."

He was so wounded, it was easy to push by him. I went into the kitchen and climbed up on the counter to find that little box and finish him off. It sailed across the room as hard as I could throw it, aimed straight for his head. He dodged the box. It hit the wall and the rattle fell out on the floor by his foot. His hand shook as he picked it up, and it wasn't because he was hungover. He held it in his hands and closed his eyes.

"All this time I thought you were drinking and grieving over her. I know what it's like to love somebody like that and somehow that made it okay. But you weren't grieving, were you? You were a drunk before Emma died, and you're a drunk now. You'll never change."

I made two more trips down the stairs with clothes and shoes while he just stood there like he was the dead one.

"I'm sorry," he whispered, as I started out the door with the rest of my things.

I looked around the apartment one last time and saw my old rag doll, Myrna, lying on a little wicker chest I'd used for a coffee table. Without saying another word, I snatched Myrna up and started out the door. Since the night Mama gave her back to me, it had gnawed at me where Mama had found her. I threw the last of my stuff in the floorboard and the minute I laid Myrna on the seat beside me, it all came back.

The day the police came to tell us my daddy was dead, Mama saw the car pull up in the driveway. She came running out of the house, screaming and crying so hard she collapsed on the ground. The sheriff and Nana took her inside. I was just nine years old; it was terrifying, watching them put her to bed.

Myrna was on the parson's bench in the hallway near Mama's room with some other dolls. I picked her up, pressed her against Mama's chest, and wrapped her arms around the doll. She just lay there, staring out into space, trembling, running her fingers through Myrna's hair.

I was heartbroken over losing my daddy, and even though Mama had never cared for me, I was worried about her. I didn't realize the doll was gone until a few weeks after the funeral. I looked and looked for her. Sometimes, after Mama had been drinking, she'd laugh and tease me. "Wonder where that old rag doll of yours up and went?" Then she'd stumble about the house pretending to search for her. "Why, she must be a magic doll because she just up and disappeared."

I knew it was Mama's lie about me that made my daddy kill himself, and now I knew she had stashed the old doll to punish me for his death.

The sound of Winston trying to open the truck door brought me back from that place in my mind that makes old wounds fresh. He was crying, begging to me to unlock the door or roll down the window. I took one last look at that pretty face and pulled out of the driveway.

32

I stood back and watched the people who loved Sara Jane pamper her day and night, preparing her for the wedding. It reminded me a lot of that old movie Liz Taylor starred in with Richard Burton, how everyone was rushing about, trying to make everything, including Cleopatra, absolutely perfect for Marc Antony's arrival. I know Nana Adams would've had herself a belly laugh at such a fuss being made over a ceremony that, when you got right down to it, amounted to two people saying two words to each other.

Most of the four hundred people invited to the wedding sent their best wishes along with a gift. There were so many wedding presents that Jimmy and Mr. Farquhar moved everything out of the living room and into the garage. The living room looked like a fine department store full of pretty gifts set out on row after row of eight-foot-long tables. Folks came by every day to drop off their gifts and to look at all of Sara Jane and Jimmy's pretty new things.

They oohed and aahed over everything, especially the grand prize, a Waterford crystal vase that was so big Sara Jane said it would make a good champagne bucket.

The wedding director and owner of the Bridal Barn, Tiny Ellison, got her panties in a knot when she found out that Sara Jane's dress was bought in Atlanta. But Mrs. Farquhar smoothed everything over by ordering the bridesmaids' dresses from Tiny and asking her to direct the wedding, which was the biggest one in Davenport that summer and maybe the biggest one ever.

Tiny was no stranger to big weddings, having directed the governor's son's ten years ago. She made out like the governor himself had sought her out, but the truth was that Tiny happened to be the bride's favorite aunt. So that was her credential to direct the biggest social event in Davenport and one that she reminded us of constantly.

Tiny would say, "we did this at the governor's mansion" and "we did that at the governor's mansion" all the time. Sara Jane and I got sick of her flaunting that around, but we didn't say anything. Tiny insisted on bringing the bridesmaids' dresses by Sara Jane's house for us to try on because she didn't want anyone to walk into the store and see them before the wedding.

"There are those," she said looking up at me with straight pins in her mouth, "who'd come by my shop for no other reason than to get a peek at these dresses. Lord knows, I'll do whatever it takes to guard the integrity of this wedding."

There were seven bridesmaids in all, me and Sara Jane's cousins from North Carolina. All of us gathered at the Farquhars' the Saturday before the wedding to try on our gowns that Tiny had altered. She swore it was a bona fide miracle that we even had dresses because they had been shipped to her store in Christmas red when they were supposed to be emerald green and had to be reordered just three and a half weeks before the wedding.

We all giggled and whirled around in those satin gowns that made swishing noises as we walked down the aisles in the living room between the gift tables. I didn't know anything about being pregnant, that I wouldn't really start showing until about midway through the fifth month, and I was sure my dress would be too small. It was a little tight up top, but other than that, it fit perfectly.

Tiny left around five o'clock with those seven dresses locked away in Bridal Barn garment bags and a look on her face like she was on a mission from God. She said that she and her most trusted assistant, Myrtle, would have the alterations done by Wednesday and to call her at home if anybody wanted her to open the shop special for them because the Bridal Barn was always closed that day for the midweek prayer meeting.

Although they were cousins, none of the bridesmaids were anything like Sara Jane. Two of them married into some religion that believed in having lots of kids but didn't believe in dancing, and the other four were in college. I was glad when they all headed back to their respective homes, which left just Sara Jane and me.

"Are you gonna take me out or what?"

"Oh, gosh, Sara Jane, I'm sorry. I didn't think about throwing you a bachelorette party."

"Come on, let's go someplace, just for a little bit. We'll tell Mama we're going over to Jimmy's."

"The doctor said that I can't drink," I said as I put on my coat.

"Well, then, I'll have to drink for both of us."

We drove to Myrtle Beach because we wanted to go to Shag

Daddy's. It was on a street near the beach with rows and rows of bars. But Sara Jane must have seen something she liked on the sign, because she whipped the car right into the parking lot of Jimmy Mack's. There was a line of girls a mile long, which didn't appeal to me at all.

"There's never a line. What in the world is going on?"

"Strippers," Sara Jane said with a wicked grin.

"Sara Jane. I never—"

"Well, neither have I. Come on, I'm getting married next week." She made the pouty smile, which always makes me say yes to her. "Jimmy's buddies took him out tonight to the Discotheque Lounge, and you know they have naked girls there. Let's just go in and see what it's like. I promise if it's awful, we'll leave."

"Any brides tonight?" A skinny little man with no shirt on and a tuxedo walked through the sea of women.

"Right here."

"Sara Jane."

"I just want to look, I'm not going to buy anything."

"You the bride?"

"And this is my maid of honor."

They let us in for free and put us at a special table up front near the stage.

"Come on, ladies," the announcer hollered as women actually ran to get a good seat. "The men aren't ready just yet. You'll have to get loud and let them know you're ready." He pumped up the crowd with dirty jokes and promises of who would be performing. Everybody there seemed to know who these guys were, and they definitely had their favorites, especially "Blaine, Blaine, the man who puts Fabio-o-o-o to shame."

When the bass started pumping, the whole place throbbed with excitement. A series of male strippers came out and did their thing, but I wasn't impressed, and Sara Jane said she wasn't, either. The jungle guy was okay, but he was greased up with baby oil and bad cologne, and was so close to us the smell made me nauseous. The police guy danced a little too well, and you could tell he wasn't really looking at any of the girls in the crowd. He just did his dance, looking over the tops of our heads, toward the back of the bar, but he still had those girls stuffing money in his gun belt like crazy.

I was glad they didn't take everything off, but they didn't leave a whole lot to the imagination, either. One of them came up and started dancing around me. I don't think he liked it when I got grossed out by the sweat he was slinging all over me, because he moved on to some of the other girls who seemed to like it.

I guess we'd been there an hour, maybe a little longer, when we both looked at each other and decided to go. The minute we started to leave, a spotlight hit each of the five bride-to-be tables.

"And now, for those girls who are going to spend the rest of your lives with the same . . . old . . . guy . . . for Sandy Deaton, BeBe Elliott, Sara Jane Farquhar, Barbie Harvey, and Jane Wilson, here's the man of your dreams, the anatomically correct Ken doll for your viewing pleasure, Derek!"

We sat back down out of sheer embarrassment as a disco version of "Here Comes the Bride" started pumping. A good-looking guy in a tuxedo walked out near a pink pulpit like he was waiting for his bride to come down the aisle. As the beat to the music picked up, he started gyrating around and stripping down to just a black bow tie and a little white pleated G-string with little black buttons. He danced by everybody's table except ours, which I thought was kind of funny, and when the song was over, Sara Jane said something to me, but I couldn't hear her.

"What?"

"I know him."

After Derek put his clothes back on, he came out to our table and hugged Sara Jane and congratulated her on the upcoming wedding. He introduced himself to me, and I know I turned ten shades of red shaking his hand after he'd just stripped right there in front of us.

"We were just leaving, before you danced," Sara Jane said. "We're going over to Shaker's for a while, wanna go?"

"I've got to dance in the second show and then I'm out of here. Do you want to grab some breakfast at Waffle House?"

Sara Jane hugged him again, and while she did some old lady pinched Derek on the butt. He just laughed and gave Sara Jane a big smooch, which made the whole place go wild.

We went to Shaker's, which was kind of dead, but a nice change compared to the strip show. I drank Coke and Sara Jane drank Tom Collinses with tiny paper umbrellas in them while we sat and talked. She told me that Derek's daddy threw him out of the house when Derek told him he was gay. I wondered if he was gay, how he could dance around those women and play to the audience like that. But then I thought about all that money those girls stuffed in his G-string and guessed that made it a whole lot easier.

We went to the Waffle House about eleven thirty, and Derek showed up around midnight. He looked different in baggy jeans and a white T-shirt, not at all like a stripper. He told us stories about being on the road with the show and how he lied about his age to get his first job. Sara Jane had told me earlier that he left home a year ago Christmas, and he talked about working since March. I asked him what he did before he hooked up with the show.

"You don't want to know," he said. "But I met Bryan, I think you saw him, the cop. He got me this job, and things have been real good."

A bunch of noisy guys came stumbling in the door.

"My Lord," Sara Jane said.

I looked up and saw Jimmy, so drunk he could hardly stand up. His buddies sat him down at a table and about five minutes later, they were so obnoxious, the cook was threatening to throw them out, but the waitress told him to let Jimmy stay since he was behaving himself.

"Is that your guy?" Derek asked.

"That's my boy," Sara Jane said with the sweetest blush on her face.

Even in his drunken state, Jimmy knew Sara Jane was there. He slipped away from those boys, came over to our table, and sat down beside her.

"Alcohol will seriously kick your ass," he said as he laid his head on the table and closed his eyes.

They must have gone at it hard because Jimmy always had a high tolerance for alcohol.

"Honey," Sara Jane cooed, "you need to eat something. How about some coffee?"

"Okay," Jimmy said and then dozed off.

We ate our breakfast and Sara Jane poured coffee down Jimmy. He ate a little grits and toast and almost laid his head in his plate twice. Sara Jane would just pull him over to lean on her, and then she said things in his ear we couldn't hear over the Waffle House clatter.

"I saw naked women tonight, Sara Jane," Jimmy confessed loudly on her shoulder.

"I saw naked men."

Then Jimmy raised up and looked at her like he was going to cry. "They got me a hooker." I could see that Sara Jane didn't take that as well as the other confession.

"What did you do?"

"We went in this room. I told her I didn't want to do nothing. I told her about you," he said. "When the time was up she made some noises like we was doing it. I could hear the boys outside the door laughing, and I was about to laugh, too, so she held her hand over my mouth and kissed me right here," he pointed to his cheek. "She told me to be good to you. I told her I didn't know any other way to be."

I left Sara Jane and Jimmy at the Waffle House and dropped Derek off at the hotel parking lot.

"I might come see you all the next time we're in town." He smiled and then looked away from me, his hand on the door. "I haven't even thought about going back to Davenport, but my folks are old. Sooner or later, I guess I'll have to."

"Well, then, come on."

He kissed me on the cheek. I could see in his eyes that he wanted to go home. He needed to know he could still go home, even if he couldn't stay. I knew this about Derek because I knew this about myself.

33

I passed the State Board examination on the first try, even though I was so nervous my hands were jittering like I'd had nineteen cups of coffee. I chose Hannah Darling to be my model because she had gorgeous thick hair, and it's really important to have good hair to work with. One of the girls brought her mama, who had the thinnest head of hair I'd ever seen on a woman. That poor girl had a time trying to roll that wispy hair onto permanent wave rods, and, at one point during her demonstration, she broke down crying.

Hannah was a senior in high school and was excited she'd been invited to Davenport High's Christmas Dance at the country club; she wanted a stylish new look for the occasion. While I was glad she'd agreed to come to the exam with me, I didn't appreciate her giggling like the schoolgirl she was, and I could tell the folks who were giving the exam didn't like it, either. One of the proctors rolled her eyes every time Hannah started up, which made me pick up the pace. I don't think I've ever turned out a head of hair so fast in all my life, and they only marked me down five points for "miscellaneous," which I'm sure meant immature model.

I finally had my temporary license; the permanent one would come after I finished my apprenticeship. Ronnie and Fontaine had agreed to take me on as a shampoo girl. They said I could do some comb-outs when they got backed up, and if any of my regulars wanted to follow me there, they were all mine. I knew that wouldn't happen because a haircut was twenty dollars at Ronnie's, and my ladies were used to paying three dollars. That was okay; I was sure I could build a good clientele there so I could take care of my baby and me.

I told Ronnie and Fontaine about the baby because it was the right thing to do. I was a little scared. I thought they might not want me after the baby came, but they were fine with it. Ronnie got all excited and showed me some adorable nurseries he had seen in magazines, while Fontaine, who never got excited about anything, had just seen *9 to 5* with Jane Fonda and said some companies let young mothers bring their babies to work.

"How do they do that, Fontaine?" I was amazed at such an idea.

"Well, in the movie, they had a day care center in the building, but we could put a little playpen in the break room. That way he'd be away from the chemical smells and we could still hear him."

"It's not a boy, Fontaine," Ronnie said, "and we can't just shove a playpen in the break room. We'll have to redo it, lots of pink. I've already started going through some magazines. *House Beautiful* has some gorgeous nurseries."

Fontaine rolled his eyes. "You're such a cliché."

"Yes," Ronnie said, "I am, and I absolutely love it."

I passed my exam on Thursday, and Sara Jane's rehearsal dinner was that Friday. I stopped by to ask Ronnie if I could start the following Monday. He said I could start any time, and that he'd kind of held the position open for me because he knew in his heart I was the right one for the job. He hugged me, which he always did, and then Sara Jane and I went to run errands.

Now, Jimmy didn't have the money to throw a big rehearsal dinner, and neither did his mama. Since the Farquhars had already adopted him into the family, like they had me, they told him not to worry one bit about any of the expenses and to just save his nest egg for after the wedding. At first, Jimmy put up a fuss and looked a little embarrassed, but Mr. Farquhar took him aside and smoothed everything over.

When Jimmy was ten, his mama sent him to Raleigh to live with his aunt and uncle. Jimmy said they were so poor in Mexico and since his uncle was making a good living with his own yard business, it seemed like the best thing for Jimmy. He became a U.S. citizen when he was twenty and that was the last time he went home to Mexico. But he wired money home to his mama religiously every Friday.

The only family Jimmy had that were coming to the wedding were his uncle Humberto and aunt Norma, but I know he would have loved for his mama to be there. Mr. and Mrs. Farquhar offered to fly her up for the wedding, but Jimmy said she'd never set foot on an airplane, not even for his wedding.

We all met at the church around six thirty for the rehearsal, and poor Tiny was about as high-strung as she could get. She was nervous and short-tempered, and when she thought Jimmy and his buddies were even thinking about cutting the fool, she hollered at them in her little squeaky voice.

Rembert, Jimmy's best friend, was kidding around with the flower girl and told her that there was a great big alligator in the baptismal pool at the front of the church. When we practiced the processional, Little Cindy would strew her petals about half-way down the aisle, turn around, and run screaming out of church.

Rembert felt bad about teasing her. He promised her he was just kidding and even got so desperate, he swore right there in church he'd buy her a pony if she'd walk pretty down that aisle. But it didn't matter because nobody could convince Little Cindy there wasn't an alligator in the baptismal pool. Even Big Cindy, Little Cindy's mother, tried to straighten her out. She threatened her, she bribed her, she even tried to make a game out of it, but Little Cindy just held on to her mama's dress screaming, "I don't want to get ate by no alligator."

When it was apparent that nothing short of a miracle was going to get that child to walk down the aisle, her mama snapped. "Well, that's a waste of seventy-five dollars, not counting the shoes." And she gave poor Rembert the eye every chance she got.

Tiny was all bent out of shape over Little Cindy and said that she knew a number of veteran flower girls that would be glad to do the job. It was at that point that Mrs. Farquhar took Tiny aside. I don't know what she told her, but it was like she had slipped that woman a Valium, because Tiny didn't snipe one time the rest of the rehearsal, and she let the whole flower-girl crisis go.

When it was her turn, Sara Jane glided down the aisle in her black velvet cocktail dress with her daddy on her arm. She literally glowed, like folks said I was supposed to. Mr. Farquhar dabbed his eyes and wouldn't look at Sara Jane, which made Tiny launch into her lecture on father-of-the-bride decorum.

"I can't look at her. I just can't. I'll break down," he complained. "I'm sorry, Sara Jane, I hope I can tomorrow."

Mama Grayson was there, feeling spry and flirty. She still made over Jimmy, but something must have clicked about the wedding, because she didn't call him her beau or fuss when he wasn't paying her attention.

"Your daddy didn't like that one at all," Mama Grayson said to Mrs. Farquhar and then pointed at Sara Jane's daddy. "If it wasn't for me, he'd have made you marry that ugly, rich boy, Lawton Berry."

After we practiced the procession three times, the minister walked us through the actual ceremony. Sara Jane and Jimmy were like two kids playing church, giggling and whispering between themselves. When they practiced their vows, Jimmy's buddies tried to crack him up and succeeded a couple of times, which nobody minded except Tiny, but she didn't say anything.

By seven thirty we were on our way to the country club for the rehearsal dinner, and everybody was starved. All of Jimmy's friends went into the bar and bought drinks since it was a dry dinner, as the reception would be. Mrs. Farquhar nearly had a fit because she was worried it would upset Mama Grayson, who could never abide liquor because her daddy was an alcoholic. So Mrs. Farquhar made them pour their drinks into coffee cups, and Mama Grayson was never the wiser.

Humberto and Norma sat at the front table where Jimmy's mama would have been. They said they had a good time, considering they really didn't know anybody except for Sara Jane and Jimmy. The food was good, but not as good as some of the spreads Mrs. Farquhar had laid out and I told her so.

We toasted the bride- and groom-to-be with sweet tea in fancy crystal glasses. Several of the guests said the most eloquent things they could think of, except for the wedding party, who told funny stories about the bride and the groom. Humberto and Norma stood up and read a beautiful poem in Spanish they had recited to each other at their own wedding and then Humberto translated it for us.

Everyone had toasted Sara Jane and Jimmy except for me, so I clinked my teaspoon on the side of my water glass, cleared my throat, and stood up. I looked at the two of them, and opened my mouth, but I was so taken with emotion, nothing would come out. I think every single soul in that room knew what I was feeling. I know many of them felt the same way, happy but longing, almost in a covetous sort of way, for Sara Jane and Jimmy's kind of love.

34

We sent Sara Jane and Jimmy off about six thirty in a shower of birdseed. They were so pretty, they looked like a picture as they got into that limousine and waved at everybody. The driver took them to the Marriott by the airport in Charlotte, where they spent their first night and then flew to Mexico the next morning for the honeymoon.

I didn't know that a Baptist wedding ceremony lasts all of twenty minutes, thirty minutes tops. A dry reception lasts a couple of hours and then folks start going home, so the social hall was empty and the wedding party was getting their things together to leave.

Mr. and Mrs. Farquhar were in the kitchen helping the caterer pack up all of the leftovers for them to take home and put in the freezer. They were just putting the top to the wedding cake in a precious little freezer box that had silver doves on top when I walked into the room.

"Thank you for the dress and everything." I kissed them both. "It was a beautiful wedding."

"It was," Mr. Farquhar said, as he hugged me. "You're my daughter, you know. And yours will be just as grand."

Every time the Farquhars talked about me being family I felt like they said those nice things because they were nice people. But that day, when Mr. Farquhar called me his daughter and talked about my wedding, for the very first time, I felt it was really true.

On the way home, Mrs. Farquhar told me that I would be able to feel the baby move soon. She said that it would feel like the flutter of butterfly wings, and that if I wasn't paying attention, I'd miss the very first movement. I told her I'd try real hard, and hoped to myself that it wasn't that night, because I was so tired when we got home, I just put my nightgown on and was dead to the world by nine o'clock.

I dreamed bits and pieces on and off all night, and then what seemed like a long dream about home. Daddy Heyward came walking out to the little shed out back where I used to hide out from the world. He walked on legs that didn't have any idea how to walk without weaving and stopped right in front of me. At first, I was afraid because he just stood there staring at me for the longest time, and then I realized that he had come out of the stupor he'd been in for the past twenty-odd years because he had something important to say.

"Did you ever want something powerful bad?" His hands were shaking and his words quivered, not knowing how to sound coming out sober. "I want—I want a boat, just a little boat. I used to fish when I was a boy, and, I don't know, I just wanted to tell you that if you ever want anything powerful bad, it's okay."

He was so pale, and his shakes were worse than when he walked out of the mist and into my dream. Then I saw him go into the house and get his little tin pint that Mama thought made him look so sophisticated and start down the road toward the creek.

I decided I'd better go check on him because Daddy Heyward never left the house to drink. When I got there, I saw the men dragging the creek for his body, scratching their heads trying to figure out the how and why of Heyward's death. Somehow I knew the reason was much simpler than they were making it out to be. Heyward just wanted to see what it was like to have his heart's desire, that's all. Nothing more. Nothing less.

I stood on the creek bank and was aware of a tiny flutter in my belly. It was so slight that when I awoke, I lay there in the darkness, wondering if it was just part of the dream, and then I felt it again.

I got out of bed, put my robe on, and went into the den where Mrs. Farquhar was knitting and Mr. Farquhar was asleep in the recliner.

"I felt the baby move."

She put her knitting down and hugged me for the longest time. As we walked toward the kitchen, she told me how much she loved me, and that she couldn't wait to be a grandma. We sat down at the table and drank warm milk together, and I listened as she told me about the first time Sara Jane moved inside her.

"Sometimes it can be scary to have a baby inside you, to be responsible for another life, but it's also quite a wonder."

She let out a little sigh and watched the last bit of milk swirl around in her glass. "You know, it's funny how I missed that kicking for the longest time," she said. She didn't really look up, and the way she said it was the way someone might talk about something sweet that doesn't last.

"Sometimes I still miss that feeling. Even now."

35

Being pregnant means sometimes all those extra hormones get together for a pity party over the silliest things, like breaking a nail or not being able to find your shoes. As I stood there in the doorway of the kitchen, watching Mrs. Farquhar making breakfast, the smell of bacon frying and the sight of homemade biscuits just out of the oven made my eyes sting and well up. By the time she touched the top of the bread to see if it was done and set the pan down on a little brass trivet, my face was awash with tears.

I know she didn't see me standing there in the doorway of the kitchen, watching her, as she began to fuss over a pie she was making for Sunday dinner, but somehow she knew I was there. "Good morning." She tasted a dab of the fluffy chocolate filling, then took one look at me and nearly dropped the bowl. "What's wrong, darling?" She set the bowl down and wiped her hands on the dish towel before she put her hand across my forehead. "You look feverish."

"I want to go home."

I don't know why I needed to. I knew I wouldn't stay. But something inside me said I had to go there.

"I was wondering if I could borrow Sara Jane's car," I said trying to get hold of myself.

"I'll go with you," she said, and before I could say another word, she covered the unbaked pie with tinfoil and put it in the refrigerator.

"You don't have to go. It takes about six hours to get there, and I'm not going to stay long. I have my first day of work tomorrow."

"Well, I sure will worry about you on the road by yourself, but if you have to go alone, I understand."

"Do you think Mr. Farquhar can get by without a big Sunday dinner?"

"Jerry'll get along just fine. Now you go on and eat some breakfast while I get dressed, and we'll be on our way."

I drove for what seemed like forever and only stopped twice so I could use the bathroom. We passed through Simpsonville and went by my old high school. The town was the same. As we drove by Mrs. Cunningham's apartment, I noticed she'd left her Christmas lights on. Little twinkly white ones laced around her balcony railing winked at us.

I stayed on the highway that went straight through the middle of town until we got to the place on the mountain where the road narrowed. A dirt road cut off to the right and straight up to my place. I had a funny feeling in the pit of my stomach and I'm sure it wasn't the baby. Mrs. Farquhar didn't say much, didn't ask any questions. I guess she knew how hard the trip was for me. The whole way there, she never did anything more for me than smile from time to time, to remind me how strong she was and how willing she was to share her strength with me. I know if she hadn't come along that day, I probably would've turned around long before the Simpsonville city limits and gone straight back to Davenport.

I let the car roll slowly over the rough spots in the dirt road. I knew the way so well, I could have closed my eyes and driven us straight to the front door. I could see the old place through the bare trees. It made me feel weak and small. As I drove into the yard, the house looked cold and lonely. I put the car in park and sat there for a minute. Mrs. Farquhar reached out and touched my hand.

I couldn't get out immediately and was almost satisfied just to see the old place and head home to Davenport. But then there was a part of me that opened the car door just enough to hear it unlatch, and I felt that cold, damp mountain air seeping into the car. I don't know what I was waiting for; maybe I half expected Nana or Mama to come out and throw their hands up like they were glad to see me. Maybe I waited, thinking I'd come to my senses and leave, but whatever had drawn me to that place continued to tug at me like the invisible thread that draws all children home.

Mrs. Farquhar got out to stretch her legs a bit. It was cold, real cold. She hugged herself and walked over to look at the old stone well with her breath trailing behind her. I placed my feet on that rocky ground, inching my way toward the house until I felt the creak of the front porch boards under my feet. I closed my eyes, listening to their strange music, wondering why I never noticed it before.

I touched the key that dangled on a shoestring from around my neck. When I was little, Nana had put the key on the string for me to play with. I wore it for years but never had to use it. I remember wearing that old string because it reminded me that I had a place where I belonged, and then taking it off when I moved to Davenport because I didn't think I needed it anymore.

The door was unlocked. I looked at Mrs. Farquhar, who had joined me on the steps.

"Honey, it's unlocked."

"I know."

"Maybe we should go into town and call the sheriff."

"It's okay. Folks up here don't lock their doors."

I pushed the door open and looked around. All the kitchen cabinet doors were open and the food was gone. There was a can of spoiled pork and beans on the kitchen table and some dirty dishes in the sink.

"My Lord, Zora, who was here?"

"Hobos, maybe somebody hiking or fishing the creek."

I remembered hearing the neighbors talk about coming home and finding hikers on their front porch. We weren't far off the Blue Ridge Railway Trail, and from time to time those folks would show up, especially in the early spring if there'd been a late snow.

"Don't worry, there's nobody here."

We walked into the room that was the kitchen and living room. I threw the pork and beans in the trash can and raked the bread crumbs off the table with an old rag. I could tell raccoons had been there by the droppings everywhere, but even they had passed on the spoiled beans. Whoever had been there hadn't left much of anything for the animals except a bag of potatoes in the bin that had long spaghetti-like eyes snaking about them. I stood there looking at the mess and shook my head before opening the door just off the living room.

"This was Mama's room." The bed was stripped, and there didn't seem to be anything left that was hers. I saw a little yellow top sticking out from under the skirt of her dressing table. It was an old bottle of Johnson's baby shampoo that had fallen back there. I picked it up and looked at the label that had faded to a pinkish color. It was sad but kind of funny that all Mama left me was an eighty-nine-cent bottle of baby shampoo.

Nana's room was right across the hall from Mama's. Somebody had taken her bedding. Her old settee was still there, but it looked like the raccoons had messed it up. If we'd brought Jimmy's truck, I'd have taken it back to Davenport and made a nice cover for it.

Her yarn was strewn about over the floor and looked a mess. We rolled some of the thread that wasn't soiled back onto cards and put it in her sewing basket. It was just a little pink wicker basket she had bought at some store for next to nothing. There was a fuzzy black poodle appliquéd on the lid with three little rhinestones on her collar. I remember fingering those things and pretending they were real while Nana crocheted.

"Let's take this home," Mrs. Farquhar said as she put the top on the basket. I guess she could see how precious it was to me. "I bet there are two or three sacks full of yarn, Zora. You could make some baby things if you want."

I smiled to myself and thought about Nana trying to teach me how to crochet and how worthless my fingers were. Whenever she put her arms around me and guided my hands, I could always pull the thread through just right. But as soon as she turned loose of me, I'd mess up. She never fussed at me, just ripped out the row I'd messed up, and showed me how to start over.

There was a picture facedown on a shelf of Nana and my grand-daddy. I put it in one of the paper sacks, along with all of my school pictures she had in little tin frames. The Bible she kept in her bedside table was gone. It was an old King James Version she kept important papers in. I suspected Uncle Heath and Aunt Fannie took it, and that was fine with me.

The old Planters Peanuts can was still there, the one that Nana kept spare buttons in. I always loved that little can, the way the buttons sounded in it, and I played with it so much over the years, the little peanut man was nearly rubbed off. I looked at the back-side of it and saw where I had claimed it for myself a long time ago by etching my name with a stickpin into the navy blue paint. I took a pin out of the can and underlined the letters.

Nana's clothes, her shoes, and old flannel robe were gone. I opened her bureau drawers and didn't see anything but three or four little pink sachet tablets I had given her for Christmas one year that had long since lost their fragrance. My baby stirred inside of me, and I touched my belly.

Mrs. Farquhar put her hand on my shoulder. "I'm sorry it's all picked over."

I nodded, set the paper bags with the sewing basket in the hallway, and closed Nana's door, holding on to the doorknob for a brief spell.

Mrs. Farquhar put her arm around me and we walked by our tiny bathroom with the little blue gingham skirt around the sink. The curtains Mama made out of bath towels were gone. There wasn't a time that I could remember when the bathtub faucet didn't leak. With no heat, the stream of water had frozen solid, extending from the spout to the drain like a great icicle. The rug that hid the bare spot on the linoleum floor was gone. I could see where a knothole had given way and wondered how long the floor had been like that.

"Is this your room?" Mrs. Farquhar opened the door at the end of the hall. I stood there frozen like my breath in the air, like the good and bad of living there was all balanced out and one false move might tip the scales.

I remembered Nana nursing me when I was sick and soothing me when life had nothing but bad for me. I remembered my daddy kissing me good night with cheap bourbon thick on his breath and giggling with me over things that only we thought were funny. I shook my head, trying to get hold of the present, taking note of real things that I could see and touch. My bed was stripped, too, like the rest of the room. Birthday cards from Daddy and Nana were still taped to the mirror over my dresser, along with a picture Nana took of me the morning of my sixteenth birthday. I looked so much like Mama it made me think of the bad men she brought into our house.

I struggled to keep my mind on the inventory. The cedar chest was open. My graduation dress was gone. My baby clothes were soiled by animals that didn't seem to miss an inch of the place. Mrs. Farquhar scooped them up in a plastic bag she found in the kitchen to boil them until they were sanitized.

My school box was on the floor. All my papers were still in it, along with precious little gifts I made Nana for Christmas and Mother's Day. A tiny pair of white leather baby shoes was there, too. I wasn't sure if they were mine, but I took them anyway.

Mrs. Farquhar put the top on the school box. "Do you want to take this, too?"

I nodded, and we started packing the car with bits and pieces of my life. It didn't take long before the trunk was full. I put the little step stool Nana always kept in the kitchen in the backseat. I remembered sitting on that thing when I was little, and I wanted my baby to sit on it, too.

When we were done packing, I took a walk around the yard. Mrs. Farquhar walked beside me in a quiet way, smiling at a bird that sang every time the sun tried to peek through the clouds. I looked down the old well and remembered it had always scared me so. A little girl had fallen down one and died when I was maybe five or six, so every time I got near that old thing, Daddy would remind me about her and tell me to get away from it. But there is something about a well that makes even scared little children peer into it. I stared at the outline of myself in the stagnant water and remembered how daring and frightening doing that used to feel.

Behind the barn, I ran my fingers over the rough, weathered wood of the little shed where I dreamt Daddy Heyward had sobered up to share the secret of the universe. How in the world could I ever be a good mother?

For the past six months I'd clung to the notion that Winston's looks made me do the things I did. The very idea that I might have the tiniest bit of Mama inside me was terrifying.

"She never loved me," I said. "What if I'm just like her?"

"Zora, you're going to be a wonderful mother. I don't know everything that happened between you and your mama. I do know that she was fourteen when she had you, no more than a child herself. I suspect she loved you the only way she knew how."

"I still hate her."

Mrs. Farquhar put her arms around me and rocked me like her own child. "My sweet girl, all the hate you have for your mother, rolling around inside you, kicking up such a fuss, is fighting to stay alive. It can't exist alongside that precious baby you're carrying."

She held me at arm's length and brushed my tears away and then her own. I knew she wanted me to pardon Mama for all her sins, but the hate I carried with me made grace and mercy for Mama like a toy put up on a shelf to punish a bad child. Not that fawning over Winston Sawyer or even getting pregnant was an unforgivable sin, but somehow knowing better and then traipsing around in my mother's shoes was.

36

⌒⌒

I'd only been working at Ronnie's for five months, but Ronnie and Fontaine were good to me from the start. They helped me build my clientele by giving me all the walk-ins I could handle and even rubbed my swollen feet in between appointments. Fontaine never got excited about anything, but I knew both he and Ronnie were as excited about the baby as I was.

One of my regulars, Charmaine Lyndell, came slinking into the shop on the wrong day. I was tired before I got up that morning and had eaten ham for dinner the night before so that my ankles were so swollen; they looked like they were going to explode. Charmaine loved nothing better than tormenting me, although if Ronnie or Fontaine had known what she was doing on a biweekly basis, they would have thrown her out of the salon on her rhinestone ass.

Right off, Charmaine and I recognized each other as mountain folk. Sometimes, after I was done fixing her hair, her eyes would narrow and she would look at me in the mirror like I'd better keep my mouth shut about where we came from. I never asked her when she left the mountains, but legend had it that ten years and two kids ago, she was a stripper in Myrtle Beach. She came to Davenport one weekend with a friend for a wet T-shirt contest, won the contest, and married the guy who owned the bar. Because of all that, and the fact she had money, she thought she was better than everybody, especially me.

When you're fresh out of beauty school, you'll put up with almost anything to build a clientele. As bad as Charmaine was to me, I was glad to have a steady patron. So I ignored her digs and her bragging and her huge store-bought tits her husband got her after she had her tubes tied to get that big tip. For a thirty-dollar haircut, Charmaine would leave a twenty, for a fifty-dollar cut and color, she'd leave two twenties. With the baby coming, I saved every cent I got my hands on, except the money Charmaine slipped into my maternity pants pocket, like I was some kind of stripper, too. I always made a point to buy something nice for the baby or myself.

Of course, when somebody hates you, truly hates you, there's a natural tendency to speculate why. I'll always believe Charmaine hated me because I have good teeth. I don't know this for a fact, but a lot of mountain folk don't have good teeth, especially the ones poorer than I was growing up, which, judging from her choppers, included Charmaine. With those big tits, nobody much looked at the one thing that gave her away, but I knew. It was stupid for her to be like that. She always wore a ton of real gold jewelry from her brother-in-law's pawnshop and could have traded it in on dental work any time she wanted.

"You're so pale, Zora," Charmaine purred. "You need some color."

I smiled and nodded at her Scotch-Irish white mountain face she'd fried crispy brown that made her look fifty instead of thirty.

"It must be hard," she went on.

I was determined not to get sucked in by her venom.

"Yeah, I bet it's hard, you being so big and just seven months. I never gained more than twenty pounds with my young'uns, but Lord, girl, you've got eight more weeks to go. If you keep getting bigger, you won't be able to get that fat belly anywhere near this chair."

Now, there are two ires you never want to raise. One is the anger that spews from a hormonal, swollen mess who's been pregnant approximately two hundred and ten days and the other is the ire of a highly protective, bitchy gay man.

Ronnie marched over to my chair and looked in the mirror at Charmaine. "Do we have a problem here?"

"Oh, Ronnie, don't be such a girl, I'm just teasing Zora a little bit."

Ronnie tilted his chin up and looked down on Charmaine. He ran his hands through her platinum blond hair like she wasn't even there and looked at me.

"Between this color and the condition of her skin, you might want to tone down the blond so she doesn't look so old."

He sashayed back to his station but kept cutting his eye around at Charmaine while he finished up his lady's hair.

"Do you?" I asked. "Want to go a little darker, Charmaine?"

"Do you want to be fat forever?" she hissed under her breath. "Because that's what I'm wishing for you right now. Get my regular color going, I've got better things to do than sit around this dump all day."

I mixed Charmaine's color and started applying it with the brush. I couldn't help but think about the client Mrs. Cathcart had used as a cautionary tale to remind us just how tricky color can be. Legend said she was fifteen and completely gray. She'd been teased so much at school, she was already damaged by the time her mother brought her in to have her hair colored, something nice and blond. Her mother said her daughter had horrible allergies and asked if that made a difference. The student didn't think to warn the girl that some people who are prone to allergies can have a reaction to the bleach and went on about her business.

Not only did the poor girl's face end up looking like the Elephant Man's, the student overprocessed the hair, so when she started rinsing the color out, it came out by the handfuls. Needless to say, if there really was a student, her calling to fix hair was revoked that very day.

Charmaine eyed me suspiciously as she dabbed at the foamy white bleach around her hairline. I smiled at her and went to the break room to put my feet up. I didn't set the timer. I could have fried her hair to match her skin, but the clock inside me that always knows how long to process a perm or let color sit said it was time to rinse out Charmaine's hair. I hauled myself up out of the chair and went back to the shampoo bowl.

Charmaine was right, my belly was big. I smiled as it rubbed up against the side of the chair and wanted to laugh out loud when the baby kicked so hard, Charmaine moved her arm away from me. When I towel dried her hair, even wet I could tell the color was perfect. Charmaine Lyndell still had fried skin and bad teeth. She was still a pitiful woman, but when I was done with her, her hair looked fabulous.

Dealing with emotionally charged women was draining, especially being pregnant. But Ronnie and Fontaine were a wonder. The most burned-out, stressed-out, miserable women could sit in their chairs and dump every care in the world on them and it didn't seem to faze them one bit. At first, I watched them, the way you might watch a magician to figure out where the rabbit went, but after a while I just gave up and asked Ronnie how he did it.

"As close as I am to my ladies, I have to envision a protective pink bubble between us, one that I can reach my arms through to fix their hair and still listen to their problems, but not take them in. If I did that, I'd be crazier than a bagful of squirrels."

It was hard enough to muster up enough energy to get through the day, much less conjure up a pink bubble to protect myself from the likes of Charmaine Lyndell. I didn't know the next woman coming in for a haircut. The day I spoke with her on the phone, she said her name was Maxine Waverly and then paused for me to be impressed. She said she was new in town and was referred to Fontaine by her real estate agent. When I told her Fontaine was booked for three weeks and she couldn't have Ronnie, either, she let out a disgusted little huff and snipped, "Well, is there anyone else who can fix my hair?"

I could tell by the nasally tension and the way she said every word just so, she probably wasn't going to be easy. I didn't tell her I was fresh out of beauty school and figured we were even.

As tired as I was, I knew the best thing for me and Maxine Waverly's hair was to call and cancel her appointment. Before I could make it to the phone to call, she pushed through the front door of the shop almost an hour early. She was a pretty woman in her forties and was dressed like a Stein Mart mannequin in a loud, expensive-looking dress. She didn't smile or say hey, just headed straight for the hairstyle books and magazines because she wanted a change.

Fontaine was running way behind because his client had just seen the movie *Big*. She'd brought a picture from *People* magazine in and the woman wasn't leaving until Fontaine made her board-straight mop look like Elizabeth Perkins's hair. I was wrapping Fontaine's four o'clock perm while Maxine went through a dozen books before pointing to the edgy Dorothy Hamill haircut Ronnie had sketched out for me and had framed.

"I want this haircut," she said to no one in particular as she eyed the pencil drawing like it was a fine piece of art.

I'd never done anything that artsy before and had no business starting on this woman.

Fontaine looked in the mirror at his client with his hands on his hips and shook his head. "Mrs. Tool, I have worked every miracle I know how to work and—"

"It's beautiful," she cooed, running her fingers through curls that would be stringy the minute she stepped outside.

Fontaine shrugged as the woman pledged her allegiance to him forever and then nodded at Maxine. "Let's get you shampooed."

Fontaine leaned her back in the shampoo bowl and she closed her eyes. He washed her hair without so much as a word while she talked on about the haircut she'd chosen.

"I like the angles," she said as he showed her to my station and shook the nylon cape open. "I'm so glad you had some time for me."

"I'm just shampooing you for Zora," he said as I took my place at my station. Maxine looked at me in the mirror all tired and young and pregnant and whipped around to face me.

"How old are you?"

"I beg your pardon?"

She turned around and jerked off her bifocals. "I said, how old are you?"

"Twenty."

"You've got to be kidding." Fontaine looked up from putting the permanent wave solution on his lady's hair. "Excuse me, sir. Your salon came highly recommended. I cannot believe you're trying to pass off this child as a stylist."

Fontaine walked over to my chair and turned the woman toward the mirror. "This child is my best stylist, ma'am. I'm lucky to have her, and so are you."

She waited until Fontaine returned to his station and watched him say something to Ronnie, who gave the woman a look that would intimidate an angry gator.

"Forget the haircut. Just blow my hair dry."

My hands were shaking while I styled her blond hair. Her roots were showing, she would need color soon. Judging from the shape of her last cut, either her stylist was less experienced than me or the right side of her hair grew a lot faster than the left. Mrs. Cathcart taught us that was normal and speculated it had someone being right-handed if the right side was longer. A magazine I read said it was all because our hearts are off center, sending more oxygen-rich blood to one side of the body than the other. By the way Maxine watched me wipe away my tears as I blew her hair dry, I don't think she had a heart.

The second the hair spray filtered through the air and onto her hair, she ripped off the cape, rifled through her purse for twenty dollars, and left out in a huff. I left out, too, wondering if answering the call to fix hair was worth feeling like I did. Ronnie and Fontaine called me at home and promised Maxine Waverly would never set foot in Ronnie's Two again. I told them I was fine, but I wasn't.

I was glad I didn't have anything on the books the next day. I restocked all the stations with towels and perm papers and cleaned a bucket of hairbrushes, which is just about the most disgusting job you could do. Not the round brushes we used for styling, boar bristle hairbrushes Ronnie and Fontaine used on their regulars who had their hair set once a week.

Just the thought of someone not washing her hair for a whole week and soldering it in place every day with Final Net made me sick. I raked through a half dozen brushes with a fine-tooth comb and had to stop before I threw up.

"Someone here for you," Fontaine said. "I went on and shampooed her."

"Thanks." I stretched and dug my fist into my back, grateful someone had rescued me from the less glamorous part of my job. When I walked into the salon, Maxine Waverly was sitting in my chair with a wet head, cradling the Dorothy Hamill sketch someone had taken out of the frame. She saw my reflection in the mirror and turned the chair around to face me, still not smiling.

"I've had nine good hair days in fifteen years," she said. "Yesterday was one of them. Fontaine said you had some time today; I'd like this haircut. Please."

After a miracle from God, I wasn't about to tell Maxine I'd never cut anyone's hair from a picture before. I was sure she'd be the only person in Davenport to wear her hair like that, maybe along the whole Grand Street. The style was artsy and beautiful, but it looked like something a runway model would wear in one of those fashion shows where they prance down the runway like Clydesdales.

During the time I cut Maxine's hair, I learned a lot about her. Her husband was having an affair, but she didn't care, she'd married him for his money anyway. Her only child was grown and gone and gay. She didn't like that, either, but she loved him and learned that whatever he was, he was hers and it didn't matter.

She looked at the severe angles of her hair and seemed pleased because they accentuated her violet eyes. She shook her head and, even wet, every hair fell into place. After I blew her dry, Ronnie took pictures to send to one of those hair magazines. Maxine reached for her purse to pay me, I thought, but pulled out a piece of stationery from a fancy salon in Dallas called Hawthorne's.

"This is my color formula from my stylist back home. If you have some time today, would you mind doing my color, too?"

Mrs. Cathcart used to say when a new client gives you the key to her color, it's a sign of the utmost trust, but Ronnie said it was more like the client was giving you the key to her heart, which sounds corny, but is really true. In all, it took two and a half hours for her color and that crazy haircut. Maxine tipped me twenty dollars and made an appointment in three weeks to touch up her color, another miracle considering most women wait at least four weeks between treatments.

A client's smile is always the best gauge to measure her satisfaction. But Maxine never smiled, which was kind of unsettling. When she surprised me with a hug, I noticed lots of feathery little scars around her hairline I hadn't noticed earlier. Maybe she'd been in a horrible accident; Ronnie guessed she'd had a botched face-lift. Whatever the case, Maxine Weatherly never smiled because she couldn't.

37

As much as I loved living at the Farquhars', I still had a little piece of a dream in my mind of a small house nearby for the baby and me. I put the dream on layaway, setting aside a little money every week for a down payment. Being so young and not knowing how much things cost, I almost cried when the place I wanted most went up for sale. So I adjusted my dream and ended up making friends with an old woman six blocks from the Farquhars who was looking for a good family to live in her home when the time came for her to give it up.

"I doubt I'll have enough money to buy your house for a long time," I told Miss Polly Jackson one day over homemade lemonade on her front porch.

"Don't doubt," she snapped like I was one of her own. "I'll just have to hold out until you do."

Mrs. Farquhar and I finished painting the chair rail in the

nursery before I went to work that morning. We called it the nursery but it was actually one of two guest bedrooms connected by a Jack and Jill bathroom. Mr. Farquhar had a carpenter come in and install shelves Mrs. Farquhar swore the baby needed and the chair rail. I picked out a simple border with pink and blue rocking horses, but Mrs. Farquhar's house was so fancy, it looked out of place. So we settled on a Humpty Dumpty one with horses and soldiers and queens in the repeat in case I had a girl.

The only picture in the nursery was the Polaroid of the sonogram the technician took at the doctor's office. I'd already heard my baby's heartbeat, which was a wonder, but taking a picture of her in my belly? Nana Adams would have laughed in that doctor's face and called him a liar. But the technician rubbed some icy blue gel on my belly and slid a microphone-looking thing over the gel until she saw what she was looking for. She pointed at the black-and-white TV screen to all kinds of things none of us could see. Arms, hands, heart, lungs. She said everything looked good and it was a girl. At first I didn't see anything but a lima bean and thought the sonogram might be a scam to separate Nettie Farquhar from her money. But when the lima bean moved, Sara Jane and Mrs. Farquhar and I were full of awe and wanting for her to hurry up and get here.

It was such a slow day that before Fontaine left to run errands, he said I should just go home and put my feet up. But I stayed and restocked all the stations while Ronnie read gossip magazines out loud and made fun of what the stars wore in public. He swore he could dress every single one of them better than they could dress themselves. I agreed with him and headed for the break room to put my feet up.

I was drinking a Coke and folding towels when he poked his head in the door.

"Another haircut for *you*."

Fontaine always quietly announced there was a walk-in waiting for me in the reception area. But Ronnie always made a big deal about it like they'd come in off the street begging for me.

"Thanks. This baby has been tap-dancing on my bladder all day. I'll be right out."

The weird thing about being pregnant and gaining weight is my weight didn't change for a long time. In the back of my mind I thought I was getting a pass on the weight-gaining thing and then one day, about my sixth month, the weight fairy came in the middle of the night, and I woke up the next morning ten pounds heavier. Not long after that, fifteen more pounds just suddenly appeared.

Ronnie always obsessed over his weight, turning sideways in the mirror a hundred times a day, sucking in his poochy belly, and asking, "Do I look fat?" I knew better than to give him an honest answer, and after the weight fairy visited me, he stopped asking.

I walked down the long hallway toward the salon and stopped short. He was sitting in my chair. His face was still achingly beautiful. He was thinner, paler, almost sallow. He looked tired, older than I remembered. His hair was longer. It was funny how just seeing little tresses of it hanging through the hammock a few months ago had moved me to tears. Now I felt nothing. He ran his hand through his hair and looked at his watch. He wasn't there for me; he was just there for a haircut.

"He's gorgeous." Ronnie's whisper was high-pitched, like he was giggling the words. "And just look at that hair."

"Why don't you take him?"

"No, ma'am. He's delicious and he's all yours."

If Ronnie knew who the pretty man in my chair was, he would have shaved Winston's head or worse. The baby kicked hard. My fingers made little circles around my belly. Sometimes I worried about seeing Winston again and having just enough of Mama left in me to be weak and foolish. But it felt good to look at him, to see how beautiful he was and know that the spell was irreparably broken.

He looked startled to see me and didn't turn around to look at me, just stared into the mirror.

"You need a haircut?"

He ran his hand through his beautiful hair. "I wanted to see you again but not like this."

I wrapped a towel around his neck like he was anybody else and set it with one of those long, pointy metal clips that looks like it could be used as a weapon. When I snapped a new cape open, he flinched like a gun had gone off. As it floated down across his broad shoulders and onto his lap, he took one of his long, slender fingers that used to make me crazy and ran it under the neck of the cape.

"Too tight?" I said, giving it a little yank.

"No," he mumbled. "No, it's fine."

"Sit forward a little bit and then lean back for me." I let the chair back so that his long neck rested in the cradle of the shampoo bowl. "Water okay?" He tried to nod but couldn't and looked away when I leaned over to wash his pretty head. My huge boobs were right in his face. If I could have pinched it off right then and there, I would have and then danced around with it like it was a prize.

But out of the seven deadly sins for a cosmetologist, a lack of professionalism is by far the worst. I had come a long way. I'd graduated at the top of my class, heeded the lifelong call to fix hair. I'd gotten a job at the best salon in town, made countless women beautiful on a daily basis, and here sat Winston Sawyer in my chair almost daring me to ruin myself again.

"How are you feeling?" He sounded like a stranger in the grocery line, trying to make conversation with the pregnant lady behind him.

I slipped my scissors out of the leather sheath. How should I go about hacking up his long pretty locks? I could forget the scissors and rip out a great big handful to give him a snatched baldheaded asymmetrical look. Or stick with the scissors and cut off his ear. At the very least, I should give him bangs. Paintbrush bangs.

I picked up a handful of hair and let it fall to see how it would lay. The texture was the same, the color was the same. But I was different.

I trimmed about three inches until his hair was the same length it was when I first met him. I brushed the hair off of his cape and bent down close to his ear because Ronnie was watching and what I had to say was private. For a moment my body remembered everything about Winston Sawyer, and then the baby kicked hard, knocking the sense back into me. I pressed my lips close to his ear so that I felt my own breath.

"I am over you."

38

❦

I don't know what it was about seeing my old homeplace and then seeing Winston Sawyer that set my feet on the path toward forgiveness. But if I hadn't walked through the past, my gaping wounds would have never healed. It helped to know that I was blessed by the love everybody around me gave so freely. All that love from my new family didn't make the walk any less painful, but it did bring the grace I'd longed for so close that I could almost touch it.

One of my Tuesday regulars, Mrs. Clara, was so heavy she'd broken my chair twice. Ronnie was always nice about it, always carrying on about how the chair was defective. But when the repairman came to fix it and I saw him shake his head at Ronnie, I knew it wasn't the chair's fault.

Mrs. Clara came into the salon bone-tired on the afternoon of July 3. The shampoo-bowl chair creaked and moaned under her weight. I shampooed her hair at arm's length because my belly looked like I was ten months pregnant and about to pop.

I tried to be quick about it so she wouldn't fall asleep, and the chair would hold up. Mrs. Clara looked like a sleepy little child when I wrapped her wet head in a towel. Ronnie and Fontaine hoisted her up from the shampoo bowl and nearly buckled under her weight. She managed to walk to my station, breathing like it was a chore. The three of us, and maybe Mrs. Clara, too, held our breath as we watched her bottom pour into my chair like thick cake batter spilling over the sides. She touched down slowly and then put her full weight on the chair and smiled a little when it didn't make that awful moaning sound it did before it broke. Ronnie and Fontaine looked at me like they were relieved.

"What's wrong, Zora?" Ronnie said.

I didn't know what to do or say. All I could do was point at the puddle of water around my feet.

Ronnie screamed and ran to the back to get the little suitcase he'd insisted I bring to work every day for the past few weeks. Even Fontaine, who never got excited about anything, was running around grabbing hairbrushes, cologne, anything he thought I might need at the hospital. He was trying to get a lipstick case that had a little mirror on it off of the display when he picked up the phone and called Mrs. Farquhar to tell her my water had broken. Then Ronnie and Fontaine helped me into their little yellow Doodle Bug convertible, leaving three wet-headed customers behind.

I was in labor forever and a day. Folks who loved me came in and out of my room like a revolving door. I knew something was wrong when the baby wouldn't come.

"Are you Zora's parents?" the doctor asked the Farquhars.

"Yes." They stood on either side of me.

"Zora, Mr. and Mrs. Adams," he began and neither of us bothered to correct him. "The baby's under a lot of stress . . ."

I knew that C-sections were done every day, but for some reason I started crying and couldn't stop. Sara Jane must have heard me because she rushed into the room and she and Mrs. Farquhar latched onto my hands. Mr. Farquhar and Jimmy, Ronnie and Fontaine, and Connie Harmon followed right behind at the foot of the bed, reassuring me all the way to the operating room.

"You're going to be fine," Sara Jane said.

"And so is our baby," Mrs. Farquhar insisted.

They let go of my hands as the gurney passed through the double doors. I was scared to death with all of those machines humming and the nurses getting me ready for surgery. One of them wrapped a blood pressure cuff around my arm without even looking at me and then turned around to do something else. I know my eyes were all bugged out as I raised up and tried to push my bottom off of the table. I wanted to run like hell. But the anesthesia had made my legs weak and lifeless, so I started crying and hollering for them to let me go. A skinny little male nurse named Don told me not to worry and prayed over me. The last thing I remember is Don asking the Lord to hold my baby and me in the palm of His hand.

I hate that I had trouble and my family wasn't there the second my baby came into the world like we had all planned. I don't remember being wheeled down to recovery or being lifted onto the bed, but I do remember waking up to the faces of the people who love me best.

"We have a girl," Mrs. Farquhar whispered with tears running down her sweet face. "A perfect, tiny baby girl."

"Gorgeous," Ronnie added, "absolutely gorgeous."

"You did good," Mr. Farquhar said and kissed my forehead. "I'm so proud, I could bust."

"Where is she? I want to see her." I was still a little groggy and felt sore from the incision.

"They're going to get her right now," Sara Jane said. "I'm telling you, Zora, she's the prettiest baby I have ever seen. Isn't that right, Jimmy?"

"Yeah, Zora, you should've seen all of us looking at her in the baby room. Kind of hogging the window. Some lady said something like our baby wasn't the only baby in the nursery and Sara Jane said as far as we were concerned, she was."

When the door opened, the six of them parted like the June Taylor Dancers as the nurse wheeled my baby over to me. Everybody oohed and aahed when the nurse picked her up. When she placed her in my arms, I felt a jolt go through my body. I guess it was the same thing every new mother feels. Love. Pride. Relief. But there was something else, too.

I heard Ronnie's squeaky voice say, "She's so beautiful."

Everybody was talking over me and the baby, looking down lovingly at us as they campaigned for their favorite name. Back and forth they went, their voices rising until they remembered the little one in my arms and started whispering again.

"Jimmy, she is not going to name that baby Katie," Sara Jane said loud enough to be heard down the hall. "I love Katie, but Zora's not going to name this baby after our dog."

The doctor knocked on the door and could barely get into the room to check on us there were so many folks in there. But I guess he knew better than to say anything. "So what is this child's name?" he asked as he lifted back the sheet so that nobody could see my incision but him.

Everybody stopped their campaigning and looked at me. He nodded and lowered the sheet. "You can't take her home until you give her a name."

"Sara," I said looking at Sara Jane, who was tearing up. "Sara Grace Adams."

"It's perfect," Fontaine said and kissed us both on the forehead.

Grace came to me, not just as a tiny bundle nestled in my arms rooting around for food. It came in the form of love and mercy. For the first time in my life, I understood Mama and how scared she must have been. Barely fourteen, with me in her arms, a mother whether she knew how to be one or not. She was all by herself with a sweet husband who drank too much. It must have terrified her just to look at me.

Even now when I look back, I'm so ashamed of the way I hated Mama for living her life like it wasn't worth anything unless she had a man under her roof, because I went and did the same thing. But then I think about Winston Sawyer, and I'm thankful for Grace and the lesson he taught me about love. Love isn't having a man. It's loving myself enough to accept love from good people in my life. It's about loving myself enough to forgive.

Readers Guide to

THE WISDOM OF HAIR

1. Throughout the novel, Zora fears becoming her mother. To what extent do you think she has inherited her mother's traits, or do you think she has successfully escaped following in her mother's footsteps?

2. Dressing up as someone else is a common theme. For example, Zora's mother dresses up as Judy Garland, and Winston first notices Zora when she is wearing Emma's dress. Do you think this signifies that the characters are striving to be something more than they are, or is it simply a sign of their insecurities?

3. Zora and Winston have a chemistry that doesn't require conversation or having anything in common other than each other. Do you think they ever really loved each other, or is it only infatuation?

4. Zora says that the reason she leaves Winston is because he doesn't defend her when John Ridgeway alludes to her being "mountain folk." How much of her leaving Winston then, do you think, is about his actions, and how much is about the actual comment?

5. Zora straddles two worlds: her life in the mountains and her life in Davenport. How much of a person's character is shaped by his/ her upbringing, and do you think it is something that can ever be truly left in the past?

6. When Zora is pregnant, she has a dream about Daddy Heyward, who tells her, "If you ever want anything powerful bad, it's okay" (p. 262). What do you think it is that Zora wants "powerful bad"?

7. Mrs. Farquhar and Zora's mother represent extremes in mother-hood. Mrs. Farquhar is a picture-perfect mother, and Zora's mother is an alcoholic who offers little love or guidance to her daughter. Zora is a product of these two extreme motherly figures by the end of the novel, and becomes a parent herself. What effect do these two parenting styles eventually have on Zora?

8. Zora says that she notices how the women who come into the hair salon "want something different, a change. They want to be happy" (p. 177). After enrolling in school, Zora, unlike the other girls, doesn't constantly change her hair. What does this say about her?

9. The novel is filled with lasting female bonds, and Zora refers to Mrs. Farquhar and Sara Jane as "the sisterhood." How do these strong female characters and their relationships with one another compare to their relationships with the men in the novel?

10. When Zora's mother comes to visit her before Thanksgiving, she says she is sober and has come to make amends for what she has done in the past, which includes confessing the real reason Zora's father died. Do you think she is sincere in her desire to turn her

life around, or do you agree with Miss Cunningham when she says, "People like your mom don't change, Zorie"? Do you think people have the capacity to make drastic changes in their lives, or are they always trapped in their old ways?

11. Zora and Emma share more than one similarity. What are these similarities, and how do you think they impacted Zora's relationship with Winston?

12. Alcoholism is a constant presence in the novel. In what ways does Winston's reliance on drinking feed his relationship with Zora, and in what ways does it pull them apart?

13. When she thinks about Sara Jane's happiness with Jimmy, Zora wonders if her "time would ever come" (p. 133). Do you think that by the end of the novel she has found "her time," in her own way? How so?

14. Several characters in the novel pretend to live different lives, including Mother Hannah, who believes she received a brooch as a gift from Florenz Ziegfeld. However, Zora is guilty of living in a fantasy world with Winston. To what degree do you think living in a fantasy is harmless, and when does it turn dangerous?

15. Ethyl Ladson seemingly hated Zora when she first came in to get her hair done, but then requested that Zora style her hair when she knew she was about to die. In what ways does something as simple as a haircut impact both the customer and the stylist? What, to you, is "the wisdom of hair"?

16. We never fully learn Winston's history with Emma, but we know he tries to drink the pain of her death away. Do you sympathize at all with Winston, as a victim of a tragedy, or do you think he's weak and unable to move on with his life?

17. Zora says it is in her nature to keep things to herself, and Sissy Carson says to her, "You're too damn private, Zora. You can't keep

everything inside of you. It'll kill you just like it did Ed" (p. 150). Has there ever been a time when you haven't told even your closest friend an important part of your life? Do you agree with Sissy that you can't hold everything in, or do you think it's okay to keep certain aspects of your life private?